A HARTLEY
BROTHERS
BOOK

# Cherish Me

## forever

### ALESSA KELLY

"I have seen your dark nights and your brightest days and I will be here with you forever waiting in your dusk." ~ Atticus

# 1

## ISABELLI LUNA MARTINS

*New York - three years ago*

A CHANCE OR A RISK?

Right now, it makes no difference to me. I've planned this for weeks, and there's no time for a last-minute 'let's think about it, Iz' jitters. I've got to get myself and my son away from Nando—far enough for us to lay low for a couple of months. Then, once I've given birth, I'll be able to move again.

"Raffi, come on, baby. It's time." I wake my seven-year-old son.

"I'm still tired!" He slithers under the covers until I can only see his crown.

"We've got to go now." I tug the comforter off him, mother's guilt swarming me.

On my phone, a notification shows Nando's flight has just departed. So for sure, he won't be back until tomorrow night.

Raffi complains some more, but he eventually drags himself out of bed.

"You've got Mr. Oreo?" The fluffy toy is tucked under his arm.

I'm just reminding him to hold on to it. Raffi won't go anywhere without his beloved toy black lab. He's hugged it, taken it for a walk (his version), slept with it—and on it—since I gave it to him for his third birthday.

We make our way down to the garage. Raffi settles himself in the back seat of my packed SUV, mumbling, "If Dad finds out, we'll be in trouble."

That man said he was going to marry me. Sweet, innocent Nando. But I never wish to get near that nightmarishly-ever-after milestone. I met him when I was seventeen and had Raffi when I was nineteen. He said finding me, a Latina with blue eyes, was like witnessing a rare flower that only bloomed one night a year. It should've been perfect. Until Nando turned my dream into hell. But I kept going, clinging to the hope that I could change him back to the man I fell in love with.

"He's not here, baby, and he won't know where we're going." I cover Raffi with a blanket and put on his seatbelt. My finger stiffens as I press the garage remote like I'm launching a bomb.

There might not be such a thing as a safe haven against Nando, but a temporary refuge is all I need until I can get help. In what form or from whom, I don't know. But there's got to be something or someone on this earth that can help me free myself from his clutch.

"Mom! Wait! Mr. Oreo!"

I sigh. "He's not with you?"

"No."

"Raffi! Where is it?" I rummage around him and through the car. "It's not here," I huff.

"Mom, find him. Please..."

He must've dropped the toy somewhere in the house. "You stay here, okay? I'll get Mr. Oreo."

A faint sound of a vehicle halts me.

Our house is perched on a cliff, facing the Atlantic Ocean.

Our closest neighbor is a mile away. Whoever I hear is driving the cliff road and can't know we're leaving.

"Wait here, Raffi. Stay quiet." I scramble to close the garage door before I return to the house.

I peep out the window. "Shit! Fuck!"

This isn't happening. That man is supposed to be up there somewhere in the atmosphere, and he seems to be in a hurry to get home.

Too late to do anything else, I head to the kitchen.

I don't need him to announce *I'm home*. The clinking sound of him tossing his keys into the bowl has primed me to heighten my alertness—and fear.

"Honey! You're back early." I throw him a surprised smile, a drink in my hand.

Nando strides to me, playing with the waves of my honey-brown hair, then circling his arms around my chest.

"Flight got canceled?" I ask, casually stopping him from kneading my breasts. His fondling hurts—an unwelcome kind of hurt because of my pregnancy. He knows it, but he doesn't give a damn.

"The whole thing tomorrow got canceled, so there's no point in me flying to San Fran." He observes the glass in my hand.

"Want some? Mock margarita."

"I don't do fakes, honey. But I'm glad you're into them." He sits down, staring at me. "Something wrong with the heater?" He questions my choice of clothes.

"No. I had to go to the shop, and I haven't had a chance to change."

"Huh." He throws a cold, scrutinizing gaze before leaving the kitchen.

His steps get heavy.

"Where's Raffi?" he yells as he stands at the bottom of the stairs.

"He's asleep. Why?"

"What's Mr. Oreo doing here?" The fluffy toy is next to his feet.

*Shit...*

"Iz, what's going on?"

"Nothing."

Nando seizes my hand, dragging me as he shoots up to the second floor. My feet can hardly keep up with him. I almost trip on every tread. He clutches my neck from behind as we stare at Raffi's empty bed.

"You're trying to run away?" He scans our son's bare closet. "Huh?"

"Nando, listen." I caress his hand despite his tightening grip. He lets me go, only to spin me around. "Nando... please." I plant my hand on his chest, trying to soothe him.

I don't have to wait to realize that nothing will ever calm his ire.

He snatches Raffi's rocket ship bedside lamp and swings it at my belly. It breaks in two. It's kids' plastic decoration—it'll hardly bruise me—but the impact is enough to push me back and stir an ache behind my belly button.

Seeing me still standing, he turns me around and presses my thirty-week bump against the wall.

"Nando! Stop!" I cry despite my hampered breathing.

"One child is bad enough. I've got no time to deal with another!" he yells when he finally relents.

I turn my head to him, but I don't dare move. He's not a big man, and unlike how he treats Raffi, he knows not to leave a mark on me. But seeing his rage-pumped fist and viperous stare, I know I'm facing an aberrant Nando. A blow to my stomach and both my baby and I will die.

He grabs the collar of my shirt. "I would've gotten rid of the first one if I'd known you'd be so difficult."

"Let me go, please," I beg when he drags me back downstairs.

"Where's that fucking rascal?"

"He's not here!"

"We both know he won't go anywhere without Mr. Oreo!"

Nando kicks the soft toy away and then shoves me to the floor. My tailbone gets the brunt of the impact this time, and the pain travels fast to my abs.

"Raffi!" he shouts, heading to the garage.

I push myself up. I've got to stop him, or Raffi will get more than just cuts and bruises.

"No! You leave him alone!" I hang on to his neck however I can, getting my bulging belly out of the way.

As I gouge whatever part of him I can lay my fingers on, he spins around like prey trying to free itself from a predator. Only this predator isn't his match. He hurls me against a mirror like I'm a useless sack. My back hits the cracked glass and then lands on the floor. Facing the hallway, I realize I've been leaving a trail of blood.

Pulsing pain turns to sharp pinches behind my stomach wall. Still, I can't let that man get to Raffi—whatever the cost. "No, you won't ever touch him again!" I crawl.

"Raffi!" Nando takes off his belt.

I gather the last bit of my energy to grab his arm. He sets himself free, then turns to me, peering down. My attempt to stop him is jeer-worthy, but I've got something else for him.

"You leave him alone!" I lunge at him.

My palm gets bloody, but the piece of broken mirror isn't in my grip anymore.

Red spreads on Nando's chest like it's been dipped in a sink full of dye.

"Fucking bitch..." The curse comes out as a huff.

I meet his eyes—a deep brown I used to admire. He was

kind, he was sweet. Until he wasn't. Was he acting when we first met? How could he have sustained his pretending for years? He always blamed Raffi for his rage, but I think it had always been in him. I was just too late in recognizing it.

Perhaps realizing that I'm simply watching him, Nando reaches out his hand. "Iz... help me..."

I step back, shaking my head. I keep moving away from him until a mighty thump assaults my belly, this time from the inside. Unable to bear my own weight, I sit down, helplessly crying over the blood pooling on the floor between my legs.

I clutch my belly, hollering for Raffi to call an ambulance for me. But the front door bursts open faster than my voice can travel out of the room.

"Iz!"

I turn my head. "Thomas? Thomas!"

"Iz!" My best friend—my only friend, Thomas Matheson—runs to me. His youthful eyes freeze in horror as he stares at the blood pool I'm sitting on. Then he glances at my dead boyfriend.

"Get Raffi and then take me to the hospital," I tremble.

"Where's he?" asks Thomas.

"In the car. Did he call you?"

"Yes. Wait here—"

Another voice arrives at the door.

"You brought him with you?" I cry in dismay.

"Iz, no! He must've followed me."

"Jesus, what a mess!" Donovan Fletcher's lanky form appears at my feet, observing the floor that has turned from red wood to blood red. He stares at Nando's dead body as his curiosity turns into satisfaction.

His eyes stir with intent as they settle on me. I've seen that look before. It's Don when he's delighted—when something has happened, and he can't wait to clean it up.

"Don... take me to the hospital. Please. Or I'm gonna lose my baby!"

Don kneels next to me. "You know how it looks, don't you?"

His statement compels me to take a second look at the corpse in front of me. Only now do I realize that Nando's stab wound isn't the only damage I inflicted on him. Whatever I did when I hung on to his neck, the skin around his Adam's apple is marred with lacerations.

"Please. We can talk about what happened later," I beg, then turn to Thomas. "Stay with Raffi. Don't let him see me like this."

Don gestures to Thomas to get to my son.

"Don, take me to the hospital. Now!"

"I should thank you. I'd wanted to do this for a long time." Don kicks Nando's body.

"We can sort out that asshole later."

"Oh, believe me, you'll want me to sort him out sooner than you're prepared to wait."

Thomas returns. "Sir, let me take her."

"Thomas, stay with Raffi!" I command.

"I'll make all this disappear," Don claims, giving Nando another glance. He then gets up as if he has to speak his next statement while looking down at me. "I'll save you, and perhaps your unborn child too. But you must promise me something."

"You'll get Nando's business. That's a promise."

"Well, that's not a promise. That's a given. What I mean, Iz. You murdered your boyfriend and the father of your child, or children, in cold blood. It'll take a lot more for me to clean it up —from this place, to the morgue, to the police. You know the drill." He pops a mint gum into his mouth. "Not to mention keeping Social Services at bay."

Terror pours into my pain-wracked body. He can take anything from me, but not Raffi!

"What do you want from me?"

"Just promise me."

"Promise you what?"

"You just have to promise, my darling."

My cramping escalates. It feels like a rake is scraping the wall of my belly. I can hardly breathe.

Don grips my jaw tightly in his fingers. "Say you promise."

My lips quiver. "Yes... I pro...mise."

The filthy man kisses me. "Good." Then he yells toward the porch. "Thomas!"

"Yes, sir?"

"Take her to the hospital," Don instructs as he saunters out of the house. His black-clothed frame moves like a shadow, so skinny it might as well be a skeleton in a robe. But I know his power. The weight of his presence is more than just a shadow in my life.

"Come on, Iz," Thomas covers me with a throw blanket to hide my stained clothes. He's about to pull me up. "Jesus, your hand... your hand!"

"Just take me to the car!" I shout at him, snapping him out of panic. The kid is only eighteen. He shouldn't have seen so much blood, but he's my only hope right now.

Thomas drags me up by the armpits. I'm standing, but my God...

I wail in agony. I can hear it trail across the hallway.

"You can do it. Come on, babe," Thomas encourages as we navigate the front porch steps.

Raffi is waiting for me in Thomas's car. "Mom! Are you okay?"

Seeing my son's face, I leave the trail of my agony at the door. I grin at him. Despite the tragedy and the unknown ahead, I have done something for him. He doesn't have to be afraid of that 'monster man' anymore. "Yes, baby, I'm okay."

"Thomas found Mr. Oreo." Raffi innocently shows off the toy he's cuddling.

"Good. Good." I caress him with my uninjured hand.

Thomas reverses the car wildly, as if it's his first time driving.

"Is baby Caili gonna be okay?" Raffi asks as we speed along the cliff road.

"Yes, she is." I maintain my smile despite the world spinning around me. "When we get to the hospital, you stay with Thomas, okay?"

The boy nods.

"Hug Mr. Oreo." I move the fluffy toy so it kisses Raffi, fishing out a chuckle from him.

So I've freed myself from the hell called Nando, only to fall into the arms of my own Grim Reaper, who will soon drag me into his lair. I've made a deal with Donovan Fletcher to save my daughter. I hope, somehow, I'll be able to free myself again— although this time, I'm up against a man who's wielding a scythe and not afraid to use it.

As the hospital 'Emergency' sign looms, my vision blurs.

"God!" I release a restrained wail, refusing to succumb as the night dips into total darkness. I swear, I will fight to the end for the precious life I'm carrying.

"Iz, hang on!" Even Thomas's voice is no more than a faint whisper now.

My body contorts, signaling the inevitable.

No...

I... will... fight...

# Present Time

# 2

## CLAYTON FABER HARTLEY

*US Air Force facility, undisclosed location – present time*

AFTER YEARS of bearing the title of 'former' fighter jet pilot, I'm back wearing the freedom green uniform, flying through contested airspace once again.

Better still, I'm getting my feet wet. Well, metaphorically, anyway. I'm taking the Snow Leopard 100 over the water. The silver beauty is a seventh-generation stealth fighter with the lowest heat signature yet—so it's literally the coolest aircraft on the planet.

After opening my comms with our sea assets, I start sharing ops pictures with them.

"Snow Leopard 100, N.E.O data received."

The confirmation comes loud and clear over the headset, but it's no time for me to release a victory grin.

First mission accomplished. One to go.

With three minutes left in my allocated time, I've got to make the best of this mighty kitty's electronic warfare system.

"Damn, you sucker. Show yourself!" I mumble to myself,

focusing on my radar. They're surely making it harder than what I was used to.

Ninety seconds to go, and—

"Tally-ho."

I lock in my target and jam their radar.

"Good work, Snow Leopard."

I grin at the announcement.

*Fuck yeah!*

"Thank you, sir. Snow Leopard 100 is RTB."

RTB, or return to base—I'd uttered it countless times during my military days. Today those three letters still give me the homecoming feeling only a combat pilot can appreciate.

I leave the contested airspace and land the jet with ten seconds to spare.

It was all a test. The Snow Leopard is still a prototype, but I can feel its fuel coursing through my blood. Not only am I the first civilian to fly the damn beauty, but I've also proven that Hartley Marine's communication gateway and locator installed in that aircraft are working as they should.

General Adler welcomes me back to the ground.

"We could do with higher image res and faster transmissions," the general complains. He was my commander when I was with the Special Tactics Squadron, and it seems he hasn't lost his urge to kick my ass.

"Unquestionably, sir, some finetuning is on the cards," I acknowledge.

He smirks, shaking my hand. "I never thought you'd find that target."

"Well, our system can track every single sea otter on the planet, and it's no different with birds in the sky," I gush about our VesslScope-AV.

The electronic locator onboard the Snow Leopard originated

from our maritime radar system, VesslScope. AV is the aviation version of it.

"I meant it when I said I wanted higher res and faster transmissions," Adler maintains.

We make our way down the tarmac toward the facility's main building.

"You still look good in sage," the general comments on my overalls.

"Always, sir," I reply as my fingers discreetly plump up my helmet-flattened hair.

Adler then rubs his chin, looking at me with a narrowed gaze. "Hey, between you and me. Keep an eye on Fletcher," he says.

Donovan Fletcher—a man with an ass bigger than the moon. He was our competitor when the military put this project out to tender.

That stray cat thought the deal was in the bag for him. He's never been a gracious loser, and when Hartley Marine was awarded the contract, he immediately claimed collusion and corruption. Of course, it helps to know people in high places. That's just the nature of business. But Hartley Marine won the contract fair and square. Adler was one of the many heads we had to convince we were the men for the job. Fletcher might own one of the largest software companies in the country, but the Coast Guard is their ceiling. They're not cut out for the real sea-sky business.

"What's up with Fletcher?" I ask.

"He's been seeking a partner."

"Are you warning me of a potential new threat?"

"I'm not your business advisor, Hartley." We take an elevator up. "I'm not warning you, but I have been warning the CIA. Fletcher is seeking partnerships in Southeast Asia. It could be a matter of national security."

I purse my lips. By Southeast Asia, I know Adler implies China. Fletcher Tech's financials have been up and down, and perhaps finding a partner in Asia wouldn't be such a bad move.

"Even Chinese technology is better than Fletcher's," I remark.

"His technology may be a few years behind, but in the wrong hands, it might create unnecessary fire. We don't want another surveillance balloon flying over Montana, do we?" he says as he walks me to the last elevator up. "Just let me know if you hear anything."

Getting out of the secret basement seems to be the cue for him to lighten the conversation. "How's Rob?" he asks about my brother.

"He has his hands full."

"How old is his boy now?"

"Three. And they're almost there with their second pregnancy."

"Phew! A handful, all right. Well, send my regards, will you?" Adler shakes my hand again. "So, what's next for you?"

"A vacation."

"Clayton Hartley is taking a vacation?"

"Work hard, play hard, General," I babble as he commands an officer to escort me out.

Adler laughs briefly, studying me as if trying to guess my travel itinerary. "The Caribbean? Spending money on over-priced cocktails? Working on your tan? Not that you need it." He glances at my rolled-up sleeve. "Perhaps falling in love, too?"

That was a high-ranking way of saying getting laid.

"You know I don't do love," I quip.

"Bullshit, Clay."

"Kenya! I'm going to Kenya."

"No kidding!"

"I don't do love." I wave at him and then give him a salute.

Oltepesi, *Kenya*

When I said I don't do love, I really meant romance. I have a heart, and I know how to love. Otherwise, I couldn't call myself a Hartley.

So far, though, knowing how to love and facing reality haven't quite married up. I used to put my heart out in the open —being accessible, vulnerable, and all that. I pursued women I was attracted to like they were all my soulmates. And I would try to please them, be the man they dreamed of. God witnessed it all. *I tried.* But when heartbreak was all you got in the end, you learned.

Nowadays, my heart is nowhere near a woman. It's with those happy faces I see coming to me.

"Clayton!" The students of Elimu Primary School flock toward me, some jumping onto my shoulders when I bend down to hug them. Those watching us laugh, especially when my ebony fringe gets messed up—I must look like a wildebeest having a bad hair day.

"You see our field?" A girl points at the newly completed sports field. I remember her. Her name is Durah. She'd told me it means pearl.

I clear the hair off my face. "I see that," I respond, watching her friends playing a game of soccer on a proper surface, with a ball that is a perfect sphere and made of quality material that will last multiple matches.

*That* is where my love goes. And these beaming children surrounding me—*they* are where my love goes.

The owner, Mrs. Nkasiogi Makena, fondly known as Mrs. Mac, has officially called the sports field Faber Park. Faber—I share that middle name with my grandfather, who was a gifted athlete and an officer in the military intelligence service during World War II. I like to think the park is named after him. At the same time, having part of me trampled by kids' happy feet playing the sports they love—I'm humbled.

Oltepesi is forty miles southwest of the capital Nairobi. It's known for being a tourist hot spot for Maasai Mara camps, but the real life of the people remains obscure to most foreigners.

I got to know Mrs. Mac on my first trip to the country. Having had enough of following a tour at the time, I ventured out by myself and got into trouble when my rental Jeep ended up in a ditch. Apparently, the pothole I accidentally drove through was a trap set by local thieves. When I saw a lady in her sixties charging at me with an AK rifle in her hand, I'd been convinced I was about to die. But then she reached a hand out to me.

"Come with me if you want to live!" she said, quoting *Terminator* in her thick Kenyan accent. Since then, we've become good friends.

"Great to see you again, Clayton," Mrs. Mac shakes my hand after she's sent the kids away. Behind her, the kids disperse to all corners of the schoolyard. She flashes her trademark grin, creasing her full cheeks. Her grandmotherly hug soon follows.

"You've done it, Mrs. Mac," I praise.

"Yeah. We still have some funds left, which I'm going to use to build two more classrooms."

"Excellent."

Mrs. Mac ushers me to the school's assembly hall, where a full traditional Mara buffet awaits. Music and dances accompany our lunch—a perfect start to my vacation. I then accept a hoop-off challenge from a couple of teachers, christening our new basketball court. Following my defeat, I say goodbye to the teachers and kids.

"If you need anything, just call me, okay? I mean it," I tell

Mrs. Mac as she walks me to my car. "I haven't received enough calls from you."

She grins, a pondering grin. "Clayton, when we first met, you were a silly blue-eyed kid trying to scramble out of trouble," she reminisces, no doubt referring to the moment she found me covered in mud, climbing out of a ditch that fateful afternoon. "But you turned out good."

Her last comment somehow exposes a deep crack in me. I turned out good, but why am I still alone?

My lips twitch. I despise that thought. Being single is an absurd barometer to measure one's goodness. But I had tasted togetherness and, supposedly, love. At the time, I told myself *a man without love is a man made of ice.*

Now I am that man.

Mrs. Mac nods thoughtfully, then says, "I hope you make time to explore the country properly this time."

I blink away my arctic thought, burying the crevasse I never thought would surface during an African holiday. "I'm off to Samburu."

"Nice. I heard the lion population is on the rise there."

"Perfect."

Nairobi airport is jam-packed and as chaotic as usual. I'm not surprised to find that my flight has been delayed. They're still weighing our bags.

Two women rush in, barely tugging their luggage. Why are they reminding me of the Hilton sisters in the nineties? *Heels? You're wearing heels to a safari?*

As they run, one of their suitcases loses its wheel. The immobilized trunk tugs the woman back, and she falls.

"Jesus, Nance!" her friend gasps.

I get up and approach them. "Ladies, can I help you?"

The fallen girl mouths a yes, but nothing comes out. I give her a hand.

She takes it and hauls herself up. "Thank you."

"Come, I'll take care of that bag." I carry the damaged suitcase. Jesus, what's in it? "You're not in the ivory trade, are you?"

The two ladies chuckle at me.

"Thank you, sir," the one owning the suitcase replies. "Is this the flight to Samburu?"

"Yes."

"God, so we're not late?" the other asks.

"You would've been, but it's your lucky day. They're running way behind schedule," I explain as I lead them to the guy who checked me in earlier. "I'm sure this gentleman will take care of you. Ladies." I nod my goodbye.

An hour later, our flight departs. It's a Cessna Caravan, and it's full.

The two ladies sit in the row beside me. With their shiny blonde hair and orange bra tops, it's almost impossible for my peripheral not to catch their movements and occasional glances.

Seeing how comfortable they look in their scanty attire, I wouldn't be surprised if they'll be wearing something similar during the safari. Someone didn't get the memo. No doubt the sand that will cling to their skin isn't the kind of paradise touch they're looking for. Besides, they'll soon find out how ferocious the mosquitoes are, especially along the river. They'd better have brought some bug spray, and I hope they're taking antimalarials too.

The women are attractive, and I was happy to lend a hand earlier. But to my eyes and my heart, they're no different than the family of four behind them or the old couple in front of me.

Halfway through our flight, the sky turns gray. We're heading straight into a thunderstorm. This should be routine for experienced pilots, but something isn't right. Passengers start gasping and whining—not over the weather, but over the limp body of the pilot.

I scan the cabin, yelling, "Is there a doctor here?"

A man sitting in the backseat answers, "Yeah." He looks to be a local guy.

"Help me out, man!" I remove my seatbelt and grab hold of the pilot's chair backrest to keep my balance. The co-pilot is frantically calling air traffic control for help.

The storm is starting to give the plane a shake. The doctor arrives behind me after struggling to navigate to the front. "Lie him here." He points to the narrow aisle, holding on to the cockpit partition. "Heart attack, likely."

The plane shudders as it rides on a strong current.

"Whoa!" I yell to the co-pilot as I peer into the sky ahead. This isn't a thunderstorm, it's a friggin' supercell, and we shouldn't fly through it at all—let alone with a frightened man at the helm.

"We've got to turn around!" I tell the young pilot.

"We're close. Doctors will be there waiting for us in Samburu."

"Turn around!" I insist. I'd head into a formation of enemy fighters anytime, but not this nasty weather band. Whoever let this flight take off was insane!

"Go back to your seat, sir!" the co-pilot shouts.

The plane goes into a nosedive following a lightning strike. The engine light comes on, and the cabin fills with screams and cries.

"Reduce power," I command.

"Are you crazy?" He trembles.

"Cut the power. We need to slow down before you level the wings," I guide him.

He listens to my advice, and the plane slows, although we're still diving. He then nods at the empty pilot chair. "Well, that seat's yours."

I jump into it, then gently pull back the control column to

raise the plane's nose. The aircraft steadies, and we gradually gain back altitude.

"Doc, how's the captain?" I glance back into the cabin.

"He's breathing," the doctor replies.

"Take a seat! Strap him and yourself up. It's gonna be rough."

For a good half hour, we're in constant turbulence. People have stopped screaming, though several are puking instead.

"We've got this," I assure my co-pilot despite the engine failing.

By now, he seems to have gathered his composure, alerting 'May Day' to air traffic control and communicating our intention.

"We're landing soon. Hang on!" I yell.

This is no Snow Leopard, and I'm not in contested airspace, but my blood thickens like I'm in battle. I have lives depending on me.

Our altitude drops faster than I'm comfortable with, but anything is better than free-falling.

"Brace, everyone! Brace!" the co-pilot shouts as I take the Cessna to the ground.

A thump draws gasps from the passengers. It's almost a dead-stick landing, but we've arrived in one piece.

Soon, fire engines swarm the plane.

"Everyone okay?" I yell.

Among the cries, I hear 'yes' from most people.

"Shit..." the co-pilot breathes when we've come to a complete stop. "Who are you?"

"Clayton Hartley. Former US Air Force." I hate to say former, but I never pretend to be something I'm not.

"I guess no flying school will teach you that."

I pat his shoulder. I've known a few Kenyan pilots, and they're some of the best in the world. I mean, bush planes are bread and butter for many of them. This kid has skills. He just needs to learn to make better decisions.

We then help everyone disembark, starting with the almost incapacitated pilot. Ambulances and paramedics gather on the tarmac.

The two ladies run to me, throwing me a relieved hug. "Thank you."

I pat their backs lightly. Curiously, they appear to be the least shaken out of anyone.

"Hey, you never said your name," one of them states as I rush away.

I smile slightly. "Met."

My callsign was Mettle—awarded to me for the guts to keep flying with a damaged engine in my first combat training.

After giving my statement to the authorities, I decide to stay in the city. I've got to find something that doesn't involve flying. Not that I'm sick of being in the air. I just can't take another day of drama.

3

___________

# ISABELLE

*Los Angeles, California*

THREE YEARS after I made a deal with the Grim Reaper, I'm still trapped in his lair. Donovan Fletcher is holding all the cards. One wrong move, and Raffi could be snatched away from me. And I can say with certainty that it's not just a threat.

I hate his power, but I have to live with it for now.

Following that fateful night, Don helped me and Raffi relocate to L.A. True to his words, he swept everything under the carpet, and my boyfriend's death record magically showed that he died in a car accident.

In evil's lair I may be, but I must say it's a hell of a bearable kind. Even though I'm at the beck and call of a forty-five-year-old man, even though I've been destroyed and humiliated as a result of my blind promise to him, my decision has given Raffi peace. No more angry shouts, backhand slaps, or belt whips in the middle of the night. We have our own house, and most importantly, my son is safe in it. I might've sold my body to the Reaper, but my soul is still mine—intact.

"Mom, you're leaving again?" Raffi questions. "I thought you had your shift this morning."

"I had class then, baby," I explain. "I'll be back tomorrow morning before you even wake up."

My ten-year-old son flattens his lips.

"What's that look?"

"I wish you weren't so busy. Uncle Don gives us money. Why do you have to work so hard?"

"Raffi, Uncle Don let us borrow this house, but he doesn't give us money. I work for us. I provide for you. I'm your mother."

Raffi doesn't respond, as if trying to digest what I just told him. I don't blame him for thinking that we live on Don's kindness, but it makes me realize how little my son knows about the truth.

Outside, I hear a vehicle approaching.

"That must be Thomas," I exclaim. He sometimes babysits Raffi, saving me from having to pay for a nanny from time to time.

The revving vehicle at my gate tells me the driver is either drunk, insane, or enraged. It pulls into my driveway fast, as if it's about to go straight into the living room.

"What the hell!" I mumble as the car finally stops.

I open the door. Like facing a backdraft, my steps regress.

"Don?" I greet him but not letting him in. This is his house, but he's never intruded like this before. Then I glance at the suitcase his bodyguard is towing. "I've gotta go to work."

Don pushes me back into the living room and lets himself in. He chews his mint gum hard, making his triangular face appear like a voracious goat.

"Raffi, go to your room," I tell him.

The boy mumbles out a few words of protest as he turns away from me.

I watch him climb the stairs, enter his bedroom and close the door, making sure he's not listening to our conversation.

My attention is back on the suitcase. "What's going on?"

"You're coming with me. That's what's going on," Don says.

"Where?"

He peers down at me. "Since when did you ask?"

Don has a steady girlfriend—well, by steady, I mean one that he keeps for a few months rather than just hours. And then he has me. But so far, he never needs me to travel—not with a suitcase that big anyway.

"Those pencil-dick Chinese will love you." Don clenches my jaw, his favorite move to show that I'm his. "To look at, of course. You're the bitch I'll never marry, but I surely enjoy fucking you exclusively."

Don gestures for his bodyguard to open the suitcase.

Shiny gowns, lingerie, stilettos, jewelry boxes, and of course, Don's favorite blonde wig for me.

"So we're going to Chinatown with all these?" I deadpan.

Don laughs. "You are funny sometimes."

Despite his takeover of Nando's business, Don's company, Fletcher Tech, has been struggling to balance its books. He's vowed not to seek foreign investments, but I won't be surprised if he yields this time.

"Chinatown via Nairobi," he jokes.

"Kenya?"

"Bravo. You know your geography. It's a fucked-up country, but it's the gateway to Africa and a gold mine in its own right. With the right kind of partner and the right level of corruption, you can make great headway."

"What happens to your girlfriend? You don't take me overseas, Don. That's the rule, right? I don't even have a passport."

Don pulls me into his embrace—a threatening embrace. "I make the rules. You don't lecture me. You're going."

"For how long?"

"A week."

I face Don, half begging. "I can't. Raffi needs me."

"Well, he ain't gonna get a free holiday. Sort it out, and I don't mean Thomas. That kid has been distracted lately—like he'd gone back to puberty or something."

I know for a fact that Thomas has just broken up with his boyfriend. Nobody else knows about the relationship—we're aware of the consequences if it ever leaked. The breakup devastated him, but in a way, I'm relieved so I won't have to keep a secret anymore. And, as selfish as I am, I need him.

Thomas and I haven't found a way to break free thanks to Don's persistent surveillance on me and Raffi. The best resolution we could come up with was that I should find a rich man who's more powerful than Don—and not a dick. I'm not counting on that scenario to come true, but my nightmare will have to end sooner rather than later, and I won't be able to do it alone.

"Don, I have my medical exam to prepare for," I say to him gently. Raffi might not be a good enough reason for him—another human being is never a good reason for him—but perhaps my study might, even though it's trivial compared to my son.

Don considers it for a moment. "When you get your medical degree, I'll be the first to congratulate you. But I'm your work, your leisure, your day, your night. That means you do as I say."

"At least give me time to prepare for the trip. I've never been overseas. Well, I was born in Rio, but that doesn't count, right? What do I know about Kenya!"

"Isabelle, I don't need your intelligence. I just need you to be by my side, to be mine. You only open your mouth to smile, drink, and eat. And to blow me."

Despite that remark, remarkably, Don never forces me to

give him blow jobs. Rumor has it that he was once hurt that way by a woman. I never ask whether it was true, hell no, but I wonder. Does he not do it at all? Or does he only trust a few—those whom he's confident will not harm him? If my assumption is right, that implies I'm not one of those few women.

He controls me, but he doesn't trust me. A bad combination.

Regardless, the absence of his oral preference is a welcome reprieve, as I can't help feeling my past sex life was all about blow jobs. Since I was pregnant with Raffi, Nando wasn't fond of having intercourse. Men like him simply want to assert their dominance. Everything is one-way—to them, for them, and about them. I'm just hoping that this coming trip is no different, that Don doesn't suddenly 'trust me.'

"Come on, get rid of that stupid clothes," he sneers at my nurse uniform. "We leave now."

Don lets me go, and his bodyguard hands me a thin knit dress. Jesus, I'm slim, but that dress is impossibly tight!

Apparently hearing my steps upstairs, Raffi opens his door and pokes his head out. His eyes are fixed on the dress I'm holding. "You're going away?"

"You'll stay with Pippa, okay?"

"Mom..."

"I need to go with Uncle Don for a week."

"A week?" Anxiety paints his innocent face. "Mom, please, don't leave."

I persevere with my look of authority, although inside, I'm going to pieces. "You stay with Pippa. That's final."

Escaping Raffi's futile defiance, I scurry to my bedroom. I call Pippa while changing. We work at the same hospital. I apologize to her profusely—apparently, I'm about to ruin her date.

"Come on, princess!" Don yells. "We're late."

Jesus, this dress is so tight I don't know how I'll survive a long-haul flight in it.

As soon as I come out of my bedroom—complete with full hair and make-up as Don always expects—he takes my hand, dragging me to his car.

I turn to Raffi. "Pippa is on her way, baby. Be a good boy, okay? I love you." Then I walk away from him, unable to witness his distraught face.

Don watches my hips wriggling in my dress as I try to sit properly in the backseat of his car. "Now, you'll be a good girl, won't you? Do as I say?"

"I've promised you, Don. You don't have to worry about me."

"Good. I'll allow you to sleep on the flight. But once we get to Nairobi, I'm expecting you to be the best goddamn escort I've ever had."

**4**

---

## CLAYTON

I've spent the last couple of days back in Oltepesi, continuing my hoop-off with the Elimu teachers, kicking balls with the kids, and filling in for their sick math teacher.

In the afternoon, I return to my hotel in Nairobi for the sake of security. An American citizen had been recently kidnapped for ransom, and it's not new in this part of the world. Mrs. Makena could well be my bodyguard, but I refrain from making myself a target.

Back in Nairobi, bored to my head, I take the advice from the front desk to tour the Giraffe Manor and spend the night in the beautiful colonial-style resort.

It's a brilliant idea—until it's time to make a dinner reservation.

I call Mrs. Makena, sitting in my hotel room chair that looks more like a throne. "Mrs. Mac, would you be my date tonight?"

"Clayton! What has got into you?"

"I'm at the Giraffe Manor. When I told the reception that I'd be dining alone, she looked at me like... I don't know, like I'd just been kicked off American Idol."

"Like a loser?" She laughs. I can imagine her belly shaking.

"Now you know how desperate I am. Please."

"I'm a busy woman, you know," she raves. "But just for you. I'll do it as long as you don't mind the age-gap thing."

"Well, I'm almost thirty-four, so that makes you—what do you say—three years older than me?"

She laughs even louder. Now that is a woman who makes me happy.

A couple of hours later, I fetch Mrs. Makena from the lobby, welcoming her as if I was the lord of the manor. She's wearing a *kitenge* dress—traditional Kenyan clothing—in bright red and yellow, while I'm wearing a suit without a tie.

One of the staff ushers us to a table, and now it makes sense why the receptionist might've thought I was a loser when I initially booked dinner for one.

"This is ridiculous," Mrs. Makena laughs as we enter a conservatory-like space, with pots of live orchids surrounding our private table. The furniture is dressed in white satin, generously lit with large candles.

I steal a glance at her creased features. "Are you blushing?"

"No." She bows her head shyly.

"You're blushing, Mrs. Mac!"

I order my favorite Kenyan beer while Mrs. Mac decides to try a Dawa mocktail.

"Clayton, stop looking at me like that, or we'll never finish the first course."

"Come on, when was the last time you had a date? At least give me points for trying."

The grandmother of six laughs heartily. "I have a date every weekend, Clayton."

"Gee, you're doing way better than me."

We enjoy our entrée over a conversation about the next stage of the Elimu school expansion. After I order more drinks, I find myself under Mrs. Mac's scrutiny.

"Now, don't look at me like that."

"You could have any woman you want, Clayton. Are you not looking?"

"To be honest, no," I admit, watching the waiter serving our mains. That is a delicious-looking fish.

"Why?" she asks, taking a piece of the dish the waiter called 'Sukuma'—which she explains is a traditional Kenyan fish spiced with cardamom, nutmeg, and cinnamon.

"A man is no good alone," she adds after the waiter leaves.

Is that her version of saying 'a man without love is a man made of ice'?

"That's why I have you," I helplessly answer.

"I'm taken, and there's nothing you can do to change my mind."

I lean back, admiring her. Stuart Makena, her husband of fifty years, is one lucky man.

Outside, through the open door of our private space, I see a group passes by the courtyard. Among the laughter, I can hear a foreign accent. From here, just looking at their backs, I think the group consists of three Asian men with their wives or partners and a Caucasian man with—

A tall woman wearing a backless yellow dress.

Her olive skin outglows her bright outfit. Her taut shoulders and traps show she takes care of her body. The skirt hugs her curves. If only that man's hand wasn't clutching her waist so tight. Excessively tight, I must say, or maybe because her waist is tiny. As she walks, her dress slit reveals her pins—so sexy especially with those red stilettos grazing the lacy hem of her skirt.

"You wish you were him?" Mrs. Mac's eyes zone in on the stick-thin figure of the Caucasian man, who seems to be leading the group.

I straighten myself, switching my focus to the meal in front of me. "No. I've had enough of being cheated on."

"What makes you think she'll cheat on him?"

"She will. Take my word for it."

"You're such a grim man." Mrs. Mac keeps observing the couple. "You know what, Clayton? I hope you never wish to be him. That man thinks he owns her."

Her remark sounds like a consolation, but she's not the type who says something just for the sake of it. "How do you know?"

"He's holding her, but her hips sway the other way," she describes. "And he keeps pulling her in."

I stretch my neck to see for myself what Mrs. Mac is talking about, but the pair have already disappeared into the main dining room.

We enjoy our desserts and tea while chatting about random subjects, from wildlife conservation to the lingering draught in the country.

A burst of laughter from the other side of the restaurant sends us cringing.

"Gee, they're loud." Mrs. Mac shakes her head.

A man's voice stands out from the noises, almost shouting like he's had one too many. "The money is on our radar, gents."

The room erupts once more, and he keeps ranting, "Radar— you get what I mean?"

Why does it sound so familiar?

He could be talking about any kind of radar, but I've heard that voice saying the word before. And if I match up that voice with the skinny man holding the woman in yellow—

"Would you excuse me, Mrs. Mac?"

"I've been waiting for you to say that." Her laugh is mixed with a challenge. She wants me to admit I'm about to check out the blonde beauty.

"I just need to visit the bathroom."

I ask a waiter to give me the direction to the gents' room, and once I know where it is, I take a detour, so I pass the rowdy table from a distance.

"Fuck me…" I mumble to myself.

It is *his* voice! It's fucking Donovan Fletcher, all right! What's the chance I meet that stray cat here? With three Chinese men?

General Adler's remark plays in my head. The Chinese have been relentless in their investment in this part of the world, and perhaps Fletcher is trying to take a piggyback ride.

The seat next to Fletcher is empty—it must be her seat. It was his arm wrapping around that stunning woman's waist. The man treats his women like takeaways, and his taste is often questionable. But that woman in yellow? Much as I want to deny my curiosity, I do want to see her face.

I trudge down the hall before the stray cat can spot me. As I make a turn into the gents' room, the adjacent door opens.

Sunshine.

Gold.

Happiness.

The woman who's starting to bend my mind has just exited the ladies' room. Her long, blonde hair dances on her equally bright dress.

*God have mercy.*

Egg.

Butter.

Banana.

Those breakfast items fail to distract me from her beauty. She's the kind of trouble I avoid—it's engrained in my system, encrypted, and impossible to unlock. Yet, her smile unsettles me, tugging me as if she has a secret I ought to uncover. And for that, my heart roars like a jet ready for combat, leaving base, flying straight into her.

I don't know how long I've been gawking at her. Or perhaps

I've only caught a glimpse of her—I don't know. Time and place are a blur right now. All I know, she's moving away from me.

"Fuck!" Her voice is muffled, but—really, she swears?

With my heart calling to me like an alter ego, I look into her eyes. Under the dim light, I can only guess that they're blue.

I continue standing like a fool, but I soon realize she's in all sorts of predicaments. Her dress strap has gotten hooked onto a protruding piece of wood. The fabric is so delicate the dress falls apart on her when she attempts to set herself free.

She releases a silent gasp.

I'm looking at her eyes.

I swear, I'm looking at her eyes.

Grimacing, her head is pulled to one side while her hands are busy covering her chest. Something else seems to be hurting her.

"Hey, you need help there?" I finally utter something.

"My earring," she mutters, fiddling with her tangled hair. Her bracelet is precariously close to the knot it may soon add to her plight.

I fly stealth fighters. My callsign is Mettle. Yet, in her presence, I'm as brave as a sedated chihuahua.

"Hang on." Despite my stiffened fingers, I manage to untangle her hair. But something is still tugging her. Her head remains in the same slanting position. I swipe her hair back to find the real source of her predicament. A faint iris fragrance drifts through my nose. If heaven has a smell, this will be it—the scent of its angels.

My mind starts painting what that heaven may look like. Even just knowing her name would take me somewhere beautiful.

*For goodness' sake!*

I save myself from further embarrassment by focusing on the problem in front of me. The longest part of her earring has been caught in the lacy strap of her dress—the one that's still intact, anyway.

She restrains her hiss as my clumsy digits tug on the diamond earring—and, subsequently, her earlobe.

"Sorry, I'm sorry." Give me radars and propellers any time. By the grace of God, my hands aren't made for this kind of delicate operation.

After a few attempts, I manage to separate the earring from the dress. "Here we go."

"Can you—" She turns sideway, hitching her bare shoulder, signaling to me to do something to fix her snapped strap.

If I was the regular Clayton, I would've asked if she'd like my help long before she asked. But I'm anything but regular at the moment. I only act on her command.

I pick up the severed strap from her grip, brushing her smooth shoulder in the process.

Had I not learned my lesson in love, I would've introduced myself or made small talk to make her feel at ease. But this not-so-little Miss Sunshine is rendering me helpless that now, it's me who needs to feel at ease.

Unable to make myself useful in dealing with satin and lace, her dress starts to unravel again.

"I'm sorry."

"It's okay. Keep going," she urges, not moving an inch as if she was a mannequin. By now, her frantic effort to cover her chest has stopped. She seems content to let me see it bare—only loosely obscuring her nipples with her palm.

I start again. She lightly tilts her face, stretching the curve where her shoulder meets her neck, giving me more room to maneuver. Her scent travels to me, and her smooth skin spreads right in front of my sight like an invitation. An invitation that's so goddamn hard to ignore.

"Here we go," I tell her.

She adjusts the reinstated strap and smooths a hand over the bodice of her dress. *If Rob saw that knot I had just tied, he would send me back to sailing school.*

Facing me, she tousles her long, wavy hair and arranges it, so it covers the repaired spot. "How do I look?"

*Dazzling, devastating.*

"Um—good as new," I answer.

The corners of her red lips lift. Then her eyes land on mine.

I don't do love, and I don't do speechless and awkward, either. But now I find myself thwarted out of my comfort zone and into a supercell of a different kind.

"Look, I—please forgive me if I ever made you feel uncomfortable."

"It's too dark to see anything here, mister." She takes a few steps away from me into the rays of a rattan-shaded lamp.

*Like hell it is!*

I blurt, "I was just looking at your eyes."

She cocks her head with an inescapable gaze, challenging me to prove my point.

I refuse to blink, accepting the challenge. Those iridescent eyes—they must be made of ocean and lightning, perhaps the aftermath of a clash between Poseidon and Zeus. They're still wide open but now no longer challenging. Instead, they're requesting a connection, as if she wants to tell me her story but needs my permission.

Her eyelids shut, and just like that, that tugging force is erased.

"You shouldn't have," she murmurs. Then she pivots, leaving me like a totem pole, standing between the ladies' and the gents' rooms.

After a couple of steps, she stops—standing as still as I am. It takes her a few seconds to turn her head to me. "Thank you, stranger in the dark."

She lopes forward like I was her distant past that'll never return.

Look at her. She's all limbs, but she has a magnificent hourglass figure. How the hell did she fall in love with a man like Fletcher? That scumbag wouldn't just tow a random woman overseas. She must be someone special to him.

I told Mrs. Makena that it would be inevitable that woman would betray her man. I fucking well wish she would—with me.

"Who did you see?" Mrs. Mac asks when I'm back at my table.

I settle myself, taking a gulp of beer. "My business rival."

"Oh... and you're in love with her?"

I give her a frowny smile. "It's a he."

She laughs. "Do you know *her*?"

"God dammit, Mrs. Mac!" I shake my head at her insistence like she hasn't already known. "It's his girlfriend."

"That woman whom you said would betray her man?"

"I guess so. And also, the one you said was swaying her hips the other way."

"Clayton Faber Hartley." She crosses her arms over her chest and gives me a slight nod as if confirming that she is judging me. "Granted, you're a good man. Ridiculously generous, and handsome—too handsome for me, which I don't say very often."

I chuckle at her assessment. The woman still attracts men's attention in her village, even decades after she was a contestant for Miss Kenya in the sixties.

She then holds my hand. "But love isn't just gonna land on your lap. You must work for it."

"I've sought, and I've failed. I've sat around and waited, and I still failed." I can't help stealing glances at the group, who are now making their way out of the dining room. There she is, her back to me, Fletcher's arm is still hooking her waist like they'll never be apart. But I see what Mrs. Mac observed. Something isn't right with the way the couple keeps pushing and pulling against each other. No one else would've noticed, but Mrs. Mac did, and now I do.

"It just means that it's not your time yet, Clayton."

I calm my rioting heartbeat. "Wise words, Mrs. Mac."

"Look, I know you're the type who wants to save the world. Perhaps you haven't been waiting for love. You're just waiting for someone who needs you, young man."

"Needs me?" I try to imagine what that looks like, and I don't think it fits my idea of forever love.

"There's a difference between being needy and needing someone," she clarifies as if reading my mind. "Listen. A woman can need a man. It's not a crime. It's not a weakness, either. As long as you need her too. Equally."

"Was that how you felt with Mr. Mac?"

"Always," she grins and then lets me have a moment, perhaps to ponder what that relationship might look like for me. "Hey, it's late. I'd better go."

I stand up with her, take her hand, and kiss the top of her palm. "Thank you for tonight."

"Take it easy. If she's right for you, she won't break your heart."

Why does Mrs. Mac remind me of Maya Angelou tonight? Before this, I always fancied her as the Swahili Terminator.

When we come out of our private table, the woman in yellow and her group is already gone. After making sure Mrs. Mac gets into her taxi safely, I walk back to the main house.

"Clayton!"

I halt my steps, knowing who that voice belongs to.

Donovan Fletcher strides toward me while gesturing to his gorgeous companion to turn back and follow his bodyguard, no doubt heading for her room—or their room.

"Clayton Hartley. What a surprise." Fletcher extends a handshake. "You should've introduced yourself to my associates earlier. We could've struck a deal."

"I thought you were here for a romantic dinner."

"I'm thinking outside the box, my friend. Why can't you have a business meeting at a resort full of the tallest animals in the world? We're aiming high."

"Too bad the giraffes have been asleep since sunset."

He releases a cynical chuckle. "How is it going with the Air Force?"

"We've reached the sky. Goodnight, Fletcher." I swing around, taking the long route to my room.

I took this vacation knowing that I would be alone, but this walk has once again exposed the deep crack inside me. I've stopped feeling the need to be with anyone since my last break-up, but now I wish I had someone in my arms.

I wish I had *her*.

No science can explain how I feel about that woman. But Mrs. Makena's wisdom might just help me make sense of it: *You're just waiting for someone who needs you.*

That stunning woman didn't say it in a word, but she yearned to tell me her story. Why didn't she tell it to her boyfriend? She needed another man to listen to it—and, dare I say, walk it with her.

Love may be the holy grail in every man's life. But bonds are formed in times of need, and strengths prevail when the going gets tough. If your partner doesn't need you, what's the point of holding her? Comforting her? Supporting her?

*As long as you need her equally.*

**5**

---

**ISABELLE**

I'm trembling. It's nothing new. When Don wants me in bed, I always tremble in disgust and hopelessness.

But tonight, something else is stirring me inside. My shivers aren't because of the anticipation of foul flesh and disgusting man breath, but I'm reacting to something unexpectedly thrilling.

That stranger in the dark came to me through some kind of godly intervention.

I've been without a man since Nando's death. And I've been without love for even longer. In fact, I've forgotten what care and love are since I lost my parents, my only protection. But that stranger's presence was soothing beyond belief, and our subsequent exchange of stares prompted me to let down my guard.

And that was the miracle that made me tremble—in excitement.

The dinner with those businessmen was a disgrace. They were there with their wives, but they couldn't stop leering at me. As Don had instructed, I only smiled, drank, ate, and talked when I was talked to. And as he had pre-empted, he hung on tight to me—those men could look, but I was his.

I left for the ladies' room for a reprieve rather than to relieve myself.

A reprieve I got, and then some.

When I opened the door, dreading to go back to the dinner that might've as well been a funeral, that chiseled, diamond-shape face appeared like a poster. Impossible, too perfect as far as my life is concerned. Then, when my eyes finally adjusted to the dim light, I saw the whole him—a man, standing like a safe house with its door open. The fire keeps the inside warm. A refuge that I desperately seek.

I could've returned to the bathroom to sort out my wardrobe malfunction, but I stayed on, unable to squash the urge to feel him and let him feel me. And I was rewarded. I even absorbed his breath when he placed his mouth so close to my ear. He smelt as a man should—the unidentifiable scent of himself, one that my brain associates with kindness and safety.

It was too intense for a first encounter—for both of us. While I did slightly better than him, he lost his nerve and never recovered.

Without knowing the man behind the face, if everything was black and white, he had all the hallmarks of a first-class Casanova. But eyes don't lie. And it goes both ways—eyes expose lies, and at the same time, the window to the soul reveals kindness too. When a man has affection, his eyes will always show.

His name is Clayton. I heard Don call him that before I was sent away. I can only speculate that he's a business acquaintance. He was alone when Don caught him, and I never got to see him at his table, so I had no idea who he was dining with.

But who is Clayton, really? Why the hell did I not blush and panic when he saw my breasts? Was it his soothing voice?

Perhaps.

But as vivid as the African sunset, it was his eyes. Before

anything else—before he spoke, before his fingers were on my skin—his eyes whispered *trust me*.

I place my hand on my chest, feeling my nipple behind the ivory silk kimono Don had chosen for me tonight.

"Clayton."

His name rides my tongue like a surfer on a wave.

I touch my neck at the spot where his fingertips landed when he tried to fix the strap of my dress. I'd be forgiven for saying he was a dream, but he wasn't.

I let him touch me.

I wanted him to touch me.

And his touch was comely and proper like it was meant to be.

When you're held hostage, you will take any reprieve you can get, and logic doesn't have to be part of the equation.

I wanted more of him—if only I could.

The door creaks open, and my nightmare enters like a rain cloud, overcoming the sunshine and rainbows that have been flourishing in my heart thanks to the stranger in the dark.

I sit on the bed, relinquishing any control as Don strips himself naked mechanically. He never shows that he wants me, but what he's going to do next will be driven by desires that know no boundaries.

He forces me down, then peels off my blonde wig, growling as he watches my real hair fanning on the pillow. It's his thing—the blonde-to-brunette transformation. It gets his prostate working, he claims.

Time to mask reality.

Where do I go tonight?

My default escape is to go back to Rio. It's an insane city, but I was happy there, a four-year-old with no care in the world.

My eyelids flutter shut when Don exposes my breasts.

Erasing him, I go back to Rio—Christmas twenty-five years ago.

Mom takes me shopping to buy a new dress. After choosing a sunflower-patterned sleeveless dress for church, she agrees to buy me another one. For whenever, she says. I can't believe it when she says yes to the Cinderella-like gown I pick. She even chooses a tiara for me. I can't wait to go home and stand in front of our Christmas tree, posing like a princess while Mom takes endless snaps with her new camera.

Mom's smile warms me, but the warmth soon turns to pain as I assess where I truly am—or rather, where Don is at. When I get to that part of my Rio story, when the force he imposes on me starts tearing my body, that filth is usually close to finishing.

But he's still on top of me, grunting like a pig. He must've taken the pill tonight, and I have to find another story to survive his assault.

*Another story*—because I don't want to go past the Christmas tree part. That's when the Rio tale takes a turn, and there is no happy ending.

I move my lips away from Don's ravaging mouth. His hand squashes my jaw to keep me in position. My breathing hitches, but that somehow numbs my senses. With that, I see Dad. He just comes home. Instead of inviting me to sit on his lap, he yells at Mom and me to pack everything.

My eyelids press hard, trying to stop the memory from playing on, while on the other side, I'm battling the current reality.

In the end, I choose reality, letting my senses take in the Reaper who's flaying me alive. This is no better than the ending of my Rio story, but I keep reminding myself that whatever I accept of this man, I do it to keep my son safe.

I pant, desperate for a new story because Don doesn't show any sign of stopping.

The dark.

Yes, that's where I'm going to go.

It's not completely dark, though, because I can see that stranger's face.

*Clayton.*

I gasp.

How did I even get here?

For once, the dark leads me to a safe place, and I'll stay for as long as I can. Clayton has got to be my story tonight because I won't survive reality this time.

Those pair of magnificent eyes...

I release a long, peaceful breath as I visualize them.

They're stunned to see me, but there's patience and graciousness in them. He touches me the way I long to be touched—like the man intends to please me because he cherishes me.

Clayton starts slow, savoring every inch of my skin when piece by piece, my clothing is peeled off. And once I'm naked, he lets his desire lead him. Firstly, he clutches my thighs to keep them parted, then he rubs the surface of my pussy, heightening my needs.

I moan.

"God, bitch!"

That voice shreds my heaven.

Worse still, I feel something crushing my neck.

"The fuck, Iz!" Don stares down at me.

What have I done?

"Is there anything you want to tell me?"

"No... why?" I gasp.

"Fuck, your cunt feels tight tonight."

I choke when he finally lets my throat loose. I then compose myself, shooting him a hungry look. "Because your cock is so damn hard."

He cracks a smooth smile like he's Don Juan. Perhaps no one ever said that to him, or I managed to convince him it was the truth. Soon he places his arm back on my throat.

"Don…" I barely huff out his name.

I shake under the ruthless force. Breathless, I dare myself to imagine Clayton. One more time. If I'm to take my last breath now, I want him to be on my mind.

But Don lets go.

Although I wish he hadn't. Because, to my horror, he ditches the condom. He hasn't come, and he has something in his mind. He had hinted at blowjobs before we left L.A., but this man isn't after my mouth.

"No! Don't you dare!" I yell and roll myself away from under his body.

He grabs me, and I kick him in the gut, then hurl myself off the bed. I crawl toward the door.

"Bitch!" He drags me by the leg, then tosses my body to the middle of the bed. He savagely falls on me, breaking my spirit like a giant hand snapping a toothpick.

I fight mindlessly.

"You're damaged goods," he growls to my ear, pinning me down. "I'm not gonna knock you up if that's what you're fretting about."

He takes time to appraise me. Apparently satisfied, he then runs his fingers along my cheek. "I've never seen you so scared. God… you're really scared. Even more scared than losing Raffi?"

"Put it on, Don."

"I know you've never been with another man, so you're clean. Are you afraid of me giving you an STD?" he jeers.

I can't beat him physically, but I've got to try something.

"I've never said no. I've kept my promise. Please let me have my way just for this one. Put it on."

"So this is how you beg?"

"Don, if you want to keep me as your whore, put it on." Those words corrode my tongue, but if they'll keep my dignity, so be it.

"Don't tell me what to do," he grumbles like a boar.

"When you fuck a whore, you always keep your condom on. Did you know that, Don? Whore—condom."

He sniggers, but that gets him thinking. Slowly he rises, his hand reaching into the bedside drawer. He rips open a new packet and then bustles to roll the rubber up his cock. I don't know how many ED pills he took. He's still disgustingly hard.

But this time, the end is in sight. He comes on his next thrust as he mumbles *fucknut* repeatedly.

When he's off me, I put on my nightgown. I won't sleep tonight. I can feel it in my crotch already. Worse still, while I anticipate him to fall asleep after such a marathon effort, he has another idea.

"Grind these!" He gives me a couple of white tablets. "Then mix it with water."

Under his scrutiny, I do as he says.

"Now drink it."

"Don... what's this?"

"Drink it!"

I'm about to throw it at him, but he reads me. He clutches the crystal glass in my hand while choking me once more. He forces the liquid into my throat. I gag, I try to spew it out, but at least half of it has already gone into my system.

Don releases me.

My lips quiver and my throat convulses, but I'm unable to get rid of what I've consumed.

"Good night, sleeping beauty."

He turns off the light, but my vision is messed up—it feels like a hundred flashlights are attacking my sight.

Eventually I pass out. When I rouse, whether intentionally or not, I feel myself thudding against the floor. I crawl, and to my surprise, I manage to reach the door without anyone stopping me.

**6**

---

## CLAYTON

*Stranger in the dark.*

That was what she called me. I don't know what to make of it, but coming out of her mouth, it sounded temptingly myste-rious—a call that describes our encounter affectionately. Far from other calls that had come my way, like the meaningless 'handsome,' 'prince charming,' or 'Captain Hot Butt.'

How on earth could Donovan Fletcher woo a woman like her? She's got class way above that stray cat's league.

I know she's his type—blonde, tall, slim—yet she's not his typical girlfriend. I'm contradicting myself. I might be clouded by jealousy, but what Mrs. Mac saw in the couple's interaction is real. They don't belong together.

'Mettle' is attached to my name, but dismally, I had also been called 'Clay the Player' in my younger days. I never cheated on my women, and despite the inglorious nickname, I never played with them, either. I simply had entertained and dated too many. It taught me a lesson, nonetheless—a lesson to see through people, particularly women.

The woman in yellow didn't appear to be the type who's happy to be in a man's arms simply for a good time or for his bank account. I was drawn to her, but she never tried to seduce me. At the same time, there was steel inside her, making her somewhat distant. But most of all, her eye contact was fierce, ridden with a story that seemingly no one would listen to. She appealed to me like she—

Needed me.

*Fuck...* she's really playing with my head.

Her smell still surrounds me, like she was here. No matter where I look, her eyes haunt me. And much as I don't want to be shallow, I can't get the vision of her boobs out of my mind.

How the hell am I supposed to sleep with my mind running like a jet? And there's nothing stealthy about it!

I sit up, rubbing my face. I'm spending the night in what looks like a honeymoon suite, with a four-posted bed, intricate curtains, and vases of roses. But sadly, the long white pillow next to me is the closest thing I have to a bride in this cold Kenyan night.

Unable to find anything else to do at two in the morning, I decide to annoy my brother. It's daytime in L.A., so he shouldn't be that annoyed.

Rob answers my call, "Clay, brother. Hang on a sec!" I then hear him telling his three-year-old son Graeme to keep playing on his own.

Not so long ago, that man's world revolved around water speed and design ratios. As if it happened overnight, nowadays, he's happy to swap them with talks of stroller efficiency and maternity yoga.

Graeme blabbers sulkily to his dad, insisting that Rob carry him.

"Hey, have I caught you at a bad time?" I say.

"No. No. It's fine." Judging by the rustling noise and the closeness of Graeme's voice, I think Rob has given in to his son's demand. Then he says to me, "Hey, I thought there was no cell reception where you are."

His voice reminds me so much of our father's. And he's got his Captain America look from him, too. Rob is fair and blonde, the opposite of me, although we both have similar blue eyes.

"I'm still in Nairobi."

"Seriously? Problem rebooking your flights?"

"I didn't even try."

"Why?"

"I kinda don't feel like cheering on the lions."

My big brother scoffs. "Since when do the African lions need cheering on? It sounds like you're the one who needs cheering up."

"Robson, my brother, tell me if this is a bad idea…" I stand by the window next to my bed, peeking at the empty courtyard below.

"It's a bad idea, Clay," Rob answers emphatically.

I chuckle. "Hey, you won't believe who I saw here at the Giraffe Manor."

"You're at the Giraffe Manor? Man! Matty is going to kill you!"

"He knows about this place?"

"Yeah."

Matty, our nine-year-old brother, whom people usually conclude is either Rob's or my son, has always dreamed about going to Africa. He was pretty disappointed that I didn't take him on this trip.

"Don't tell him, please. I'll take him next time."

"So, who did you see?"

"Donovan Fletcher."

"Fletcher Tech Donovan Fletcher?"

"Yeah. Adler has been warning me about him. He had dinner

with three Chinese guys, and it wasn't about importing live giraffes into the United States."

"Huh... new investors?"

"Maybe. Get Blake to snoop on him, will you? If his new venture will affect Hartley Marine, we've got to know now. If it's got something to do with national security, Adler will take care of it."

"Good idea."

"Talking about Hartley Marine, is everything okay?"

"Brother, you're on vacation. The only thing you need to worry about is the fact that you've used up your annual leave," Rob deadpans.

I feel better already.

"So, what was your bad idea?" Rob probes.

And just like that, my feeling better is canceled.

"Never mind," I say and change the conversation. "I had a date with Mrs. Mac tonight."

"Oh, bless her. How's she?"

"She's good. She said I'm waiting for someone who needs me."

"Clay, is that bad idea a woman?"

I sigh out my admission. After all, I do want to tell my brother about her.

In the background, I can hear Rob persuading his son to play on his own again. This time Graeme seems to listen to his dad. Rob then asks me, "Someone you met there?"

"Yes."

"A local?" my brother drawls.

"Fletcher's girlfriend."

"Fuck, Clay! That is a *terrible* idea!"

"It is, brother. I know."

"Since when did you lay eyes on someone else's girlfriend?"

"Don't say that. It sounds so bad."

"Because it is, Clay. Don't dig your own hole again. I don't think you can survive another relationship drama, or a love triangle for that matter."

My big brother has been through what I went through in the desolation department, although that lucky ex-frogman has found his soulmate. He deserves Amber—hell, they deserve each other—but heaven knows if I'll ever be so lucky.

"Turn away, do you hear me?" Rob warns me again.

"Yeah." I rub my chin.

"Graeme! Stay in this room," Rob calls his son. Then he talks to me again. "What are you gonna do tomorrow?"

"I don't know."

"You sound like the most miserable tourist in Africa."

"Perhaps."

"Forget about her. I never want you to get hurt again, Clay."

Rob is as good as a big brother can be. We are each other's rock, but mostly, he's been my rock. I should really listen to him.

I yawn.

"Am I boring you?"

"No, you've just put some senses into me." I stifle another yawn. "Hey, it's late here. I'm gonna crash. Say hello to Matty, Graeme and Amber."

"Good night, brother. Dream about giraffes and lions—I mean, not one eating the other."

I lie on my stomach, one ear firmly on the pillow—a position that usually gives me the best chance to fall asleep. And it seems to be working.

Until a thump ruins my way to slumber.

I sit up. Sometimes pillows and mattresses can amplify surrounding noises because of the vibration. It's an old building, and that could've been nothing more than a heavy step.

But something in me refuses to let it go.

"Ah, fuck it," I murmur and swing out of bed.

The hallway is quiet and looks like a resort is supposed to at this hour—except for a bare foot poking out of a corner.

"Jesus..."

As soon as I round the corner, I see a woman in her nightgown lying face down on the parquet floor.

I kneel next to her, flipping her body.

Jesus Christ! It's her! What the hell happened to her blonde hair?

More worryingly, what the hell happened to her neck? It's bruised, and she's breathing laboriously.

"Hey, can you hear me?" I tap her pale cheek, and she responds with painful moans.

I place her head on my lap. There's no one around, and for now, I'm going to keep it that way. She's barely dressed. I wouldn't want anyone else to see her like this.

"Clayton..." Her call is barely audible, but there's no mistake. She just said my name!

"Sweetheart, I'm going to carry you to my room, then I'll call a doctor, okay?" I squeeze her hand. She has soft skin, but I feel a couple of bumps on her right palm—two lines of stitches run from below her ring finger to the base of her thumb. Those must've been some deep cuts.

With her head resting on my chest, I fling her arm around my neck. It falls delicately, but to my surprise, she tightens her grip. As we move, she buries her face in between my pecs as if refusing to look at whatever we're passing.

"It's just me," I whisper as I carry her to my room. "The doctor will be here soon. You'll be okay."

She's as light as a feather, but I must admit it feels good to have her hanging on to me.

"Clayton..." she moans in her weakening state.

I rest my face on her crown. There's no sign of her iris scent, but I sense something else—the smell of woman that instantly tugs me into her. It's like a connection has just been restored, that brief connection we shared when we first locked eyes with each other.

At my room door, I use one thigh to steady her as I struggle to find my key. "We're almost there. Hang on."

As soon as I step in, she falls still.

"Sweetheart?" I wish I knew her name so I could call her—because she's stopped fucking breathing!

"No, no, no! Stay with me! Stay with me, damn it!"

I lay her on the rug.

"What did he do to you?" I mumble as my hands go to her breastbone, performing CPR. I blow life into her while listening for the tiniest clue that can tell me she's still alive.

A few seconds later, she gasps. Her eyes flutter open, but she's still struggling. I give her another lungful of air, helping her to get over the line so she can breathe by herself.

She chokes, followed by a few short breaths. She squeezes my hand as if trying to tell me that she's back

I huff a sigh of relief.

But then her body twitches, and she gags. I immediately turn her sideway. Water and saliva spill out of her mouth. There's a whiff of chemical in it. Looking at her bruise, I can only speculate that she's been drugged.

I move her to my bed and cover her.

"Sweetheart, what's your name? I'm going to call a doctor now, okay?"

She looks at me, dazed, but she shakes her head, snatching my hand when I'm about to reach for the phone.

I sit next to her. "I know you're scared, but you need a doctor. You may have been poisoned."

She keeps shaking her head.

"I won't leave you alone, I promise."

Slowly she releases her grip on me.

After two attempts, a man from guest services answers my call, and he tells me a doctor will come within the hour.

"How are you feeling?" I dab a wet towel on her lips, cleaning traces of her vomit. She touches her mouth as if trying to recall what has just happened. I can still taste her on my lips, and I hope she does mine—because as much as I kept her alive in that moment, I felt that life had just given me another chance.

The aftermath of my CPR must be hurting her that she's rubbing her chest now. As she lowers the cover, I realize I've ripped part of her gown. The neckline is already low, and its material is thin. With that rip, half of her chest is exposed.

"I'm sorry, I had to."

She looks around, and without warning, she gets up too fast. I fail to stop her.

"No, no, don't get up so soon." As I predicted, she loses her balance. I catch her mid-fall and then guide her back to bed. "Sit down."

I throw a blanket over her shoulders as she sits stiffly at the edge of the bed. Her fingers shake when I offer her a drink. She can't even hold the glass.

"What's... this?" she quavers

"It's just water. You need it." I hang on to the glass while she tries to grip it. "Let me," I murmur. She's too weak, so I take the glass up to her mouth, placing the brim in between her lips.

She only takes a sip.

"Drink some more," I encourage her.

She does, and after a couple of gulps, she moves her mouth away from the glass.

"What's your name?"

Her lips release a couple of last quavers, but she's not giving an answer.

"He did this to you?" I point at her neck. "And he drugged you?"

Her head falls limply, escaping my scrutiny.

"You don't have to go back to him. I'll help you."

"You don't understand," she finally breaks her silence.

"No, I don't. But this—" I point at her neck again. "Whatever happened between you and him, this is not okay. You stay here and let me deal with that man."

Her gaze holds me hostage. She's a Latina. Her natural brunette hair makes her even more stunning, trumping the torment on her face. And those blue eyes. Rob warned me to go the other way, but with her looking at me like this, how could I?

I still feel her resistance, but as her eyes gradually mellow, I know the distance she's set between us is shrinking.

Her plump lips slowly form a gape. They look rosier now, but the sensation of my mouth trembling over them is still fresh —when I thought I was losing her.

Then she falls onto me, latching a fierce hug around my waist. "Clayton." Her whisper-faint voice goes straight to my core.

I put my arms around her. It's like the pieces of my life finally fall into place. When something so profound strikes you, every organ in your body knows. It's no illusion. It's no game.

"Stay, please," I murmur as she sags in my embrace. "That man has no right—no right!"

She stays silent, but her body responds to my plea. Her fingers cling to my back as she straightens herself. Her shoulders curve toward mine, letting her breathing lead her body forward, erasing the slightest distance that's left between us. I hold her right there, because I never want us to part.

Before I can declare my intention to protect her, someone is at the door. It's not very often efficiency in this country makes an impression on me, and it comes as I'm starting to truly feel who the woman in my arms is. But her welfare is more important than my urge to keep comforting her.

"Mr. Hartley?" A deep voice calls.

"It must be the doctor," I murmur.

Her arms slide down my sides as she breaks our embrace.

A man in a suit stands by the door. There's no sign of his medical kit, only a phone in his hand.

"Where the hell is the doctor?" I stop the man from entering.

"He's on his way. I'm here because I've got an important phone call for the lady."

I turn around. Her face blanches even more than when she wasn't breathing.

"Mom!" I hear a boy's voice coming out of the speaker.

She has a son?

"Raffi!" She thrusts past me, as if she had leaped across the room in one go. She rushes toward the man who has let himself in and snatches the phone off him. "Raffi, are you okay? Where's Pippa?"

She grimaces in distress, pacing the length of the room.

"You'll be okay, Raffi. I'll be home soon."

The call ends when the man takes the phone back off her. He holds her, and she walks out with him as if she's been brainwashed.

I stand in their way. "You don't have to come back to him."

"Mr. Hartley, let us pass," the man insists.

But I stand my ground. He doesn't seem to be interested in picking a fight with me. He simply lets her take half a step closer to me.

She clutches the blanket I wrapped her with, covering her chest. "We never met. Got that?" Her ominous voice lances me. "If you come near me again, I'll report you to the Kenyan police. I'll tell them you tried to assault me."

"No, you won't!" I reach out my hand, trying to convince her to stay with me. But she pushes me with her two open palms.

Jesus! I've never been shoved like that by a woman before.

What happened to her calling my name? Not once, not twice. But three times!

And that fierce hug?

"I will!" she insists. "And trust me, you won't' want to mess with this country's judicial system."

I stay back—not because of her threat, but the reason behind it. Whatever it is, I should heed her warning. This isn't about me or her. It's about that boy on the call.

I watch on as she's ushered away by her minder, who looks more robot than human.

A sense of emptiness crawls over me, yet I feel an enormous weight. I'm never a sore loser, but witnessing her slipping away from my grasp has awakened my belligerence.

This is far from over!

## 7

## ISABELLE

Don's bodyguard drags me along the hallway.

"Is my son okay?" I ask him. I wish I could reach out for that phone in his pocket and call Raffi. "Tell me he's okay!"

But as usual, the man keeps his silence. He clutches my arm. I can barely balance myself, let alone run away, so I don't know why he looks so worried.

"You yourself have a son. I know that!" I persist. Someone else replaced him for a couple of days not so long ago, and Thomas told me his wife just gave birth to a boy. "What if Raffi was your son?"

The man doesn't change his expression, let alone his actions. He keeps dragging me as I flounder along the hall.

"How would his mother feel if he was snatched away from his home?"

With a growl of frustration, he mumbles, "Your son is just fine. Now shut up before I gag you."

It turns out I had come two floors down from Don's room. Did I walk? Run? Crawl? I can't remember a thing. And how the hell did I end up in Clayton's room? In his bed?

Don's bodyguard called him Mr. Hartley. So he's Clayton

Hartley—and in close-up, out of the dark, he was even more impressive. His thin pajama top didn't leave much to the imagination. The man has broad shoulders, a tight waist, and strong arms that can be gentle when called for. Yet, his eyes remain the part of him that holds his aura together.

Despite his anger at what Don has done to me, kindness oozed out of him like he had an abundance of it.

Never mind my initial Casanova verdict. He was a hero whom everyone would say 'doesn't exist.' But he was as real as my hell, although the only thing I have of him now is the blanket he gave me to keep myself decent.

In the short span of time between me knowing his existence and now, Clayton has saved me twice.

Without him as my story tonight, I would've broken when the Reaper imposed his savageness on me in bed. Then, in that brief moment of freedom—albeit a moment when I literally stopped breathing—the stranger in the dark brought me back to life.

If only I could stay with him just a while longer.

I passed out a couple of times then, but not all of the events that happened with Clayton escaped my consciousness.

As we approach Don's room, I think about how my savior's lips felt on mine. It wasn't a first-kiss kind of ferocity—he was simply trying to keep me alive. And from the sweat coating his face, his panting, and his tense eyes, I know he gave everything he had.

That man was exactly the safe house I had been imagining. Its door was wide open—too inviting that I gave in and entered. The fire was burning, warming the inside.

That was how I felt when I hugged him.

I might regret my audacity. But the moment called for it. I had to thank him for what he'd done, and I craved him like nothing else in my life. I had to feel him close. And in that moment, I felt him giving himself to me. Every muscle in his body was for me. Every inch of his skin was for me.

Every ounce of his heart was there on offer.

All that might've just been the embodiment of my helplessness. But it can't be denied that for the first time in my life, I felt safe with a man.

So, do I really regret my audacity? No. I regret nothing. Come what may, that moment will stay with me forever.

I could've gone one step further and accepted his offer. He said he didn't understand my situation, but he would help me. I believed him, and I had my hopes up.

If only Don didn't hold all the cards.

Hell, if only Don didn't hold that one crucial card—my son —I wouldn't have left that safe house that is the warm and alluring Clayton Hartley.

The creaking of the wooden door and the sleaze-smelling air I'm entering compel me to bow helplessly.

*Welcome back to the Reaper's lair.*

"There you are," Don speaks flatly.

I simply tighten the wrapping of the blanket, trying to savor the smell of Clayton to counter the foulness surrounding me.

He then asks his bodyguard, "Did you cancel the doctor?"

"Yes, sir."

Don rips the blanket off me. Disgust flies out of his eyes as if I'd just been fucked by a dozen men.

I wrap my arms across my chest. After being so close to Clayton, having experienced his hold and care, it just doesn't feel right for any other man to look at me, let alone touch me.

"I just needed fresh air," I reply.

It's true. Whatever drug he gave me, it suffocated me. I wouldn't be so stupid as to run away in my nightgown without a passport in a foreign country where the kidnapping of western citizens is a common occurrence.

"You choked me, Don. You fucking drugged me!"

"I'm allowed to do anything to you."

"Where did you take Raffi?"

"Oh, he's fine. He's just being a pussy," Don sneers. "He's fed, and he's done his homework. You've got nothing to worry about."

"You took him to a stranger's place, for god's sake!" I bark. "Take him back to Pippa's."

"Of course, darling. When we land in L.A. Right now, though, he's my insurance policy, and he's staying where he is."

"I won't go anywhere."

"Of course not. I just want to... rattle you a little." He curves his lips sideway.

"I've never broken my promise. I just went out for fresh air," I tell him again.

"Yeah. I believe you."

"At least let me talk to Raffi, please. Just to assure him."

He bites dead skin off his lower lip, ruminating on my plea. "All right." He gestures to his man to dial a number. I can immediately hear my son's voice in the background while a man mumbles to answer the call.

"Put my son on!" I demand as soon as Don passes me the phone.

The man on the line simply lets out a heavy breath, and then I hear Raffi. "Mom... I don't know where I am. I'm scared."

"You're safe, baby. Uncle Don just moved you to his friend's place. Don't be scared."

"When are you coming home?"

"Soon. Do as you're told, and you'll be fine."

"Are you okay, Mom?"

My boy is always thinking of me. He's little, and his fear is justified, but he never loses his protective instinct. Before that fateful night in New York, he'd never stopped talking about being a big brother, but it was just not meant to be.

"I'm fine, baby," I reply. "You take care of yourself, okay? I'll see you soon. I love you."

"I love you too, Mom."

Don's bodyguard snatches the phone off me, and Don coos. "How lovely!"

He hasn't mentioned anything about Clayton, but his forbidding gaze tells me he has a plan. He then hands me another nightgown with a dirty smile. "Wash up."

There's nothing I can do now. Clayton is a grown man. He'll be able to handle Don if the Reaper decides to go after him. All I need right now is to get back to L.A. and be with my son.

8

———

## CLAYTON

If you ask a Giraffe Manor guest about their highlight, it's got to be the breakfast.

There was no Mrs. Mac accompanying me the next morning, but it was far from a lone experience. A pair of giraffes took turns to poke their heads through the windows, enjoying their share of fruits and other treats from my table.

Unfortunately, though, there was no sign of the woman in yellow, or Fletcher. So I was itching to go home that day, but air travel dramas seemed to follow me like a heat-seeking missile. The flight was canceled twice—leaving me wishing I had flown my private jet from Cali.

Three days after my intended return date, I finally land in L.A.—half awake, half jetlagged. Out of all souvenirs that I got from Kenya, the only one I care about is a bracelet. It's of jade hearts with links made of sterling silver, which I found in my bed at the manor. It's all I have to remember her by.

Knowing I'll go stir-crazy staying in my house, after taking a long shower, I drive to Newport.

It's not business as usual at the Hartley Marine HQ. As soon as I step in, I'm greeted by tense shoulders and tight jaws. This is not how I left the office before Kenya.

"Where's Rob?" I ask his assistant.

"IT," Kylie answers in her thick Irish accent. She's been Rob's right-hand woman since Hartley Marine started. She's known for being an office clown, and I don't know what tricks she's been training my new assistant, but today, there's no sign of her usual I'm-in-control face.

"What's going on?"

"Cyberattacks."

"Shit…" I rush to the IT quarter. Rob is standing next to the lead software engineer's desk. "The fuck is going on?"

"First, DDOS, then injection attempts," my brother answers. "We've quashed the attacks, though. At least for now."

"Do we know who's responsible?"

"Likely from China," the lead software engineer voices his verdict. "From the code pattern, I bet they're aiming at VesslScope."

The statement hits my head like a baton.

Rob motions me to follow him to his room. Worries clutter his Captain America face. Although with his neatly-combed hair and impeccable suit, he still looks every part the boss of Hartley Marine.

He sinks inside his executive chair. "Anything you wanted to tell me?"

I take a seat in front of him. "You think this has got something to do with Nairobi?"

"You tell me."

"She came to me," I admit.

"Clay, all you had to do was to turn away."

"I couldn't, Rob. Fletcher strangled her, and he drugged her! Even if she was someone else, and I wasn't attracted to her, I wouldn't have turned away. The woman needed help."

Rob's head bobs up and down as if trying to convince himself I did the right thing. "Well, this could be a coincidence, but something is happening. Stay vigilant."

"Anything from Blake?" I ask about our PI.

Rob hands me a folder. "The three Chinese men dining with Fletcher are from a Shanghai-based infrastructure development company. They're partnering with various African organizations to build roads, railways, and airports. Fletcher is aiming to win a contract for supplying traffic control systems."

I read the report and frown at the last paragraph. "Military? Is that Fletcher's final aim?"

"Looks like. Military systems for the major hubs in Africa."

That stray cat uttered 'radar' a couple of times in his dinner conversation with those men. It's not farfetched that he was referring to installations on a large scale.

"I'll relay the news to Adler. He'll deal with the CIA, and no doubt they'll find more. Africa may just be the start."

"So, what's happening between you and her?" My big brother can't hide his concern.

"She didn't want anything to do with me. She went back to him. They were gone before I woke up."

"And?"

He knows me too well—it's not the end of it.

"I've asked Blake to dig into her records."

I'm desperate to find her again. When a man loses his treasure, he's got to keep seeking. She is that—a treasure. Because everything fell into place when I was with her, despite her resistance. Or maybe it's because she resisted that my urge to find her compounds.

Most of all, though, I want to help her find her freedom.

Rob draws a breath. I can almost see red lights and exclamation marks floating around his head. Yet he refrains from telling me to stop pursuing her.

I continue, "I haven't got much so far, but her name is Isabella Martin."

"That name doesn't mean anything to me, but okay," Rob says tentatively.

"I've asked Blake to find whatever there is to know about her. I'm doing everything I can to protect myself, Rob."

Even though logic can't explain how I feel, it doesn't mean my head has stopped working. I've learned my lesson, and I'm not going to rely on my judgment alone.

My 'Clay the Player' days had taught me to err on the side of caution rather than regret. Not all of my breakups were nasty, but those that left a scar are enough to condition me to adopt a 'guilty until proven innocent' approach. When your assets are in the billions, angels can turn into thieves, and sweethearts into cheats. I'd been amazed by how good an actor some women could be, tricking me flawlessly even after we'd spent intimate time together—and I don't mean one-night stands.

My assessment of Isabella may still be right, that she's a woman with no money motives and that she isn't the type who uses men for her advantage. But no matter how much I've learned, a master manipulator might still outsmart me. So, while I unintentionally extended my vacation, our PI has been gaining intel on her.

Rob softens. "I guess that's why Blake has been looking for you like you were his new master."

"Has he?"

"She's that beautiful, huh?" My brother appraises me.

"Fletcher doesn't deserve her." I purse my lips in frustration.

"No woman deserves Fletcher."

"Especially her," I emphasize. "She's not like the others, Rob." I pause, contemplating my own statement. "I know every new girlfriend is different. But—I wasn't looking. I wasn't even thinking of love or whatever it is. I was with Mrs. Mac, for goodness' sake!"

Rob chuckles.

"She just came to me," I tell him as plainly as I can.

My brother casts me a helpless stare, like a teacher who knows their student will do whatever they're set to do no matter how much advice has been given.

Then a text message arrives from Blake. "Hey, I've gotta go."

Rob gets up and pats my shoulder. "Well, good to have you back, brother. But don't let me lose you."

"No. You won't."

My last breakup almost killed my spirit. Although I kept it airtight inside me, my big brother knew. To say that I was distracted at work because of it is an understatement. I was useless. But one good thing happened during that spirit-breaking period. A miracle. Separate from my struggle, my brother found the love of his life, Amber-Rose, who is now his wife and the mother of his child—soon children.

I hope this is my time, although no doubt it's going to be a turbulent flight.

Simon Blake is already waiting inside my office, donning a country look with his navy cotton shirt and chinos. Far from the notorious description of Alaskan men, 'the odds are good, but the goods are odd,' the former trooper is a dark, entrancing guy who proves that a man can have it all—brawn, brain, moves and mental toughness.

Back in his twenties, he was apparently scouted by a well-known modeling agency. Lucky for us, he shunned the promise of glitz and glamor. Now, the private investigator has worked exclusively for Hartley Marine for almost a decade. His job description is pretty loose. As long as something needs investigating, be it business or personal, he's our man.

Despite his sharp face and toned physique, the guy has mastered the art of not standing out in the crowd. He's a chameleon, always looking the part, whether in a tuxedo or a t-shirt and jeans, blending in with a crowd of high-flying socialites or street criminals.

"What have you got?"

"Isabella Martin." He swipes an envelope across to me.

I open it. The first thing that comes out of it is a photo.

My knees go weak.

Look at her and her magnificent eyes. She's wearing a green dress, plunging at the front, tight everywhere else. The background indicates the photo was taken at a hospital fundraising event.

"Twenty-nine years old, born in Rio. She immigrated to the US with her parents just before she turned five and spent most of her adult life in New York. She now lives in Los Angeles, working as a pediatric nurse in the UCLA Children's hospital, and also a second-year student at the university's med school."

"Criminal records?"

"She's clean."

"What's her tie with Fletcher?"

"Now, that's where things get interesting."

That makes my gut twist.

Blake explains, "It goes back to her parents. Her father got into trouble with a Brazilian mob. He leaked information to the authorities after a couple of boys were murdered. Guilty conscience, I guess."

This is bad news. Right now, my conscience tries to weigh in with my decision to pursue her. There's a fine line between the past and the present. If I want Isabella in my life, her whole timeline will tangle with mine—no exception. Am I prepared?

Blake surveys me. He knows what I'm thinking.

"Go on," I urge.

"He was a brilliant computer scientist, but nobody could protect him in his own country—nobody even tried. Fletcher senior got to know him prior to the debacle. In fact, Isabella's mother was a capable programmer too. So they were like Fletcher Tech's golden geese. Senior helped the family immigrate to the US. Illegally at first, but eventually the whole family were naturalized."

"So you think Isabella is paying his father's debt?"

"Maybe. Or she may simply be in love with Donovan Fletcher."

I growl under my throat. What does he know? I refuse to entertain his provocation, so I continue. "Is that Brazilian mob still at large?"

"He's in jail for life, no parole."

"Where are her parents now?"

"Deceased."

"Suspicious circumstances?"

"Her mother died of pneumonia complications, but her father—well, maybe, maybe not. Heart failure from a drug overdose."

Not a happy past, and her present may be even worse. "She has a son. Raffi. Is he Fletcher's?"

"No. Rafael Martin is her boyfriend's son."

"Her boyfriend? As in... another boyfriend?"

"Technically, Donovan Fletcher isn't her boyfriend. The Don has got a girlfriend, an 'official' one," Blake explains. "He was good friends with Martin's boyfriend, though."

"So, where's her boyfriend?"

"Dead. Car accident."

I nod with a sigh.

Blake adds, "It didn't sound suspicious, but after his death, Fletcher acquired his company. This was three years ago.

Fletcher was the tech king on the West Coast, and Martin's boyfriend's company was based on the East Coast—pretty successful, too."

"Total domination?" I comment.

He shrugs, as if reminding me that anything can happen with Fletcher.

"Is Raffi her only child?"

"Yes."

I swivel my chair. "So Isabella is Fletcher's mistress?"

"Unfortunately, yes."

*Bastard.* That stray cat really doesn't deserve her!

"Any other boyfriends that I should worry about?"

"No. She's never been with anyone else since her boyfriend's death. I guess she's devoted to her son."

"Is Fletcher abusing Raffi?"

That disturbs Blake's neutral face. "What makes you think so?"

"That night at the manor, she got a call from her son. He was in distress."

"So far, I haven't found anything that points to Fletcher hurting the boy. But it doesn't mean he hasn't—I just haven't focused my investigation on that. Martin and her son live in a house owned by Fletcher, but as far as I know, The Don is hardly there—too busy with his work and his girlfriend, too, I guess. So I don't see a reason why he would want to abuse the boy."

"Maybe Fletcher simply uses her son to keep her obedient." I tap my fingers together, recalling how she changed that night after the call. "Why didn't Fletcher take his girlfriend to Kenya?"

"His last known official girlfriend is a daughter of a Wallstreet financier. I heard their relationship is on the rocks."

"You do know everything, don't you?"

"Well, I don't know what's on your mind."

"I think you do."

"Love?"

"Not quite there, but close to," I confess. "Is Fletcher putting surveillance on her?"

"Yeah. This man," Blake reveals, pulling out a photo from the envelope. It's the guy who fetched her from my room that night.

"Twenty-four-seven?"

"Not really. She often has night or early morning shifts at the hospital. The man usually skips those hours. Even during her normal-hour shifts, sometimes he's assigned somewhere else. Fletcher isn't exactly overflowed with cash at the moment. So he's starting to cut corners."

"He always cuts corners," I banter.

"I guess you're right."

"You've got other photos of her?"

"Just look inside, Clay."

I empty the contents of the envelope.

My God. There she is, with her son. Their eyes are almost identical, and so are their smiles. She's wearing the jade bracelet there.

My heart is engulfed with desire that I don't recognize. It's hasty, it's rash, and it's uncontainable.

"She's a stunner," Blake comments. "By the way, she usually goes by Isabelle, or Iz."

Isabelle. I like that.

"Anyone following me?"

"I don't think so."

"The next time she's not watched, call me."

"Okay." Blake gets up and pats me on the shoulder. It seems that everyone is wishing me good luck today.

"Am I making a mistake?"

Blake waves me goodbye.

I fling my head back, brooding over what I'm about to get myself into.

My eyes gradually lower, catching sight of the photo lying on the table. The mother and son stare back at me and something shifts in my chest. The crevasse has opened up again, deeper than ever. Isabelle and her son aren't going to mend the crack, but for once, I don't feel the need to hide it.

9

---

## ISABELLE

My shift was supposed to end a couple of hours ago. But into my tenth hour, dealing with staff shortage, I'm still on my feet, trying to be a nurse, a mother, a counselor, and a peacekeeper—often at once.

But I wouldn't have it any other way.

Winter is always a busy time in the ER—severe flu and other respiratory illnesses being the most common culprits. But right now, the two-year-old girl crying in the temporary bed in front of me is battling with a different kind of emergency.

"She could've swallowed anything!" the mother cries.

"How long ago was it?" I ask.

"Probably an hour or two. Where's the doctor?" she insists.

"The doctor will be here soon. In the meantime, we'll take some X-rays." I'm really hoping the girl hasn't ingested something seriously dangerous, like batteries or sharp objects.

An orderly helps me wheel the bed to the X-ray room.

"I want a doctor to see my daughter," the mother shouts, grabbing my arm to stop me from moving further.

I face this every day—parents or patients dismissing me just because I'm a nurse. My colleagues and I are highly trained for these kinds of situations, but unfortunately, a lot of people think we're just PAs to the doctors.

"Mrs. Chelsea, I understand." I try to calm her down. "The doctor will be here soon. But right now—"

The little girl convulses. We haven't even left the hallway.

"What's happening?" The woman howls, trying to handle her daughter.

"Mrs. Chelsea, please step aside," I assert. The girl can't even cry anymore. I'm towering way above her—sometimes, being tall can be a challenge when your patients are kids—but she keeps extending her arms to me as if adamant that she'll need to be as high as me.

Ignoring the mother's curses, I take the little girl in my arms, resting her on my shoulder, stroking her back to help her vomit. Her stomach contracts, her mouth gapes, and—

I've never been so happy to have vomit spewed all over my clothes. And soon, what she had ingested becomes clear.

The girl spits out whatever is left in her mouth, half crying, but she looks at me with wide eyes, and her face has brightened up already.

"It's okay, sweetheart. You've done well." I wipe her mouth.

"What have we here?" A doctor finally takes over, to the delight of the mother. He studies an object among what looks to be the little girl's dinner or breakfast. "Is that a pom-pom?"

The mother drops her stare to the wet clump of fluff. "Oh, my God!" She shakes her head in disbelief. "Yes. It's from her sock."

"We'll take X-rays anyway," the doctor states. "As a precaution, in case there's something else in her system."

The mother peers at my puke-covered uniform. "Thank you. Sorry for earlier. I was just panicking."

"It's okay. Your daughter will be all right. That's all that matters."

Another nurse joins us, and my supervisor gestures to me to wrap up my shift.

Every case in the ER is tense, some stay with me for a long time, but the girl has made a different kind of impression on me. Not the impression of her puke on my uniform, but the way she held me and the way she almost begged for me when she lay in bed convulsing. She was beautiful and courageous.

That's how I imagine baby Caili would be.

I head to the staff room and take a shower. My feet are aching, and my heart is still pumping. In saying that, the ten hours have passed in a flash, and I'm looking forward to lounging around at home until I need to pick up Raffi in the afternoon.

Yet, I dread to think about what the day has in store for me. Because once I'm out of the hospital, I'm in prison.

Don has officially broken up with his girlfriend following our Kenya trip, and that's bad news for me. He has been demanding more of me, and time spent with him never flashes by—it drags on like a never-ending nightmare, and I'm exhausted.

On the bright side, though, the more he expects my presence, the more slack he gives me when we're not together. And the brightest side of all, his attention on Raffi seems to have waned.

Despite having almost no time for myself, somehow, I still manage to keep Clayton Hartley on my mind. Our story is over, but more than two weeks after our insane encounter, I've failed to unlearn him.

The stranger in the dark turns out to be one of America's richest men, co-owning a yachting empire. He officially became California's most eligible bachelor after the previous title holder, his older brother Robson, got married three years ago.

I don't know how God works, but the Hartley brothers are

certainly blessed with premium genes that ninety-nine percent of the earth's male population can only dream of. Better still, they're apparently well-known philanthropists.

Go figure.

According to gossip, though, the younger Hartley has dated some of the most beautiful women on the planet. The fact that he was prepared to defend me makes me wonder what he saw in me.

"What was that about?" Pippa approaches me as I open my locker. "Another angry mother?"

"A mother in panic, that was all," I reply. "Her daughter swallowed a pom-pom from her sock."

Pippa shakes her head.

With my controlled life, I don't have many friends. Pippa and I are as close as I can be to having a good friend. Still, she doesn't know half of my story. I met her at nursing school back in New York, and we were reunited when she moved to L.A. last year following her meeting with her current boyfriend. She's three years younger than me, and the world is still her oyster.

"Hey, you finishing up?" She leans on my locker door, tucking her black bob hair behind her ear.

"Yeah. What's up?"

"Um... can I please ask you for a favor?" Her begging face presents itself. "Pretty please?"

"Fire away." I owe her for a lot of unexpected babysitting nights, especially when the Reaper dragged me to Kenya. She even had to deal with the trauma of Raffi being taken away following that night at the Giraffe Manor, and I had to lie to my teeth that Don's man was my uncle and there had been a misunderstanding.

"My honey butter biscuit is leaving for Switzerland this afternoon. I won't see him again for a month. Would you?" Her cherry lips stay puckered.

"Of course, I'll cover you. What time does your shift finish?"

"Midday. So, you can still leave in time to pick up Raffi and drive him to basketball."

I acknowledge her preparedness. She knows my son's schedule as well as I do.

"Go! I'll cover you."

Pippa hugs me. "Thank you, Gizzy Belle."

I smirk. Sometimes people call me 'Gizzebelle' because of my disproportionately long legs—although I'm nowhere as quick a gazelle nor am I graceful.

She's about to leave but quickly stops. "Oh, this also means I need my car today. Sorry. You should get the garage to hurry up and fix your wheels."

"Yeah. I've been calling them every day!" I fret. "Don't worry about me. I'll take the bus."

I put on a fresh uniform and go back to the floor. My supervisor agrees to Pippa's shift swap, but she insists I take my break now.

As I make my way out, I receive a call from Thomas. Now, this guy is one that I can call my best friend, although we don't really spend as much time as besties should. We don't take road trips together or create troubles in town. Thanks to Don, we limit our interactions to avoid suspicion.

Everything always goes back to Don.

"Hey, you wanna get breakfast?" Thomas proposes.

"Where are you?"

"I'm just around the corner."

"What happened to being enslaved in Fletcher's sweatshop?"

"The Don is away. Back in Kenya."

"Oh? I did not know that."

"The contract with Nairobi Airport is in jeopardy, so he's trying to put out fires at the moment."

I'm hoping this means I'll get some reprieve.

"Maybe not breakfast. How about coffee?"

"Sure. We can go to the gym together later, too, if you're up for it."

"You're on! I miss kicking your ass," I chuckle. "I'll see you soon."

I've been on graveyard shifts for most of my working career, but stepping into the morning sun—after leaving the outside world in the dark of night—is one of life's little joys that never grows old.

I stretch my arms as I amble toward the café where I'm meeting my bestie.

"Isabelle!"

The call halts my breathing. Has my long shift taken a toll on me, and I'm now hearing things?

"Isabelle, wait up!"

That smooth, masculine voice is as real as the noise of L.A. morning traffic.

Every muscle in my body tightens—with excitement, doubt, and delight. It feels like I've just found a lost friend—or in this case, stranger—who never had a chance to hear what I wanted to say.

Just around the corner, a man wearing a checkered shirt saunters along as if he has forever to get to me. The stretch of sidewalk hedges obscures my view of him waist-down, but once he's out in the open, I know this isn't going to be an ordinary morning.

So this is Clayton Hartley in moderation—his look between pajamas and a suit. Despite the abruptness of his presence and the boldness of his guts, I give myself permission to indulge in him.

"Nurse Isabelle," he calls as he increases his pace.

His hips sway. I nudge myself away from his path, observing

him from an angle. At this time, I've only one objective—to relish the sight of his perky, jeans-clad ass.

Having him standing in front of me now, I tuck my fervor deep inside my pocket. I haven't forgotten what's at stake—the reason why I rejected him that night at the manor.

"Are you out of your mind?" I tell him off.

"Good morning." A full grin stretches across his face. His dental assets compete with the sun shining from behind him, taking his *buenos días* greeting to the next level.

"I told you not to come near me."

"That was Kenya. We're in the land of the free now, and I have faith in this country's judicial system."

"What do you want?"

He dips into his shirt pocket and takes out a jewelry box.

I release a silent gape.

A small chuckle leaves his mouth. "No, I'm not about to propose to you." He's clearly enjoying my nervousness. He then opens the box, presenting it to me.

"Oh..." I wind back my fake annoyance. I thought I'd lost that bracelet forever. "Thank you."

"Allow me." He takes my hand gently.

As if he had practiced it many times, he elegantly encircles my bracelet around my wrist and clips it securely—maintaining a light contact between his fingertips and my skin. The man is trying to wake up my craving. He almost succeeds!

I beam, relieved that the heart of jade is back where it belongs. "This bracelet means a lot to me. So thank you."

"You're welcome," he replies, unleashing his charm with his eyes. "One of the chains broke, so I sent it for repair and cleaning. It's good as new."

I admire the green stones. I've never seen them so bright.

"Thank you, I really appreciate it. But I have to go."

I gnaw my lower lip because I can't say anything more, and he doesn't seem to be in a hurry to leave me alone.

But soon, something catches my attention—and it's not part of his body.

That motorbike travels awfully close to the sidewalk. It's zooming in at speed, although it doesn't make much noise. Right behind Clayton, the rider lifts one hand off the handlebar, picking up something from his jacket pocket.

That man has a fucking knife!

"No!" I scream, hurling myself to cover Clayton. I don't know how the hell I've done it, but I manage to knock the six-foot-three hunk down onto the pavement—me cocooning him like I was his mother.

"Whoa... Isabelle!" Even the man himself seems baffled.

I'm almost five-foot-nine, but against his mass which is mostly muscle, this gazelle shouldn't have had a chance against the full-grown grizzly.

"Are you okay?" I pat him all over with my trembling hands, trying to find any sign of injury. God forbid, I won't forgive myself if anything happens to him because of me.

"Whoa, whoa, are *you* okay?" His thick brows arch low as he tightens his gaze. He's so close to me I can feel his breath.

What would I do to have those lips on mine again? Not to wake me up from unconsciousness, but to free me from the invisible prison Don has sentenced me to?

And more?

I escape his touch to stretch my neck, trying to catch where the motorbike is going. But it has disappeared among the traffic.

Clayton examines me.

"I'm fine!" I get up, and so does he.

"What's wrong?"

I squint, planting my focus far into the road. "That man..." I murmur, recalling the disturbing scene that must've just lasted for seconds.

That man's hand... his glove was disturbed when he drew his hand off his jacket pocket. I saw some sort of green tattoo on the top of his palm.

I draw a shuddering breath. "He had a knife."

I inspect myself, back and front, hoping to see a cut on me or my clothes. Not that I'm worried about being wounded, I want to prove that motorcycle man was real.

Dismally, not even a scratch!

Clayton is left baffled as he watches my angsty move. I say to him, "Clayton, listen. You can't see me anymore."

"Do you think someone was trying to kill me?"

"I don't know! It could be just a warning. It could be just Don's game. But I'm not about to test it!"

"Did you see his face?"

"No, he was wearing a dark helmet."

"Isabelle, I can take care of myself—"

"Did you see him coming at you?" I challenge his confidence. "Did you?"

"No, but I would've reacted. And he could've been just—"

"Don't say he could've been just a thief!"

His groan affirms that was what he was thinking. "Isabelle, I'm here because I chose to see you, and I'm not afraid of Donovan Fletcher!"

"You should be. He's watching."

"Let him."

I cast him an astute gaze. "What do you know about Donovan Fletcher?"

"Enough to know that his attention is not on you at the moment."

So he knows Don's movements. But it doesn't give me any

comfort. I'm still engrossed in the vision of that man with a green tattoo.

Clayton seems to know what's playing on my mind. "That rogue biker wanted to get *me*, Isabelle. Not you. Fletcher wants me. He's always wanted me."

"And what do you know about me?" Waves crash against my ribcage, anticipating a big reveal that will push me into a corner.

"I know about your parents and the Fletcher family. You don't owe Donovan anything."

So he has dug into my past? I glance at my bracelet. He even knew to put it on my left arm, above my watch. My tongue is eager to curse at him, but a part of me wants him to know who I am.

"You think with your money and power, you can buy me?" I serve him a sinister look.

"Isabelle, I'm not trying to buy you!" His wide eyes tell me he thinks I'm unbelievable. Whether he knows my true or fabricated past remains to be seen. "Yes, money and power help my cause, but I've got a heart, too. I genuinely want to get that bastard out of your life. You know damn well he's not a good man!"

"You want to wage war against Fletcher?"

"Oh, we're already at war."

My phone beeps. It's Thomas, and he's waiting for me.

"I'm sorry, I must go."

"Isabelle—"

"We've never met," I clip out.

"Donovan Fletcher is threatening you with something. Don't try to deny it, don't try to protect him."

"We've never met. Got that?"

"It's too late for that."

"You know nothing about me, Mr. Hartley. Please, for the sake of all of us, leave me alone."

My heart tells me to trust him, just like I trusted him to touch me and fix my dress in that dim space between a reprieve and a torturous night. But I can't afford to be foolish. Don's attention might not be on me at the moment, but it won't be long before he watches me like a hawk again.

I sidestep Clayton. My feet are aching, not because of my shift, but because the whole weight of me is screaming at them to stop and turn back to the man who was once my savior and comfort.

**10**

---

**CLAYTON**

My head is filled with images of Isabelle, and I have no hope of erasing them. I thought I'd been in enough kinds of romantic pickles that the rest of my life would feel like a walk in the park, but this—wanting a woman who wants nothing to do with me— is turning me upside down, shaking me to the core.

If that's not enough, what I know about women has been flung out the window.

Hell, *she* protected me.

If that man on the motorbike was really gunning for me, I could've taken him down. I would've felt him against me, and I have no doubt my instinct would've kicked in.

But it didn't matter what I could've done. The fact remains that Isabelle put herself in harm's way—*for me.*

At that moment, I was at the receiving end of her incredible determination. She shielded me with all she had—or what she didn't have. I mean, where did she get that strength from? She was a wrecking ball when she shoved me. I guess desperation can drive anyone to possess power beyond their normal limits. But did I mean that much to her?

A woman could spend day and night trying to convince me

of her loyalty and undying love, but what Isabelle did in that split second was more than what any other woman is capable of showing in her lifetime.

And that's more than enough reason for me to love her.

Maybe love is too strong a word and too soon a feeling. But what I have for her is more than lust, infatuation, or impulse. It's coming from a deep place; it's grounding me as much as it's lifting me up.

Day one of my quest has certainly given me a glimpse of what's to come.

So, Fletcher sent me a warning, just like the cyberattacks on Hartley Marine. Cheap! And I'm not going to be intimidated. I'll deal with that son of a bitch—I will—but firstly, I have to win Isabelle's trust. I've got to convince her that from now on, *I* will protect her.

But how?

Her son.

He's the key to her. It crossed my mind to bring him up in our conversation earlier—to somehow convince her that I had what it took to protect him too. But putting a child in the spotlight while his mother feels cornered is never a good idea. And I should know—even though her son is the key, he's not a pawn.

So how the hell am I going to earn her trust?

Two coffees after being left bewildered by her, I still don't have the answer—not even a plan on how I can see her again. God have mercy, I'm still trying to figure out what to make of my day!

As I continue driving aimlessly around L.A., the best I can do now is to wash myself in nostalgia. Even though the moment that buoys me only happened hours ago, starting from me waking up at five in the morning to see her.

When Blake told me last night that Donovan Fletcher and his men were off to Kenya again, I decided today was the day I was going to pay her a visit. I never anticipated the ending, but the start certainly warmed me.

I was going to say hello to her as soon as I arrived, but seeing her tending to those young people with a smile and a reassuring voice no matter the situation—I stood mesmerized, helplessly watching from a corner. Ten minutes turned into an hour and an hour into two.

How she cared for her last patient at the time—a little girl who was in all sorts of pain—summed up what Isabelle is made of. Behind the glamor she exuded when I first met her, beyond the helplessness when she was lying unconscious in my arms, she's a gentle, caring human whom the world needs. Isabelle comforted the girl, despite her mother screaming at her and despite the girl unleashing a hefty pool of vomit all over her.

Call me a stalker, but the connection between her and me is real, and my intention is just. I want her, but if she doesn't want to do anything with me, I'll be happy to let her go—as long as she's free from Fletcher's control. Seeing firsthand how much love she has in her, I'm more adamant that I've got to do it.

It's apparent now. My biggest challenge is not Fletcher himself but Isabelle's resistance. I must admit a little bit of my ego was dented this morning. Very rarely women rejected me— if at all. Isabelle has done it twice now. I haven't forgotten her firm push and her threat at the manor that night when I tried to convince her to stay. Then, in front of the hospital this morning, once again, she insisted on her 'we've never met' stance. She even called me Mr. Hartley at the end of our conversation.

Am I embarrassing myself?

Perhaps.

Maybe because she's in Fletcher's grip that my desire to have her is raging like a dam has burst in my heart. But truly, past the noise, my feelings for Isabelle surpass any of my experiences with other women.

Am I wasting my time?

I don't believe so.

I won't be able to live with myself knowing she's giving up her life because of that stray cat.

Isabelle Martin—she's too good a person to be with such a rotten man.

I'm a man of logic. But I give myself permission to rely on fervent faith this time. Bringing her into my life is the path I've got to take.

Still driving around in circles, I'm back at the hospital complex. Perhaps I need another coffee. Maybe she's still there, and I'll apologize to her and ask how I can make it up to her. But I give it a pass.

Traffic piles up in front of me. At this time, the route to Newport is always a pain in the ass. I ask Siri to check my messages, and so far, there doesn't seem to be anything urgent for me to handle. I hope my assistant is holding the fort back at the HQ because I'm not up for more drama today.

As I stop myself from thinking about Isabelle again, my mind goes to Fletcher and *his* drama. I try to conjure up why his deal with the Kenya Airports Authority fell through. Perhaps General Adler did contact the CIA, and Fletcher's so-called new investors smelled trouble and got cold feet. From what my PI Blake has gathered, there are signs that the Chinese developer Fletcher Tech is looking to partner with is going to withdraw from Africa altogether.

I'm not sure if Fletcher knows this yet. So far, the chaos he's trying to put in order seems to confine to the Nairobi Airport contract only. I guess time will tell.

As my stomach starts asking me, 'what's for lunch,' an incoming call flashes on my dashboard screen.

Seriously? Matty's school?

"Mr. Hartley." I recognize the principal's voice. "Matty isn't feeling well. We need you to pick him up immediately."

"Is he okay?" I ask nervously.

"Yes. It's just a headache, and we've given him acetaminophen, but your brother insists that you pick him up."

"I'll be there soon."

This isn't the first time Matty complains about a headache to get away from a lesson he loathes. But I suspend my suspicion. If he's really ill, I won't hesitate to take him to the hospital and ask for Isabelle.

## 11

## ISABELLE

"Babe?" Thomas greets me with a frown. "Why are you looking like Heath Ledger?"

Am I really looking like a scary clown?

"Sorry I'm late. Had to deal with a difficult parent," I huff out my lie.

His hooded eyes follow me as I put my handbag on the café chair and sit down. It's a January day. L.A. is overcast, around fifty degrees, and slightly breezy. Yet, hot flashes rise in my chest. The walk between here and where I left Clayton felt like a walk of survival.

"Oh! You found your bracelet." Thomas studies my wrist under the light. "How shiny!"

"I found it and got it clean. It was in my bag all along."

"See! What did I tell you? You just forgot where you put it. All those tears!"

"I know!"

I came home from Kenya whimpering like a child and I blamed it for losing my bracelet. It was true, I was terribly sad about it, but the pent-up stress, confusion and fear just broke me. Moreover, seeing my son again—after apparently being hidden in Sacramento while I was away—just made me realize how close I was to losing him. When we picked him up, Raffi stopped talking to Don, and somehow that rattled the man. I guess the boy was the only one who hadn't seen him as an enemy, and when that changed—miraculously—the Reaper showed remorse. His stance softened as he tried to win my son back. When talks failed, he put forth a different kind of peace offering.

Don gave us a couple of VIP tickets to an L.A. Clippers game with backstage access. My son worships that team like they were gods. For the sake of Raffi, I accepted Don's offer and let him be the hero. I even let him tell my son lies. About how wonderful our trip to Kenya was, that he'd take him there next time, and that he transferred him to Sacramento that night for protection because some bad guy wanted to hurt him.

Had I stayed with Clayton that night, defying Don, things would've turned out differently. So I made the right choice. Because I swear, I wouldn't be able to live without Raffi.

After fidgeting for a few seconds, Thomas sits tall. He then leans forward. "Hey, I think it's time for us to start preparing our getaway."

It's taken us too long, but his statement terrifies me.

He had his twenty-first birthday just last week. The guy has a brilliant mind. If only someone else had spotted his talent. He won a programming contest that Fletcher Tech organized despite having no formal qualification. He was sixteen, broke, and lost. He had a rap sheet like a small-time thief but got tangled with the big guys—enticing enough for Don to intervene and take control of his life.

"Tell me," I urge.

"Look, I know someone in the immigration who knows someone who can give us new passports."

"Thomas, I don't want to mess with immigration."

"They'll be legit passports issued by the Department of State, but the records will be like ghost records."

I shake my head.

He presses, "It's the only way we can get out of here, out of Don's reach."

"Where to? We'll be forever fugitives!"

"We can go to Thailand or Cambodia."

I puff. "You may be able to survive living there. You'll even love living there!" He's told me his ideal place to live is by an exotic beach where coconut cocktails are served in abundance, and people speak a foreign language. "But can you imagine me and Raffi?"

"I would've said the Caymans or Virgin Islands, but Don has got contacts there. Even in Mexico or Brazil."

The last country makes my skin itch all over. My parents and I left Brazil in the middle of the night, not knowing if we'd arrive in the United States alive. We were packed like cattle, transported in a windowless cart, sitting on a floor coated in human excrement.

"No. I wouldn't go near South America," I maintain.

"You can make it temporary. You can always move to Singapore or even Australia," he argues further. "Don is distracted at the moment. It's a perfect time to make our move."

I agree about the timing, but his plan is even worse than maintaining the status quo.

"Iz, we can't just sit around here. Our chance will never come if we don't create it. Raffi is ten. He still thinks Don is a friend. It won't be long before that bastard uses him, just like he did me. Think about it!"

His compelling argument is stopped by a waiter taking my order.

Thoughts are competing in my head, like race cars making crazy laps, overtaking each other. I lean back, pressing my lips together. After a few seconds of silence, I slant forward, challenging him, "What happened to plan A?"

"What plan A?"

"Finding a non-dick who's richer and more powerful than Don?"

"You know that was just a joke."

"What if it's not?"

His eagle eyes raise to me. "Iz? What happened in Nairobi?"

"I met someone."

"Wow!" He looks into his coffee cup like it's a crystal ball. "Wow..."

I wait for him to say something else, but he falls quiet.

I continue, "He and Don know each other, though."

"God... who's he?"

My eyes wander around the room as if someone might be overhearing us, then I whisper, "His name is Clayton Hartley."

Thomas' jaw drops.

All this time, I've felt that he's grown up too quick. He's built up muscle, and he grooms himself well, making him as swoonworthy as Shawn Mendes. But that look when he heard Clayton's name—that was his teenage-babe look.

"Hey, you know him?" I try to take my bestie out of his silly state.

"California's most eligible bachelor? Dolce and Gabbana's muse? My God, Iz! Why the hell did you never tell me that you met Clayton Hartley?"

"It was nothing."

"Nothing?" His mouth gapes. "Babe, he's my soulmate!"

I shake my head in a laugh. "He was outside the hospital waiting for me just now."

"Fuck... is this real?"

"What do you know about him?"

"The Hartleys are certainly richer than Don, and arguably more powerful. How much does Clayton know about you?"

"He knew about my parents and Don senior."

"And Nando?"

"I don't know how much he knows about him."

"Hmm... I don't think he's dug that deep yet. Your Isabelli Martins records are supposed to be invisible."

"He called me Isabelle—so whether he knew me as Isabelli Martins or Isabella Martin, I really don't know. But maybe you're right. He wouldn't be pursuing me if he knew that I killed my boyfriend in cold blood, would he?"

"Ergh... don't say that cold-blooded thing. It really gives me the creeps. It was self-defense!"

"Well, that cold blood thing was what Don put in my records."

"I know. I know. Just don't say it out loud," he protests. "So, knowing this new fact, plan A is a brilliant idea then."

"I told Hartley to piss off, though."

"What?"

I put my face in my hands, a dull headache forming behind my brow. The vision of that green-tattooed hand clutching a knife behind Clayton flashes at me. "You know what, forget about it. I don't want to use him."

"*Use* him? You're in love with him, babe." He lifts my chin up.

I escape his scrutiny. "No, I'm not!"

"You friggin' are!" he teases. "So once Clayton has sorted Don out, you two will ride into the sunset—with me, of course. A perfect happily-ever-after! How will you use him exactly?"

"I was besotted. I can't deny it. But in love? I don't know..."

"Come on, Iz!"

"What if I'm in love with him only because of his looks and because he was there when I was wrecked? What if when everything goes back to normal, I find that I'm not attracted to him after all?"

"How could you not be attracted to Clayton Hartley?"

"Really, if anything happens to him, I won't forgive myself."

"You care about him that much?"

"I do."

"So, in other words—you're in love with him?"

"I'm not in love. I'm not in anything other than Don's control."

"Babe, the Hartley brothers are rich and powerful because they're smart and able," Thomas argues. "If anyone can put Don in his place, it'll be Clayton Hartley."

"Everything is happening so fast. I—I'm not sure about this. I don't want to bring trouble to his family. Or even danger."

"Isabelli Martins," Thomas says in his stoic voice. "Robson Hartley was a Navy SEAL, and your Clayton was a US Air Force fighter pilot. They ate danger for breakfast. Probably still do."

*My* Clayton?

I release a long, helpless huff. That man is certainly capable of defending himself. My fear of that knife-wielding biker is probably unfounded. But I still don't feel right about getting close to him just so that he can save me from the Grim Reaper.

"I don't want him to do everything for me, and then—what happens if I'm really, really not in love with him? And even if I am, love isn't everything."

"How? Gah! You're impossible!"

"What if he ends up being a pain in the ass?" I sip my coffee, mundanely watching people pacing the street so I don't have to front Thomas, who's evidently thinking that I'm being absurd.

But there's nothing absurd about my logic.

Behind his formidable physique, Clayton Hartley is a man, a human being who breathes, thinks, and feels.

I straighten myself and resolve, "No. Forget about it! Forget about plan A—*and* forget about your Thailand idea. Well, maybe do it for yourself. I'll support you, but not for me and Raffi."

This conversation has had my heart beating painfully—a terrible, guilty kind of pain. I need my freedom. Clayton Hartley may be my ticket out. He may be powerful, but he isn't a tool. He's too good a man to be used like that.

## 12

## CLAYTON

"What's up with you?" Matty asks when we walk out of the principal's office.

"Well, pal, it's me who should ask you that."

My baby brother is as healthy as an ox. He pretended that he wasn't feeling well so he could escape his athletics session this afternoon. I'm sure the boy just wanted to stay home playing Minecraft.

"Please don't tell Rob," the little mischief begs—putting on his most pitiful expression. His beady eyes remind me of *Shrek*'s Puss in Boots.

Following our parents' deaths, Rob has been one hell of a brother, and father, to Matty. After he and Amber got married, Matty has been living with me full time, although the boy spends time with them most weekends. Needless to say, Rob wouldn't have let Matty get away this easy. I know I'm being soft, but I understand what it's like with school sometimes.

"Don't do that again, okay? You can't just pretend that you're not feeling well. Sometimes you've got to do things that you don't want to."

"Athletics is no good for anyone! You run, you jump, then

you're pooped," Matty justifies. He uses his fingers to comb his light brown hair, which is overdue for a cut.

"It's good for your stamina."

"Meh!" He looks out the window, escaping my stare. After sensing that I'm not going to go on about his friskiness, he repeats his earlier question, "So, what's up with you?"

"Nothing. Why?"

"You look so nervous."

Luckily we're stopping at a red light so I can see my brother's expression. He looks dead serious, as if something is really wrong with me. I reply, "Nervous? No. I was just worried about you."

"Really?"

"Of course I worry about you, pal. If it was true that you fell sick, it could be anything. I would've scrambled to get you to the hospital."

Matty reaches out his hand, placing it on top of mine. "Sorry."

"It's okay. Now that you skipped class, you have to do something for me."

"What is that?"

"We're going to get a healthy lunch."

"Eww... salad?" He puts on his bunny face, tapping his teeth in quick succession. "I'd rather go back to school!"

"Okay!" I step on the brake, ready to make a U-turn.

"Clay! Nooo!"

I toss him a 'gotcha' smile and then drive on. "We'll get some quesadillas, but with a lot of greens."

"Fried chicken?"

"Nope. Fish."

As I promise my brother, I give him lots of vegies for his lunch. He still has the guts to bargain with me. But when I say I'll tell Rob about what he did, he licks his plate clean.

"Good boy, Matty. That wasn't so hard now, was it?"

"So where are we going?"

"Home."

"I thought you could take me to Disneyland."

"Matty!" I raise my voice. I really should stop being soft with this boy. "You will stay home and do your homework. And I need to do work, too."

He purses his lips.

Ten minutes out, I spot something. In fact, it's two people who are too familiar for me to ignore. Isabelle is waiting at a bus stop with a boy who I recognize as Raffi. He's dribbling a ball, and every now and then, he glances far away, as if trying to see if a bus is coming.

Noticing I'm driving toward them, Matty asks, "Who are they?"

"She's a friend. And that's her son."

Matty smiles at me.

"Be nice, okay?" I don't know what he has in his mind with that cheeky grin.

I pull over. She instinctively stands in front of Raffi as if someone would get out of this car and snatch her boy away. She may not be able to see me behind the tinted windows, but... Is she that scared of being watched?

As I wind down the passenger window, I observe her. Her beauty never fades, but look at those tired eyes. She wasn't like that this morning. Perhaps the long day has finally taken a toll on her. When was the last time she slept?

"Hi there," I call.

"Hey," Isabelle responds hesitantly. "How's it going?"

"Yeah. Good. Can I drive you somewhere?"

The wind is picking up, blowing her hair against her face. "No, we're fine."

Raffi whispers to her, apparently asking who I am—and she answers discreetly, 'a friend.'

"I really don't mind," I insist. I then look up at the sky. "It may rain soon."

"Mom..." Raffi looks at her impatiently. I know he's begging her to accept my offer.

"The bus ain't coming," I try to convince her.

"Mom, please..."

"Are you on the way to practice?" I eye the ball in Raffi's hand.

"Yes," he answers.

"Come, I'll drive you. The least I can do." I send a smile her way, offering my apology. I think she's still annoyed about this morning.

"Hi, I'm Matthew," my little brother joins in. Damn, the boy looks so sweet like that. Is he trying to be my wingman?

He doesn't know it, but my baby brother has had prior experience with that.

"I'm Clayton's brother," Matty continues. "Nice to meet you."

The usual reaction when people hear that statement is apparent on Isabelle's face. The age gap between us usually makes people think Matty is my son.

As always, though, my baby brother has the answer. "And I'm his real brother, not stepbrother or secret brother."

Isabelle releases a chuckle. "I guess you got asked that a lot, huh? I'm Isabelle. Nice to meet you too."

"Come with us," Matty persuades.

Look at her! She's melting all over.

"Mom! Please..." her son begs.

"Okay," she relents, and the boy grins in relief.

"Hi, I'm Raffi," the boy introduces himself to me, and then to Matty.

"I'm Clayton. Great to meet you, Raffi," I welcome him.

Raffi is quick to dive into the back seat of my red Porsche, beaming. In the meantime, his mom surveys the traffic, pondering, clearly uncomfortable—slightly frustrated, I must say.

Having the Martins on board my car perks me up like a refreshing morning shower. On the other hand, meeting Raffi for the first time fills me with pride and a sense of responsibility. It's not just about me and Isabelle. Whatever I do, it'll be for him too. I can't muck this up.

"So, what position do you play, Raffi?" I ask.

"I'm point guard."

"Nice. Me too."

"You play?" Raffi asks.

"Sure do. So where's your club?"

"Culver City."

"Ah, I know where it is. What's the club's name..." I think hard. "Um—don't say it, um—Wolf Club?"

"Wolfpack!" Raffi responds.

"Yes, yes. That's it. West Coast National Champions?"

"You got it, Clayton!" Raffi can't hide his enthusiasm.

"Great club."

Raffi spins the ball in his hand as Matty watches on. My brother seems impressed.

"I'm joining the Junior Clippers next year," Raffi announces.

"That's awesome, man!"

"Clay is a Lakers' fan, though," Matty interjects, looking proud that he can be part of the conversation. "You'll be in trouble, Raffi."

Raffi giggles. "Well, Clayton, we'll just have to agree to disagree when the time comes."

Isabelle glances back at her son as if not believing what she's just heard.

"So, how did you know my mom?" Raffi asks with a cautious tone.

"Raffi!" Isabelle blushes.

Not surprisingly, the boy has questions about me and his mom.

"We met in Kenya," I answer before Isabelle can say anything further.

"Do you know Uncle Don?"

"Who?" I gulp, not expecting to hear the name. But I reply, "No."

"Raffi, why don't you talk to Matthew?" Isabelle suggests, clearly trying to prevent her son from finding out anything more about her and me.

"Hey, you wanna see something?" Matty says. I realize he's showing his stitches to Raffi.

"It's a long scar!" Raffi follows Matty's finger trailing the stitches. "What happened?"

"Car accident."

The accident is behind him now, but from time to time, it still makes him think of our parents.

The slow traffic is allowing me to keep glancing at the kids through the rearview mirror.

Raffi looks at Matty, concerned. "Does it still hurt?" he takes my brother's arm very gently. Like mother like son? And do I see a hint of a big brother instinct?

"No, it doesn't hurt anymore," Matty declares cheerfully. It sounds like he's trusting Raffi. "It did hurt a lot back then, though. My teddy bear got crushed too in the accident, but Amber fixed him."

"Who's Amber?"

"I have another brother. Amber is his wife. She's a bear doctor. People call her Amber the Mender. She's cool."

"Does your teddy have a name?"

"Bjork."

"Cool. I have a toy dog. I love him. His name is Mr. Oreo because he's black. I've had him since I was three."

"Same! My mom got me Bjork when I was three!" Matty says as if he's just found a soul brother.

"Cool! I know I'm supposed to have grown up and stuff, but Mr. Oreo is still with me," Raffi admits with a degree of embarrassment.

"I still have Bjork too. Although I don't bring him everywhere now."

I turn to Isabelle. "How old is Raffi?"

"Ten."

"Ten? He's so tall!" But I shouldn't be surprised. I don't know what his father looked like, but I'd like to think the boy has his mother's genes.

A proud smile hangs on her face as if wiping her tiredness. "I guess he's tall for a boy his age. How about Matthew?"

"Ah, call him Matty. He's nine."

"He's a smart nine-year-old."

Yep, and a troublemaker.

"Clayton, what do you do?" Raffi's attention is back on me.

"Raffi!" warns Isabelle.

"It's okay. I run a yacht business with my older brother."

"You're a sailor?"

"Well, my brother is more of a sailor. He was in the Navy. I used to be in the Air Force."

Once again, I glance in the rearview mirror.

Raffi's eyes flare with eagerness. "You're a pilot?"

"Yeah."

"Why do you run a yacht business, then?" Raffi probes.

"It's just how we set up the company."

"Wow... your brother is way cool," Raffi tells Matty.

"He is. He flies our plane when we go on holiday."

"That's way cool!"

We arrive at the club with five minutes to spare. Some kids gather around us, and some watch us from a distance.

"Thanks for the ride, Clayton." Raffi waves at me.

"Thanks, *Mr. Hartley*," Isabelle corrects his son.

"Come on, Clayton is fine," I counter.

"Dime, ma man!" Raffi joins his friends, and they do a hip-hoppy greeting. "Spreadin' the jam?"

"Rafael Rebel!" the boy called Dime replies. He then admires my car from where he's standing. "That's a bomb!"

Isabelle rolls her eyes. "That boy's name is Eric. I don't know why they call him Dime," she explains to me in amusement. "And I swear, my son doesn't talk like that at home."

"Boys gotta do what boys gotta do," I respond.

"I'll see you soon," Isabelle says to Raffi as he and his friends troop along to the court. She then readies herself to leave my car.

"Wait, can I drop you off somewhere? Or, I'm happy to wait with you so I can drive you two home."

"Um, don't bother. I'll take the bus home."

"Are you trying to minimize your carbon footprint?"

She glares at me playfully. "If I wanted to reduce my carbon footprint, I'd live in Nepal. My car is at the shop. They told me they were struggling to order the spare parts."

"Ah, yeah. The supply chain is in disarray at the moment."

"Tell me about it," she says. "Well, thanks for the ride. I appreciate it." She then swivels and hops out.

"Wait." I jump out and round the car to get to her. "Your car —it isn't under repair because of driver's negligence, is it?"

She chuckles, looking so irresistible I just want to take her waist and pull her to me.

I extend my key to her. "Take my car."

"What?" Her eyes pop wide.

"You can have it until you have yours back."

She stares at my hand. "I... I can't!"

"Of course you can. Please. Take it."

"How about you?"

"We're big boys. We'll sort out our own transport."

She twists her mouth. "Well…"

"I know you want to," I persist, putting the key in her hand.

Her fingers furl halfway, touching my palm—and they stay there. For the first time I feel her warmth. She then mutters, "I… I don't know what to say."

"You don't have to say anything," I reply evenly, although the sensation from our hand contact is spurring me to do more than just talk.

In the end, we both withdraw at the same time. But before she completely retracts her hand, I give her my name card. "Just in case," I say.

She accepts it then raises her eyes to me. "Okay. Thank you."

"Matty, come on."

I rest my arm on his shoulder as we stalk off, giving Isabelle a few backward glances while calling for a taxi.

"She looks happy," Matty comments when our ride arrives.

"Yeah, she's happy. You're a good wingman."

Matty squints at me. "What is that?"

"Like a partner but cooler."

"What do you mean?" he probes.

"You helped me talk to Isabelle. You helped me make her happy," I explain. "Just like what you did for Amber and Rob."

If it wasn't for him, Rob wouldn't have met Amber. Following a car crash that killed our parents and seriously injured Matty, the boy had a hard time coping. We all did, but being only six at the time, compounded by his injuries, the loss completely crushed Matty. Amber played a big part in his recovery—and it all started with Matty's teddy bear.

It's a love story for the ages, and it will be a hard act to follow.

"Oh, that!" Matty seems to have an a-ha moment. "Do you love Isabelle?"

"Maybe, pal."

Matty looks at the time. "Don't you have work to do?" The boy is surely keeping me honest.

"Later."

"You're lying, Clay!"

"Hey, I'm not!"

"You have time for her but not for me?"

"We're not going to Disneyland if that's what you're thinking. You want me to spend time with you? Fine, I'll stay with you while you're doing your homework."

He flashes me his bunny grin—but this time, it soon turns into a grimace. "Clay..." His voice is almost inaudible.

"What's the matter?"

"When you marry Isabelle, can I still live with you?"

"Hey... Matty." I hug him. "Isabelle is just a friend. I'm not marrying her."

Yet.

I add, "If I get married—whoever she is—you can live with me for as long as you want."

"Promise?"

I give my baby brother a pat on the shoulder, assuring him that I'll never abandon him.

We gave Matty a choice when Rob and Amber got married, even though the couple was happy for Matty to keep living with them. In the end, Matty chose to move in with me of his own accord.

I ask him, "Did you regret leaving Rob's place?"

"No. I like living with you. Rob can sometimes be too intense."

The day has gone better than expected. I had anticipated Isabelle's resistance, but I'm making headway. Whatever

Fletcher is doing to her, I'm going to kick his ass out of her life. It doesn't take a scientist to figure out a woman in distress, no matter how much she tries to hide it. And it doesn't take a Simon Blake to know what kind of man Donovan Fletcher is.

My hand is still on Matty's shoulder, but the warmth from Isabelle's touch still lingers. My heart is beating for her. But dare I give it to her?

## 13

## ISABELLE

Once you go Porsche, you won't look at another. When they say it's 'driving at its finest'—you'd better believe it.

Unfortunately, tonight, I did have to look back. Very reluctantly.

After my shift, I handed over the sleek red baby to Clayton's driver. The man himself had an urgent meeting with the Air Force, apparently, but he sent a pack of chocolates to apologize for his absence.

So our story isn't completely over. Barely a month ago, that man was simply a fantasy, an escape from enduring Don's savagery. Now, as real life takes over, I can't believe that he's actually still in it.

Clayton's little brother. Even without knowing his name, I would've known that boy was a Hartley—*that* Hartley family. I've dealt with children almost all my life—starting from babysitting when I was a teenager, to a stint as a kindergarten teacher, to now. I've always been fascinated by family resemblance in kids. If I mix Robson's eyes with Clayton's nose and lips, that would be Matthew.

I must admit, seeing Clayton interacting with his hybrid

Hartley mini-me, I felt all warm and fuzzy, like I had found a father figure for Raffi—and a manly figure for myself. Crazy, but it happened.

Thomas notices me pulling into my driveway. He stands by the door, goofily jeering at my Toyota.

"Don't say anything," I warn.

"I'd say it's great that you have your car back, but gee... I must say, I'm sorry," Thomas consoles me, slightly exaggerating. "Hey, maybe one day you'll get to own one. Maybe a wedding present?"

"Shut up!" I grumble. I found out that Clayton's set of wheels is a limited edition that costs about two-hundred-eighty grand. But I guess it's nothing to him, considering some of his yachts sell for more than half a billion dollars a pop.

"Hi, Mom," Raffi greets me, donning the same look as Thomas when he sees my car.

"Done your homework?" I move his attention away from my chariot, which has just changed back into a pumpkin.

"Yes."

I turn to Thomas. "You didn't do it for him, did you?" I know Raffi had a big math homework.

"I just helped," Thomas reveals in a neutral tone.

My car lock beeps, and he laughs at me. "You still bother to lock that old junk?"

"Hey, it's mine, and it still works fine."

"Whatever!"

"Did you see Clayton today?" asks Raffi.

"No. He had a meeting."

"Clayton looks like a kind man. I like him."

"You do?"

"He's not like Dad."

I cross my arms. "Raffi, don't start comparing people."

"He was nice to Matty, and to me. So definitely, he's not like Dad. If I could choose my own father, I'd choose him."

"Raffi…"

"He's a pilot, he plays basketball, and he's kind. He let you borrow his car without knowing how you drive."

"Hey, I'm a good driver."

Raffi shrugs.

"I am!"

"She is, Raffi," Thomas supports me. "You should've seen how my mother used to drive. Now, *she* was a terrible driver."

"Anyway." I put my arm around Raffi. "Don't think about Dad anymore, okay? What he did to you was wrong. But we have a new life now."

"Sorry." Raffi kisses me on the cheek. "I love you, Mom."

"Love you too."

"I'll see you later!" Raffi heads upstairs to his room.

Thomas and I stay in the living room. I open a bottle of wine for us and the box of chocolates from Clayton.

"Do you know when Don is coming back?"

"Tomorrow," Thomas confirms, chewing on the chocolate. "Gee, this is good. And he'll be coming home pissed."

Jesus, I'm not looking forward to it.

"Any chance he's falling in love again soon?"

"Who do you think I am? His matchmaking agent?" Thomas then leans back, his hand pressing at his temple.

"What's wrong with you today?" I query his unusual moodiness.

"Randy wants us to get back together."

"No, not again!" I make my stance. "Don't entertain him. He left you, and you weren't yourself when you were with him."

"I know."

"You'll find someone else. A man who isn't in it just for the good time. You want someone who takes care of you as much as you do him."

"With Don shadowing me, I'm not that optimistic. We really need—"

A pair of headlights shine into the room.

"Shit! He's early!" I grumble at the disaster arriving at my gate.

Don enters without even knocking. "Thomas, leave us," he orders.

"I'll be fine," I tell my bestie. "Go."

Thomas' prediction on Don was spot on. The bastard is angry. Once we're alone, he throws himself at me and starts touching me.

"Not here, Don! Raffi is upstairs."

"You smell different," he sneers as his foul breath smears my face.

"Just tell me what you want."

"What happens to 'Welcome back, Don. How are you, Don?' Huh?"

"Since when do you expect niceties from me?"

He chuckles cunningly. After studying me like there's an entire island missing from a map, he sneers, "Clayton Hartley."

My gut tightens, and my fingers tingle with nervousness. Don already knows about Clayton and me, but for him to say his name in front of me, I fear for what's to come.

"What about him?" I deadpan.

"Sit down."

I do as he says, and he keeps his vicious eyes on me. He lets silence linger, playing with my psyche. Finally, he discloses his demand, "I want you to pursue him. Or at least entertain his pursuit."

"Why?"

"I need something from him, and you'll get it for me."

"And what is that?"

"I'll let you know. For now, gain his trust if you haven't already. Then, when the time comes, I don't care what you do. Seduce him, drag him to Dungeon East, put a knife to his balls—I don't care, as long as you get me what I need."

I stay quiet.

"Bear his child if you must."

I pant in anger.

He laughs. "We both know that's not gonna happen. Well, didn't the doctors say so? But hey, you can fantasize."

"Fuck you!"

"Watch your mouth!"

I let his warning pass me by. "Once I get what you want from Hartley, set Raffi and me free."

"Negotiating, are we?"

"Stop giving me shit, Don. You've been controlling me because you have all the cards. But Hartley isn't stupid. I need to know that I'll get something out of it, and only then will I try my best. No half measures."

"You know what will happen if you betray me, don't you? Have you seen what I included in your criminal record? I mean, Isabelli Martins' record? The NYPD uses my software, Iz. I have full access to it. I can do anything to it."

"It was self-defense."

"You've never wanted to challenge me all this time, for a good reason. If you're smart, you'll keep it that way."

I know he has the power to manipulate anything, and Raffi is still the main card he's holding. But what he's asking of me is almost beyond my capability.

"You killed your boyfriend in cold blood. And it's only me who can keep that record buried."

"What will I get out of it, Don?"

"Well, you'll get to fuck that lover boy, of course."

"You think that's all I want?"

"You don't fool me, Iz."

"I'll do it for you. I'll get what you want. On two conditions."

"Two now?" he sneers.

"You need me on this. You know no one else can get you what I can off Hartley. After you've got what you want, let Raffi and me go. And stop fucking me—starting tonight. Those are the carrots that I'm asking for."

Don grabs my jaw, but I whip my face away from him. For the first time, I feel I have some kind of leverage.

He grunts but doesn't attempt to grab me again. "Your carrot is Raffi. And this." He slaps a stack of bills onto the coffee table. "Buy something nice. You'll need it."

Two thousand bucks. Perhaps I can buy a new sexy dress or lingerie to bring Clayton to his knees. But I'm going to save it for something else.

**14**

———

## CLAYTON

Love is a game. And after trying every trick, I've learned that the most effective is to stay out of it. Never make yourself a contestant, let alone a contender.

But Isabella Martin has torn away my rule book.

Mrs. Makena said I was waiting for someone who needed me. *Needs me*—not needy.

I'm ready to extend my hand to whoever needs my help—for love or not. But there's something about Isabelle that changes my outlook on relationships. When I think of her, I feel that I'm more than just a man, like she's part of my life purpose.

So far, she doesn't want my protection. She doesn't want anything to do with me. So, Mrs. Mac was right again when she said I had to work for it.

"What did Adler say?" Rob checks on the outcome of my meeting with the general.

"We're ready for round two," I reply, looking around my office as if it was a foreign space. "Hey, what do you think of putting more fresh flowers around our HQ?"

"Fresh flowers? We've already got fresh flowers."

"Maybe more roses? Lilies?"

"If anything, we need anemones around here."

"Oh, come on, Rob!" I look around my office again. "At least in this room."

"Well, it'll come out of your budget." Rob nudges his chair closer to me. "Come on, focus! What else did Adler say?"

"All right," I claim. "The Air Force is still finalizing the date. The fully built Snow Leopard will be ready then, no more a prototype. One of their combat pilots is going to do the full testing. We have four candidates, and I'm going to train them first before the whole shebang begins."

"We've doubled the image quality and resolution of the N.E.O., and the transmission speed is like nothing Adler has ever seen," Rob affirms.

"That's way cool."

Rob examines me. "You sound like Matty."

"Oh... he got that from Raffi."

"Who?"

"Isabelle's son."

"Matty has met her son?"

"Well, we drove past them when they were waiting for a bus that never came."

Rob smirks. "Metro Bus—or the lack of it—made your day? Doesn't happen very often."

"Good things happen to good people," I argue, swiveling my chair. "Hey, how's the new engineer going? What's his name, Stefan Boss?" The 300-footer and 700-footer Pentela Next-Gen are complex machines with advanced AI embedded in most of their components. With the development of Hartley Marine's upcoming collection falling behind schedule, we need an extra brain to support our lead marine engineer, Rocky, and his current team.

"He's friggin' great," Rob responds. "But Rocky has been calling him an imposter. I really hope they can get along."

When it comes to marine engineering, Rocky is our alpha. He's Hartley's first engineer and has been with us since it was just Rob and our father running the business. Perhaps it just takes time for those two to warm up to each other.

Rob adds, "And the newbie's family name doesn't help, I guess."

"Stefan Boss, who's not quite the boss," I quip. "Well, they're big boys. They'll sort it out. What we need to worry about is our system security."

Rob moves his gaze to blink up at the ceiling. I know I've just reminded him of something he'd rather forget. "The DDOS and injection attacks seem to have stopped now. Well, they never stop, but nothing like that day," he remarks.

"Thank God for that." I share his sentiment. I'll never want that day to repeat again—what a welcome it was after my first vacation in... I don't even know how long! "But it's a matter of time before it happens again. Our team is still too small. Why is it so damn hard to find a good cyber engineer?"

"Every company is headhunting cyber engineers. It's dog-eat-dog. But we're still keeping at it."

"By the way, our old friend Neo is back," I tell Rob about one of our best customers, Prince Yiannis-Andreas of Greece. "He's coming next week to take a look at the Pentela Next-Gen. He sounded keen to check out the floor plans too."

"About time! Where has he been?"

"His divorce got nasty. He lost a lot of money for the settlement," I explain.

"And he thought it was going to be forever," Rob scoffs.

I bow my head. "Well, talking about forever... well, not forever yet. But I'm going to ask Isabelle out."

My brother leans back, his steepled hands covering his mouth.

I fiddle with the silver ball on my desk. He gave it to me years ago, and it's still my favorite office toy. When it spins, it creates an optical illusion like the ball was cascading into my desk.

With that illusion, my mind starts to picture what my war against Donovan Fletcher will look like. The anatomy somehow resembles that of the legend of Troy. I'm Paris, who stole Helen from the king of Sparta—and Rob is the big brother Hector who was left to defend the kingdom.

The possible consequences of my endeavor won't be an illusion. Rob has every right to veto my decision if he wants to.

"I know you have your reservations," I say to Rob, who's looking at the same spinning ball. "But I'll beat myself up if I don't give it a go."

"It's your life, Clay. I can't tell you what to do."

"I'll be careful."

His big-brother look of wisdom rises on his face. "I'm with you, Clay. I want you to be happy, and we both know happiness doesn't just arrive at the door with your name on it."

I toss him a slight smile. I know he'll always have my back. "Thanks, Rob. That means a lot, but I've got to do this alone."

Hell yes! I'll make damn sure my affair is between me, Isabelle, and Fletcher. No one touches Rob or his family, or Matty, or even Hartley Marine, for that matter. No Trojan horse will ever bring us down. Not on my watch!

"So, when's the date?" he asks with interest.

"I'm hoping this weekend."

"Good luck."

I wink at him as he steps away from my desk.

Unexpectedly, he turns back. "You know, Clay, women who reject you don't usually betray you. So you've got that going for you with Isabelle."

"It's resistance, brother, not rejection," I reply, spinning the silver ball.

I LINGER at the UCLA Children's Hospital parking garage. I don't even know when Isabelle is finishing her shift, so I could still be waiting for hours yet. I don't usually have the patience, but waiting for Isabelle is unexpectedly bringing out the calmness in me. Besides, I'm being entertained by the latest season of *Yellowstone* playing on my phone.

Who needs meditation when you can use your downtime like this?

A tap at my window un-Zens my moment.

*Shit!*

Where did she come from?

"You just don't give up, do you?" Isabelle complains as soon as I wind down my window.

I maintain my sanguine face until the adverse vibe oozing out of her eases a notch.

"How did you know I'm here?" I state my curiosity. She was stealthy. I'll give her that!

"I could see your red Porsche beckoning from a mile out!" She crosses her arms. "What are you doing here?"

"How were the chocolates?"

She tips her head sideway. "Nice. What do you want?"

I hop out of my car, and she takes a couple of steps back. "Relax. I won't bite, but I want accountability."

"What accountability?"

"You see, Isabelle, you returned my car with scratches on it."

"Clayton!" She glares.

That's the name I long to hear—not Mr. Hartley, as she called me the last time.

I offer her my most charming smile. "Good to see you again."

"Good night, Clayton." She spins around, abandoning me. She has no idea how long I've waited for her!

"Isabelle, let's stop this nonsense."

She strides back to me. "Yes, let's. You and I—we can't happen."

"You're still afraid of Fletcher?"

"I told you that night that you didn't understand. You still don't."

"It's about your son?" I have to bring this up now. She's got to know that when she's with me, Fletcher is never a threat.

"Don't bring my son into this!"

"If you want us to happen, I'll protect you—and Raffi."

Her face twists, as if trying to quash her own thoughts. But she refuses to let me see her struggle. She spins around, marching away from me.

I rush to block her. In the duel of wills, I brace myself to take her hand.

Despite her surprise, she doesn't protest. Her blue eyes haven't settled, though, telling me she's still fighting with herself.

"Isabelle, tell me you don't have feelings for me, and I'll leave you once and for all. Don't use Fletcher as an excuse to walk away."

"I don't have feelings for you," she maintains, her chin up. Yet, her hand is still in mine, with not a hint of an intention to remove herself from me.

"You've got to do better than that!"

"I don't. I don't," she utters with difficulty as if her tongue is contorting against her.

"I've been a fool before, but I know you're not just another woman."

"You'll regret ever asking me."

"I've had a lot of regrets in my life. But I know this won't be one. Regret, is something that you can taste in your mouth even before it happens, but you play it down. I know what I'm in for.

Us—you and me—isn't going to be easy. But never have I had that taste of regret. Not anywhere within me."

"What do you want from me, Clayton?"

"Just give me a chance."

I feel a tiny squeeze on my hand, and it's not nervousness. Her eyes relax somewhat. Right then, I know she's let me in.

**15**

———

**ISABELLE**

When life gives you a chance, you seize it.

When a man who's prepared to risk it all for you asks you for a chance, you give it to him with both hands.

Chances and risks.

Life has taught me that they always go hand-in-hand, and sometimes you don't know which is which. But with Clayton, when his eyes brim with kindness, you accept whatever is ahead with gladness.

Don's threat is graver than ever. He still holds all the cards, including Raffi. But thanks to his own plan, time is on my side.

Clayton offered me a bodyguard to watch over Raffi, which I refused. He doesn't know that I'm dating him with Don's blessing, and the last thing I want is to stir the peace. The Reaper is desperate for something only I can get, and he will give me time. I will ride this calm for as long as I can. Then, when I've figured out my options, I'll decide on my next move.

Thomas whistles at me as soon as I'm out of my room, taking my hand, so I do a spin for him. I'm wearing a teal see-through evening dress, the low bodice suspended by a couple of spaghetti straps forming an X at the back, with a reasonably snug skirt on the hips. It flows right down to my ankles. The hem is finished with generous lace trim.

"You could convert a gay man with this dress," he quips. "Let me guess. Prada?"

"Marchesa, pre-loved." It was a bargain, so I didn't have to dip into the two-thousand-dollar carrot Don gave me.

Thomas looks closely at my hair which I've tied back in a sleek ponytail. "Sexy. Mysterious."

I play with my earrings, the same ones that inadvertently played matchmaker at the Giraffe Manor. "That's the idea. You don't reveal everything on your first date, do you?"

"With Clayton Hartley, I'm not sure you'll have enough self-control."

In other words, he thinks I'm too horny.

I dismiss his verdict as I hear Raffi coming down the stairs. My son studies me from head to toe. "You look nice, Mom."

"Thank you, baby."

"I'm happy for you. Don't be so nervous. He likes you," he encourages me.

I feel my smile gleaming at him. He's given me his blessing to date another man after what he went through with his father. I wish it were just a normal date, and I could see a clear path ahead for the two of us...well, the three of us. But if everything had been normal, I wouldn't have met Clayton.

Raffi adds, "Say hello to him."

"I will. Feel free to give Thomas a hard time tonight." I kiss my son's forehead as my bestie glares at me.

I rush to my car, followed by Thomas.

"If there's anything, call me immediately. Got it?" I remind him. "Immediately."

"Go on! You're gonna be late."

"We'll find a way to get rid of Don. This is just the beginning."

"Babe, tonight is your night. There's no Don, and there's no me." He plants a light kiss on my cheek, careful not to smear my makeup. "Have fun."

I can't remember the last time I associate 'fun' with anything that involves a man. But with California's most eligible bachelor as my date, I'm prepared for any eventuality.

***

Clayton has asked me to meet at a spot near Franklin Canyon. The closer I get to my destination, the more I question my choice of apparel. If he's thinking about taking me deep into nature, I'm certainly not dressed for it.

But when I see my date waiting for me in his navy suit and tie, beaming, I know I'll be just fine.

Balmy California spring air presses against my face.

"You look lovely," Clayton welcomes me in his smooth voice. There's confidence in his grip, with a touch of possessiveness which, I'm sensing, he's still testing on me.

He brings our chests together, his jacket soft against my cheek. It may be the wool, or it may be his huggable nature. Whatever it is, my arms spontaneously wrap around him. Maybe a little too tight for a first hug because I feel a chuckle of amusement gliding over my crown.

"Shall we?" I stand tall, recovering from my involuntary eagerness. I could do with indulging more from that hug, but I don't want to get carried away. At the same time, I can't wait for him to show me what it feels like to be his—just for tonight. I've given him a chance because I have feelings for him, but after Nando and Don, I have no intention of becoming another man's possession.

"We have all night, but sure," he responds with a degree of curiosity.

He slides a glance at my sky-high shoes. The path ahead of

us is stony and uneven, but I won't embarrass myself. I'll have to negotiate it.

Clayton offers his arm. He even lets me lean on him to use him as a safety net. "Hold on to me, baby."

Baby? Coming out of his mouth, with his muscly arm securing me, it sounds affectionate yet deep. Different from how I use it to call Raffi or Thomas. Clayton's 'baby' feels like I've been stripped and then slowly wrapped in a roll of luxurious blue velvet.

We follow the path lined with lavender bushes and sage-brush on either side.

"Raffi says hello, by the way." I relay my son's message.

A grin stretches across his handsome features. "That's nice. Say hello back."

At the end of the path, the land opens up as if nature has just revealed its treasure. A blue lake spreads in front of me, and just to my left is a magnificent wooden cottage perching on a little hill. The air is so still. I can hear a calling, as if from an old spirit that has inhabited this secret place since its inception.

"Clayton...this is beyond amazing!"

He gently rubs my spine as we gaze up. "My father built that place when he was a very young man. He did it for Mom."

"Now I know how you became a romantic."

That remark earns a smile from him. He's clean-shaven today, looking fresh like a dew-covered meadow. I take time to peruse his cleft chin. It's subtle but adorable for a man of his stature.

"You okay to walk up?" Once again, he glances at my shoes.

"What? Are you gonna carry me?"

"I'll save that for when you're too drunk to walk."

I'm not much of a drinker, but I don't think he's talking about that kind of drunk.

I hold on to Clayton a bit tighter as we start making our way up.

He explains, "It was a humble cottage back in the day. Dad was a boat builder, but he did a decent job building this beauty. Needless to say, Mom was impressed."

"Now you're trying to impress me? Without having to hammer a single nail?"

"Fair point," he accepts. "But I've made my mark, you know. Over time, Rob and I did a series of renovations and turned it into our holiday home. We haven't used it much since Mom and Dad died, though."

Halfway up the path, I smell food. "Who's cookin'?"

"Well, I'm not much of a cook." He sends me his admission in a wink. "So I hired someone for tonight. You don't mind an early dinner?"

"No, not at all."

The hill and my heels turn out to be accepting of each other. We get to the top without any podiatric drama. Maybe because the master of the house is by my side, the earth decides to be kind to me.

The entrance to the cottage is a rustic, thick wooden door. "My dear." He pushes it open.

A fire is burning. Mixing in with the cooking spices, the smell of cedar wood and wildflowers assaults my senses. Going past the living room and into the dining area, I can only gape at what this man has prepared. The table has been set—a large oak table, lightly polished, almost raw, decorated with a white runner. Several candles are placed in the middle, accompanied by roses in small metal vases.

"Clayton, you've gone through so much trouble."

"I was happy to prepare all this for you. Now, that, I can claim I did myself."

I guess this is how a man shows how much he appreciates his woman. But how? Why? I'm not used to this.

Reflections of the candles twinkle in his eyes, complementing that projection of kindness that can only come from his heart. It's his constant. It's who he is.

A figure in a chef's uniform enters the room. "Ma'am. Clay." The man offers a polite smile. His white top fits him like a suit as if he's just come out of the White House kitchen.

"Isabelle, this is Guillaume, the man of the moment," Clayton introduces me to him.

"Nice to meet you. Whatever is cooking, it smells divine," I compliment.

"Thank you, Ma'am." He takes my hand and kisses it.

Clayton then helps me with my dress as I sit down.

I left my dream of being a princess on my last Christmas in Rio. Now, being treated like royalty despite the lack of a tiara and Cinderella dress is making me see pink.

We start with warm bread and a glass of red. I smile at the label—*Product of Kenya.*

Moments later, Guillaume returns with a tray in his hands. "Oysters Florentine."

Clayton looks at me, waiting for my reaction. I ignore him and thank the chef instead.

"Anything you want to say?" Clayton provokes as I marvel at the spread.

"I'm allergic to these," I whisper.

A panicked expression flutters across his face. "Oh, God! I'm sorry." He shuffles himself out of his seat. "Gui—"

"Relax! Relax, I'm kidding." I revel in the moment Clayton Hartley loses his cool.

"Jesus, Isabelle." He sits back down with a huff.

"I love oysters." And the one that has just touched my palate is friggin' delicious. I take my time, then add, "I won't comment on *that* association. But I must say, it's a bold choice for a first date."

He slurps the supposedly aphrodisiac shellfish, then cocks his brow to give his approval. "I didn't pick the menu. Guillaume has been our guy for almost twelve years, and he never disappoints."

While I keep going with my entrée, Clayton pauses. Something on the table seems to be bothering him.

"Excuse me. I'll be back." He dashes into a room adjacent to the kitchen.

A moment later, he emerges, hauling a long bench that looks as old as anything in this cottage. He positions it along the length of the table. He disappears again into the same room and returns with a pile of thick, fluffy throws, covering the bench with them, then rearranging our plates and cutlery.

"I'm sorry for the interruption." He reaches out to me, helping me up, drawing the heavy chair out so I can step away. "Please." He guides me to the bench, helping me sit and arranging my skirt. He then perches himself by my side. "You were too far from me."

We enjoy the view of the lake reflecting the twilight sky, framed by the window in front of us like a painting. His arm hooks around my waist, pulling me as if there was still a gap between our hips. That possessiveness—it's official.

There should be some kind of caginess building in me. Something like how I felt when Nando's arm was tight around me as if I was his birthright. But the firmer Clayton's hold on me, the more I want to dive into that possessiveness. Truly, what would it feel like? Belonging to a man whom I once fantasized as a safe house?

I start my exploration by putting an arm loosely around his hips. What if I want to own him too?

My arm drops lower until it settles at the top of his mounds. Damn, that is one tight ass!

Guillaume smiles when he sees the change in our table arrangements. He announces, "Our main entrée tonight is a creamy chicken stew with rice." He then puts the serving bowls in the middle.

Clayton scoops some onto his plate. Then, instead of serving mine, he removes the empty plate in front of me, cutting a 'trust me' glance.

He dips his fork in and gets a healthy serving of stew and rice. "Open your mouth."

The buttery gravy brushes my upper lip, thanks to Clayton's deliberate move to smear it. Never mind the chicken melting on my tongue, his stare voluntarily prompts me to lick my gravy-streaked lip.

He hums out his satisfaction. That was his intention. Not to find an excuse to wipe my mouth but simply to watch my tongue doing the job.

"This is the best chicken I've had," I murmur.

"Chicken, or *chicken*?"

"Chicken."

He smirks and keeps feeding me, and occasionally himself. We nudge ourselves closer to each other. I don't know how, but we keep finding space we need to fill, and we never seem satisfied that we're close enough.

I don't think we'll last till dessert, but we do.

"Fancy going out into the water?" he asks when I lay my head on his shoulder, soaking in the lake view from the window.

"Why not!"

Before we head down, I take off my shoes.

"Had enough of holding me?" he teases.

"I just want to feel the earth," I claim. There's something about this place that tugs me in. I don't know what it is, but I know it's beyond the beauty of its surroundings—and it's not just because it's my first time here with Clayton.

"Actually, I should ditch this, too." He loosens his tie.

We make our way to a jetty, where a rowboat is waiting. Clayton jumps in first, then helps me aboard, lifting me by the waist and setting me down like I'm his—well…princess.

"It's magical," I mutter, feeling the connection to this patch of heaven even more now that we're in the water. "I thought I knew California, but I never thought I'd find a place like this."

"I've done well, then?" he gushes.

A breeze sweeps across the lake, pushing the clouds over the setting sun. I unpin my hair, then remove the tie around my ponytail, letting the wavy ends bounce against my shoulders.

His ass fidgets while his gaze cuts to the tree line along the shore.

I'm a fan of nature, but I won't be outdone by some distant greenery. I fiddle with a few strands of my fringe, my foot brushing his ankle.

Catching a breath, he drops his resistance to take in my seduction. "Are you trying to send me to ICU?"

I shake my hair playfully, spreading it across my back.

Before he decides what my real intention is, the heavens open.

"Whoa!" Clayton looks up as he scrambles to ditch his jacket, then spreads it across my shoulders. The lining is still warm from his body heat as if the man himself is hugging me.

"Is this part of the plan?" I squint.

He bores into me as his shoulders rise and fall. "Well, I shall make it part of the plan." He swallows the distance between us, taking my face in his hands, his veiny palms covered with the gift from the heavens. His drenched fringe drops, wrapping his forehead as water batters his diamond-shaped face.

That's how a hero is supposed to be. Raw, hasty, and sexily sodden.

The intensity in his eyes sharpens as his gaze dips to my slightly parted lips. Strangely, I don't mind if he parks his kindness now because what's taking over is hunger—one that shouts he can't wait to have me.

His hand shifts to the back of my head. A groan vibrates against my lobe as his fingers dig into my hair, indulging in the texture despite the rain steadily soaking every strand. He draws me to him, and his lips press to mine.

I welcome his pucker. It's softer than I anticipated. Heat coats my lips despite the pelting rain, quickly becoming a need in my core.

Clayton Hartley has been my fantasy, but I never actually imagined our first kiss. It was never relevant. But here it is, I'm kissing the man who should've been out of my reach and out of my life. It sets me on fire, but he's not the flame. He's the oxygen that keeps it alive.

In fact, the man *is* the oxygen I breathe. My lungs can testify to that.

Clayton opens his mouth wider, relishing my lips. I part them, inviting his tongue to sweep mine. With precision and authority, he teases my palate.

I nudge myself to kneel right in front of Clayton without breaking the kiss, then brush my pelvis against his.

That makes him release a feral grunt. He pulls me toward him as if I'm still too far. My breasts press against his chest. With the lacy material of my dress soaked in water, and his thin shirt laminating his torso, the contact is almost like a skin-to-skin.

He pants, his face flushed. "Let's go back."

I hesitate. I haven't had enough of him. But he's already started rowing, and as I watch his arm muscles swell inside the wet sleeves, my reluctance evaporates with the wind.

We reach the jetty in no time. I don't know how he balances it, but with me securely in his arms, without my feet touching anything, he carries me back to dry land into the sheltered warmth of the cottage.

The only noise I hear is the crackling of wood. Apparently, Guillaume has left.

Clayton lays me down on a wooly rug right by the fire. Fragrance from the cedar wood and wildflowers infuses the smoky air, bringing out the sacredness of this place. Even if Clayton and I don't end up together, I feel we somehow belong here.

By now, he has ditched his soaked clothes and stripped to his underwear. His briefs are just slightly wet, but I can see the contour of his formidable cock. His six-pack abs glisten with sweat, moving in and out following his breathing. He places himself on top of me. Water drops from his fringe onto my face.

His restless hold declares he has to have me now, and there isn't a single fiber of me saying I shouldn't take him. My body begs me to, to the point that I get weak with impatience.

Clayton plays with my dress strap, pulling one of them down my shoulder, pondering.

"Going to recreate our first meeting, are you?" This cottage is almost as dim as the space of our first meeting. But tonight, I see the stranger in the dark in a new light.

"No." He sweeps his thumb across my cheek. "I'm going to create a new chapter." My earring clinks as he unhooks it off my lobe, observing it closely as if the process is a ritual that arouses him. Because soon he nibbles my bare ear as he hums erotic moans.

His touch sends my eyes closed with a sigh. I feel his palm pressing against one of my breasts, his thumb seeking my nipple. He strokes the tip—twice, three times—and I purr like a contented kitten.

Clayton shifts himself up. Something draws a grunt out of him—it might've been my thigh brushing on his manhood. He then pulls me up, supporting my back so he can unzip my dress.

I square my shoulders, rolling them in a smooth motion so my dress drops to my waist, giving him an unobstructed view of my breasts.

"Jesus, Isabelle."

He drops his head on my shoulder, his face turned to the side of my neck, kissing it thirstily as his hands mold my breasts with ardor. "Damn, you're so sexy, Baby Belle."

Baby Belle?

Sweet, with a touch of naughty. And with that, he licks my nipples softly as if savoring their taste. I project my chest forward to give him better access, and he starts sucking them. He does so with much adoration.

If this is how he shows possessiveness, the safe house I pictured is still standing. Whatever this man is doing to me, I feel nurtured and admired. I bloom. And God help me, I don't want it to be just for tonight or one night a year, like the rare flower Nando once compared me to.

The constant fondling sends me writhing, releasing wild moans.

"Goddamn!" he hisses out his satisfaction, massaging my breasts a little firmer this time. He then pushes me back. His mouth moves to my lips, kissing me vigorously like a man intent on giving his woman a night to remember.

His fingers start flicking my erect nipples, gradually pinching them. He stays there as if knowing to let the pulsing sensation disperse to all parts of me. Right when the unfamiliar bliss is about to fill my body to the brim, I feel a nip on my left nipple and the tip of his tongue pushing against it. He keeps at it while his hand rubs my other breast.

Something like an electric current travels down my belly. By and by, it bursts into waves, lapping at my center from the inside, crashing my defenses.

My mouth gapes but I'm unable to utter anything.

Fuck... I just came.

A satisfied smile plasters his face. So nipple orgasm isn't a myth. But seriously, that shows more than a glimpse of how well-versed Clayton is with the female body.

He gives me a moment, which I need and don't need at the same time. My seared lips gape, still releasing steam from the unexpected beginning. But I want more.

My legs under my dress skirt get restless, calling for the man who just made me come to dip in between them. Clayton senses it. He nudges me to lift my ass, and once I do, he pulls my dress —and my panties—down.

"I will die for you, Isabelle. Do you know that?" He gazes at my nakedness, following every curve.

I shake my head, telling him don't even go there. It's too dangerous even to consider what he would sacrifice for me when death becomes an imminent part of us.

He bends down and slowly blankets me with his body. Nothing is covering him now, and his skin is wet with more than just the remnants of the rain. His manly scent overrides the fire-wood and flower fragrance. My senses heighten. For him. And only for him.

His hardened length lands on my pelvis as he dips a finger into my pussy. He should know I'm drenched down there. He tries to obscure my view, but I won't let him deny me visual access.

I scoop his waist up, forcing a gap between my belly and his crotch.

God, he's huge.

I've never made love to a man so well-endowed. I should be concerned about how I'm going to accommodate him, but my core is pulsing with need. I don't care if it hurts.

He lines himself up, only supporting his upper body lightly with his arms. "Is this what you want?" he whispers.

"Hell yeah," I huff.

His lips are back on mine—hungry. My eyes fall closed once more, absorbing his aggression. Our first kiss has kindled a fire. Now this continued contact is fueling it to burn even higher.

In this magical place, in the company of a man who's giving everything to me, nothing else matters.

Nothing. Not even Don and his threats.

"Clayton..." I moan out his name.

I feel his weight on top of me, gentle but enough to warn me this is a point of no return. I shift my hips, affirming that I don't intend to look back.

He pushes one of my thighs up, getting it to bend to give him room. He glides inside me on a slight angle and then nudges my bent thigh toward him, making sure his entrance is tight and creating as much friction as possible.

This is pain, but not as I know it. It binds me to him. It turns sex into something so goddamn beautiful.

He's in me, the stranger in the dark who's no longer a stranger. He's a man I'm holding onto with both arms, a man I'll cling to as long as possible. I gave him a chance. Now I'm giving myself a chance to be satisfied by a man who wants nothing else of me but *me*—the person, the woman.

Suddenly I feel a sweet kiss lands on my gaping pout.

The man had woken me up with his lips before—long before I knew what they were capable of. I tasted his resolve to keep me alive then. Now, I'm satiating myself with his urge that is as carnal as a man can have.

He kisses his way down to my neck and my cleavage. My hand follows his movement, clenching a fist of his thick hair.

The pleasure he's granting me is incredible, more than what my imagination can contrive.

He thrusts his intensifying erection inside me again and again. For the first time, I feel his size and solidness.

"You know, Isabelle." His elbows straighten, creating a distance between our faces so he can gaze at me. "I won't die for you." He's still in me, but he's stopped moving as if wanting to separate his statement from the heat of the moment. "I'll *live* for you. For who you are, for whatever you need from me."

It's the most profound thing anyone has ever said to me.

Apart from his godly body, constant kindness, and sheer desire, I don't know much else about him. Yet, I believe he meant every word he said.

Getting a long silence from me, he lowers himself, showering me with kisses hotter than any he has given me today. His cock sinks deeper, stretching me. Every burst of pleasure feels like a tiny piece of his heart has been planted inside mine. Deliberate, selfless.

Most of all, at this moment, he holds me with such care and tenderness as if I'm his most cherished person.

A rush of emotions knocks me back. I wish I could sit up, embrace him, and cry in his arms. Instead, I clamp his sturdy hips with my thighs, my eyelids shut tight.

**16**

---

# CLAYTON

"Clayton, don't stop," she sighs.

This woman is certainly challenging my willpower. I'm turned on like I've never been before. With that squeeze, I could come right here, right now.

But I haven't had enough of her.

"Shh, keep them wide." I pull out slightly, shifting her thighs outward so they're not pressing me so tight.

Her mouth releases a conspicuous moan. Her eyes are closed now, but earlier, I saw them hazy. Hazy from euphoria, which she obviously has never tasted before, let alone thoroughly enjoyed.

But I stop.

I soften my hold. Is that a tear escaping?

"Baby? You okay?" I murmur.

Her eyes bat open with a sigh. "Yeah. What's the matter?"

"Am I hurting you?"

"God, no!"

"Were you—well, you'd tell me if I did, right?"

"Clayton, I'm almost there. Don't let me lose it."

There's something that she doesn't want to admit. But I let it slide before her impatience turns into frustration. I can only hope what I saw was a tear of joy—perhaps for what I've given her so far.

I sink into her again. I've sheathed myself this time. She's damn wet—hell, she has been since the start of our foreplay—but I know I'm spreading her pussy even more because of my swelling cock. Her resistance only adds to the friction between us. The sensation makes her buck out of control, her fingers digging into my traps.

She's panting, calling out my name repeatedly. I lower myself even more, forcing her ample breasts to rub against me. Her nipples are teasing the blooming pores across my skin. They're impossibly tense. They must be aching!

Isabelle widens her thighs, but she's still fucking tight. Despite her slight bucking, she lets me dive into her deeper. I cast a glance at her eyes. There's no sign of her tears. She seems too busy taking in the pleasure I'm milking out of her. There's no faking it.

Seeing her satiated face, I feel something tugging my chest—an attachment of some sort, as if she's where my heart moors.

I've had sex for the sake of sex, and there were times when making love had dismally turned into a burden—expectations and imminent judgment raining down on me like it was a contest. But with Isabelle, everything is natural and effortless, and what I've been granting her comes from the deepest part of me.

"Clayton..."

That's the voice of a woman begging for a climax—it's agonizing and incredibly arousing. I'm going to give it to her, and I'm going to ride it with her.

She lifts her head, reaching for my lips. I place my hand on the back of her head, pushing her to me. My fingers interlace with her wet yet bountiful hair. It's as if I can grasp her femininity in my hands, like silk yarns waiting to be weaved. Smooth. Lustrous. Seductive.

I glide as deep as I can, driving her to gasp. Her eyes are fixed on me, connecting to mine. I've never seen a woman so lost in pleasure. Her blue eyes sparkle sharply. Her hold on me is unabating. I can feel her orgasm unleashes itself as if it was mine.

"Isabelle..." This time I moan her name as I come. My body shudders, releasing more of me into her.

I collapse, my heart walloping behind my ribcage, my elbows barely supporting myself. My head falls next to her. For a few moments, I lie still, puffing right under her ear as pleasure courses through my body.

Slowly I roll off her, discreetly discarding the well-filled condom. I never mind condoms, but with her, I wish I didn't have to use them.

I lie sideways, pushing myself against her because I don't want to lose contact. In return, she angles herself toward me, burying her face in my pecs, rubbing her pelvis gently against my softening cock.

I run my fingers along her spine, the tips feeling her shivers.

"I'm glad you're here," I murmur.

She's sobering up, but her pleasurable gaze is still evident. She lifts her arm sluggishly as if she barely has enough energy. Her hand lands on my cheek, and I angle my face to kiss it.

Now I realize she's not completely naked. I stripped her off her clothes and earrings, but something still clings to her.

I play with her jade bracelet.

I don't mind it a bit. That bracelet is part of her, and she looks intriguingly sexy wearing only that.

"You said this was from your mom?" My voice is so hoarse it's barely audible.

"Yeah. Her nickname was Jade because she had green eyes,"

she replies. "This bracelet was a gift from my dad to her for their first wedding anniversary. Just before she passed away, she gave it to me."

"So you've got your blue eyes from your dad?"

"Yes. It's not very common for a Latina, I know. But hey, Latin genes are the most diverse."

I stretch my arm, reaching for a blanket folded on the side of the fireplace. I spread it across the both of us.

"So, Clayton Hartley, now that we've got to know each other's bodies, I want to know about *you*."

I chuckle. "What do you want to know about me?"

"What do you do? I mean, I know about your extravagant yachts, but what do you do exactly?"

I stretch and lie flat on my back, inviting her to come to me. She crawls and lays herself on my chest.

I explain, "Well, my formal title is Chief Operating Officer. But I do all sorts, really, and so does Rob. I do a lot of testing, I guess."

"You test drive your yachts?"

"Yeah, pretty much."

"Raffi actually brought up a good point. Your job is very different from your Air Force career?"

"In a way, yes. However, the technology isn't that much different, whether you're in the air or on water. Like the radar systems, for example. I'll take you to the HQ sometime."

She grins at me. "What else do you do?"

"I guess the thing that I do which others tend to run away from is marketing."

"Kissing people's asses? Of course people would rather avoid that."

"Come on! I'm not that bad. I schmooze, yes, but I don't kiss ass. I'm too rich for that," I banter.

She giggles, writhing on top of me, which is seriously waking up my cock.

She asks, "What is it like to be a billionaire?"

"What do you think?"

"It's like a fantasy. You roll in money, and you kiss people's asses to get more."

"One last time. I don't kiss people's asses, Isabelle."

"All right, all right." She lifts herself up. Her hair falls gracefully, teasing my cheeks. "I can't even think about a life like yours."

"Look at this." I point at our surroundings. "Do you see a fantasy here?"

"Hm... no. I'm in it."

"We're billionaires, but we're humans first and foremost. I breathe, I eat, I have a house. I work. I—"

"Fuck," she completes my sentence.

I shake with laughter. "Yeah. I do. So this is my life."

*With you in it.*

I shift myself up, nudging her so she's under me again. "Now, it's my turn to get to know you better."

"Huh?"

"What's *your* fantasy?" I challenge her.

"Clayton Hartley. First, it was the oyster entrée. Now this question. Should I remind you this is only our first date?"

"I'm the bold kind." She doesn't know it, but fulfilling a woman's fantasy is a shortcut to a man's success.

Following her lack of response, I brush her neck with a finger, up to her chin, then tease her lower lip. "Come on, what's your fantasy?"

"You."

I appraise the fire in her eyes. She's not lying, but it's more than just *me*. It's what she wants me to do to her or what she wants to do to me.

"Me what?" I probe.

"Not telling."

"You're not that cruel, are you? Keeping me hanging?"

"I can be," she utters. "Perhaps I'll send it in a letter. When you least expect it."

"You are cruel."

"It's called maintaining the suspense."

She runs her fingers through her mane as her tongue sweeps her lower lip.

Never mind my new hardness. What should I do with her? What *could* I do? Isabelle has taken me deep into dangerous territory. It's too late for me to bail out, but despite the suspense she boasted about, I haven't forgotten that she's scared. And she's scarred. But I've got to have her and keep her.

Just by imagining what her fantasy might be, I'm trapped. I've already promised myself that whatever it is, I'll make it my own as soon as I know it.

**17**

———

## ISABELLE

The sun rises, reminding me that all good things must come to an end—including my time with Clayton.

My heart is rebelling like a teenager being told they've been grounded. I'm sore but hungry—and it's not for breakfast. My core is still pulsing from too much pleasure. The moment when I told myself 'just for tonight' seems like a distant past.

How am I going to survive today, and tomorrow, without him?

Unable to deal with my helplessness, I let myself fall onto him. He responds with a tight embrace—dare I say he's as helpless as I am. But we both know that much as we want to go back to bed and ravage each other again, I can't miss my shift.

"I wish we could stay here forever," I murmur.

"You're welcome here anytime. We have plenty of opportunities to recreate last night," he whispers.

I'm hopeful but realistic. There are forces around us that might change our destiny, but I can't help letting myself get lost inside his safety.

"Or, creating something even better?" He runs his fingers

across my cheek, which I'm sure is a hint about the fantasy that I haven't revealed yet.

I'm here because I wanted to be with him. I want nothing of the man other than his affection, but imagining him and me doing what I had in mind, is more than a carrot for me to keep going with him. Oh, that man has no idea!

He scoops my chin up and gives me a kiss. "For now, your patients need you."

My lips pout in a smile. He's still close, so I twist them slightly, hinting I want that kiss again. And he gives it to me.

He then offers, "Come, let me drive you."

Tempting, but I hang on to my keys. "I need my car."

"Well, I'll drive your car then."

I grimace. I know he's not a snob, but him driving my Toyota? For the sake of keeping my vision of Clayton Hartley as the ultimate billionaire hero intact, he's got to stay within the boundary of my imagination. Besides, that red baby is calling.

Catching me wondering, he places a playful kiss on my crown. "Tell you what. I'll get my driver to drop off your car at the hospital so you'll have a ride home after your shift."

"Okay. For now?"

He tosses me his Porsche key. "Swap ya."

I give him mine, which he leaves under the mat for his driver to pick up.

Although my dress has dried overnight, thanks to the warmth of the cottage, the breeze out here makes me shiver.

"Here." He gives up his knit cardigan and helps me slip into it.

God, I can get used to this.

"Did you ruin your suit?" I ask, at the same time admiring his t-shirt-clad torso. His muscles stretch the material, revealing how ripped his trunk is. How I want to tear it apart and repeat last night all over again.

"Fine wool and rain don't mix, but I don't think it's a write-off. It was only the first time it got drenched like that."

I chuckle, glancing at him, warning him that there may be more times to come.

I dive into the driver's seat like the Porsche was mine. Taking in the leather smell, I clutch the steering wheel as if I'd just met an old friend.

*Hello, baby.*

I reverse, then make a three-point turn, and we hit the road in no time.

He watches me. "You're good."

I shrug.

He adds, "I'm surprised you didn't have to adjust the seat."

"I'm almost as tall as you are."

Perhaps sensing my cockiness, he places a hand on my thigh, tracing my leg under the skirt of my dress. "You have long legs, that's why." He then drives his hand back up, resting on my inner thigh.

"Clayton, I'm driving." This is too close! If he moves just half an inch, I'm going to let go of the wheel.

"Not so good now, are you?" he whispers.

I extend my arm, slap my hand against his crotch and fondle his balls.

"Ugh..." he groans.

Fuck, that makes me horny! I saw his morning wood when we woke up, but what's growing against my palm right now is almost as hard as stone. Where it starts and where it ends, it's beyond what my mitt can handle.

For the sake of my own sanity, I withdraw my hand. "Now we're even."

"Revenge, huh?" he fusses, adjusting his pants. "By the way, how did you sleep?"

"Not so well."

"Oh?"

"I was hungry."

"Why didn't you tell me? I'm not much of a cook, but I could've fixed you something or heated up the leftovers."

I look at him, hinting he's got it all wrong. Then I gnaw my lower lip, clarifying what kind of hunger kept me up all night.

"Baby Belle, not now," he grumbles as I pull up into my driveway.

"Pity," I deadpan, and then hop out of the car.

When we get inside, Thomas is making breakfast while Raffi is still in bed.

"Hey," I greet my bestie, entering with Clayton in tow.

"Hey, did you have fun?" Thomas asks, bustling at the stove without paying any attention to who's watching.

"It was *fucking* fun."

My word choice finally prompts him to turn around. He drops the spatula he's using to make his omelet. "Iz! I didn't know..."

"Clayton, this is Thomas. Thomas, Clayton."

"Hi there," Clayton greets him genially.

"Hey..." Thomas finally extends his hand after glaring at me, clearly, for not telling him in advance about my guest.

Seeing his comical face, I can't help it. "Thomas thinks you're his soulmate," I blurt.

"Iz! How dare you!" Thomas demurs with a concoction of emotions—perhaps surprise, embarrassment, and titillation. Whatever they are, he blushes like a crab.

Clayton smiles sweetly. "Sorry, man. She's beaten you to it."

Thomas gathers himself, picking up the spatula and wiping some clumps of omelet off the floor. "Would you like some breakfast?" he offers.

"Gee, I'd love to, but I've got to go. Maybe next time," Clayton answers. "And I'm sure Isabelle needs to go soon, too."

He grabs my waist, spins me around, and then kisses me on the lips.

"Oh God, get a room, you two!" Thomas banters.

Hearing the commotion, Raffi comes down. "Clayton!"

"Hey, man!"

Raffi offers his hand, which Clayton takes, and then my son draws him into an embrace—man-to-man. He then peeps out the window, clearly checking if it was a chariot or a pumpkin that took me home just now.

"Are you staying?" Raffi asks in anticipation.

"Not today," Clayton replies. "But I've been thinking—"

I tip my head sideway, anticipating what he's about to say.

"Will you play basketball with me sometime?" Raffi requests. He told me that he found an article about Clayton playing hoop-off with a Greek prince aboard one of his mega-yachts—both were wearing their tuxes.

"Of course I will, Raffi. But what I have in mind is way cooler."

"Really? What is it?"

"How about I keep it as a surprise?" Clayton decides. "I'll pick you up next weekend."

"Cool!" Raffi offers him a fist bump, which Clayton accepts with enthusiasm.

"Make sure it's your day off." He nods at me. "It's going to be a whole day kind of outing."

"Okay. I'll try."

"Where's your commitment?" he criticizes.

"Okay, I will get a day off."

"That's the spirit! Can I take Matty too?"

"Of course!"

I pause. Why am I feeling happy? Not the kind of happy like you're going somewhere with a special someone or happy that you're being treated kindly. But happy that something is coming true. Not just 'something'—it's actually one of my long-running fantasies.

To have a family again.

Two kids going on an outing with me. Imagine that. And beside me will be my own hunky boyfriend—who is a fantasy in his own right.

"Ready whenever you are." Clayton hints that it's time.

"Oh, yes. Let me get my bag and uniform." I head upstairs.

Thomas rushes to follow me.

"Iz..." He draws my hand and puts it on his heart. "Do you feel it?"

"Yeah. You're still alive."

"What kind of a nurse are you? I'm about to have a myocardial infarction!"

I cackle, pinching his cheek like he's my son.

"How was it?" he asks.

I simply give him a long sigh, eyes rolling as if painting the Franklin Canyon sky over me.

"So, you revealed everything on your first date?"

"A lot. But not everything." I look at my watch. "Hey, I really have to go, but I'll tell you all about it later."

I change into my uniform in a flash. As I lay my teal dress on the bed, my body weakens, reminiscing all the things Clayton did to me on, in, beneath, and without it. God, save me. That man is really taking over me.

I close my bedroom door, then rush back downstairs. "I'm ready!"

Clayton stops to look at me.

"I'm no Cinderella, you know."

"I never wanted Cinderella," he conveys, opening the car door for me.

He turns on the engine, but he anchors his attention on me. It strikes me that perhaps one of his fantasies is me playing nurse with him—wearing a mini white skirt and barely-there top, my breasts spilling out of the cups.

Sexy—but not as spicy as mine.

"So, does Thomas live with you?"

"He's my best friend, but if he lived with me, we would be sworn enemies. He sometimes babysits Raffi, that's all."

"He looks like a Care Bear." Clayton watches me laughing. No one has ever called Thomas that. "Don't you think?"

"I thought he looked like Shawn Mendes, but Care Bear is a better description of him."

"He works for Fletcher, doesn't he?"

I bite my lower lip, wondering what he's hinting at. "Yes. Have you got a problem with that?"

"No."

"He's not like Don, okay? I've known him since he was sixteen. And he's close to Raffi."

"I don't have a problem with your friend, Isabelle."

As we arrive at the hospital, he looks at me, straight faced. "Look, I know Fletcher is going to come after us."

I wish he hadn't brought it up, but I guess sooner or later, reality will catch up with us. "Are you still worried about Thomas?"

"No. I trust you. I trust him. I'm just stating a fact," he emphasizes. "When that time comes, let me protect you. Let him come to me. Do you understand?"

"Clayton..."

"Do you understand?"

I take his hand without confirming anything, but 'I've got to go.'

## 18

### ISABELLE

"So, what's the surprise?" I query, watching Clayton's hair blown by the breeze as he drives. We're in his Bentley, going—somewhere. Even after almost an hour on the road, he still hasn't told us.

"Can you be patient like the kids?" He fixes his fringe, which the wind instantly messes up again. Messy or sleek, Clayton Hartley has a healthy head of hair that smells delightful and makes you glad that men exist.

I watch Matty and Raffi. They're busy catching up with their Minecraft strategies. The boys have been playing online together, with Matty giving loads of tips to Raffi that my son apparently got to his best position on the leaderboard yet.

So Clayton is guarding his surprise. He's not the only one who's capable of devising one. Wait until he receives mine—although right now, that surprise is at the mercy of the U.S. mail.

"Are we flying somewhere?" Raffi asks.

Now it becomes clear. We're going into Clayton's domain.

"Better than that, buddy," Clayton replies, driving around the airbase. "This is the back way. Actually, I prefer to call it 'the VIP way.'" He parks near a hangar.

"This is way cool!" Raffi exclaims, realizing this isn't going to be an ordinary day. People are here to fly fighter jets!

"Is Raffi going to be flying in one of those?" It is 'way cool,' as my son says, but I can't help thinking that he's just a kid, not yet made for that ominous machine.

"That's the idea."

"Okay..." I go along with it, seeing how excited my boy is. "Who's flying that thing?"

"Yours truly, of course."

I feel better then.

"Wyatt!" Matty calls, running toward a man wearing a pair of aviator sunglasses and pilot overalls. He must be in his fifties, but he looks pretty dashing. What's with these pilots and their sex appeal? Because those overalls actually look hideous on their own.

"Hey, champ!" The pilot called Wyatt hugs Matty.

"Isabelle, this is Wyatt, a former US Navy pilot and Hartley Marine's current official pilot. But when the corporate world becomes too much for him, he comes here doing his side hustle as a tour guide."

"Tour guide? That's an insult, Mr. Hartley!" Wyatt banters, taking off his sunglasses. Then he extends his arm to me. "Hi, Isabelle. Nice to meet you."

He's got a firm handshake. The man is certainly well trained, but that disarming smile couldn't have been part of the aviation curricula.

"Nice to meet you, Wyatt."

"Wyatt is one of the casual pilots here, showing tourists how it's done," says Clayton, gazing at the military jet being tugged out of the hangar. "Raffi, you're ready?"

"Yeah, but—" He looks at Matty. "Matty, you go first."

"No, you go. I'm not tall enough," Matty says slowly, perhaps not wanting to show his disappointment. "But I'll go on the simulator. It's cool too."

"You're not far off, pal. I think next year will be your year," Clayton reassures him, putting his arm around his little brother.

Matty gives him a wordless nod.

"Good boy," Clayton pats his shoulder, then he turns to Raffi. "Come, Raffi. I'll get you geared up."

"Is he old enough?" I whisper.

"When I fly, no one's too young. It's the height that matters. Your Raffi is tall enough," he explains. "In saying that, I do need your consent."

I smile. "Tell me where to sign."

I then wait outside with Wyatt and Matty.

"Your son will be just fine," Wyatt assures me.

"Yeah, I know." I try to calm my motherly jitters.

"You wanna go on the simulator now?" Wyatt asks Matty.

"Um... no, I want to see Raffi fly."

"All right," Wyatt agrees. "We'll stay here then."

Moments later, the two flying boys join us. Side by side, in their matching overalls, they epitomize what father and son would look like in my dreams. Raffi even mimics the way Clayton walks, holding the helmet on his hip.

I melt like a weeping candle. Hiding my brewing tears, I hold my phone up to take a few snaps of the two cuties. And before I embarrass myself—and my son—I replace the vision of my silly dreams with thoughts of jet engines and oil.

"I'm surprised they have his size," I nod at Raffi's overalls.

"What can I say? I came prepared," Clayton gushes.

Did he get them custom-made?

Seeing my questioning gaze, Clayton simply winks at me. That man is impossible!

"How do I look, Mom?"

"You look like a pilot," I respond proudly.

"Good answer, Mommy," Wyatt teases. Maybe because of his age, but this 'tour guide' surely knows how to push this single mother's button.

I kneel in front of Raffi, mundanely touching the zipper of his overalls. "Listen to Clayton, okay? If you get sick—"

"He'll be fine. I'm not Tom Cruise." Clayton rolls his eyes.

He's not—he's a real top gun. On him, the lowly green overalls don't just look good. They have become a symbol of his undisputed masculinity. Now *that*—is some sex appeal. To think that he was single when we met baffles me.

"What kind of jet is that?" Raffi queries.

"It's an L-39 Albatross, my man. And we're gonna jump in shortly."

Then he turns to Matty. "Stay with Wyatt, okay?"

Raffi flashes a backward glance at me as they get ready to climb aboard, then he looks over to Matty, who's giving him a small wave. He stops as if considering the little boy left behind. He then tells Clayton, "Hey, man, actually, I'll stay with Matty. I want to go on the simulator too."

"Raffi, it's okay," Clayton assures him.

It's not fear that's stopping my son—it's his character.

"No, I'll stay with Matty. Why don't you take Mom?"

Clayton's gaze lingers on Raffi as if commending him. "Are you sure?"

"Yeah. Take Mom." Raffi walks back to Matty, who's beaming like he's not alone anymore. They give each other a fist bump.

"Come on then, boys!" Wyatt leads the kids into the building next door.

Clayton watches Raffi in admiration. "Wow... that was the sweetest thing I saw a boy do. Wonder who he got that from?"

"He's always wanted to be a big brother," I murmur as my eyes blink furiously and a sniffle escapes my nose.

He turns to me. "Hey... are you crying?"

I am—I can't even stop myself.

"Come here, Mama." He draws me, letting me dry tears with his clothes. "You've done well. You know that?" He rubs my side. "You know that, Baby Belle?"

I nod, but inside, I'm dying to say he doesn't know half of my story. Caili would've been three years old now. And Raffi would've been a big brother to her. That's a dream that won't ever come true.

Clayton nudges my chin up, and then he thumbs my remaining stubborn tears. "You're a great mother."

Raffi suffered under my watch, and that would never make me a great mother. But in Clayton's embrace, with his eyes telling me that what he said is no lie, somehow there's peace rising within me.

He continues, "He's so sweet. I don't think any other kid would do that."

I shoot up an eyebrow. "Would Rob have done it with you?"

Clayton considers it. "Well, I guess. Yeah, I guess he would've."

"There we go. We come from good families, then."

He lets me know that he agrees with a kiss.

"My dear?" He leads me into a corner and helps me gear up. "Sorry, they haven't got your size here," he says. The overalls fit my hips, but when the zipper reaches my chest, he stutters. I'm wearing a tight tank top, and the overalls are squeezing my breasts. These must be a boy's size!

"Admit it. You were looking at my tits that night in Kenya!" I taunt him.

"I was looking at your eyes," he insists.

I shoot him a smile, giving him permission to drop his denial.

His eyes flash me a lascivious look. "But it doesn't mean I

didn't see your boobs." He places his hand on my chest so he can fasten the zipper all the way up.

We cross the tarmac toward the steel albatross. Clayton is in his domain, but ever the gentleman, he helps me climb onboard as gracefully as he lets me into his Porsche, strapping me up like a leader as much as a lover.

"How good are you with motion?" he queries.

"I've never tested myself."

"Well, today's the day, then."

And we're off. I can't help feeling like a princess on her first magic carpet ride, but braver—and rougher. Clearly, there's a reason why it's called a 'jet' and not a coaster. Clayton soon maneuvers the aircraft, reminding me that it's a thrill ride and he's in charge. I can't imagine what it was like when he was in the Air Force. He must've been a chick magnet.

"Whoa!" I cheer when we land.

"My dear," once again Clayton offers his hand.

"I enjoyed that."

"Good."

My hand in his, we make our way back into the hangar.

"Clayton, why did you take Matty today? You knew he couldn't fly."

"Well, I didn't want to leave him behind, and he's been asking about catching up with Raffi again. He understood that he couldn't fly yet. It's not a problem. I wanted us to be together."

"Testing the dynamics between the boys?"

"Well, kind of... but I did it because I wanted Matty to be with someone his age and not get jealous. He's been like an only child, you know what I mean? Rob and I are always protective of him. It's time for him to grow up."

This man knows a thing or two about parenting.

Clayton adds, "And I think he learned exactly what he needed to learn today from Raffi."

As a souvenir, Raffi and I got to keep our overalls.

Raffi is proud to leave them on. On the other hand, I'm still in them because Clayton insists—although I have to zip it down a bit. What's with him? He's prying me in these overalls, and it's not just my cleavage.

We then have dinner at an Argentine steak restaurant, which reminds me so much of my mother's cooking. That man sure knows how to entertain a lady—and the boys. Raffi and Matty dig into their dinner with gusto while they keep boasting about their records on the simulator. Apparently, Wyatt set the difficulty level high, but the boys were up to the challenge.

Almost immediately after we leave the restaurant, the boys fall asleep in the back seat. My phone buzzes inside my handbag. I know who the text messages are from, but I ignore them.

"Hey, how about you and Raffi spend the night at my place?"

"For real?"

"Of course. Catch a glimpse of how I live and all that."

"Okay," I respond in a seductive sigh to his virulent smile rather than his explanation.

"Next time, I'll take you to Hartley HQ," he proposes. "Just you and me. Get to know my world a little bit more. And you'll see that I don't kiss people's asses."

"I'm looking forward to it!"

Arriving at his Beverly Hills mansion, I can't help looking around like I've just entered wonderland. So this is how a billionaire lives. Nando was well off, and we had a nice house. Don is filthy rich too, and his mansion is pretty impressive. But this? With a driveway that goes on forever, surrounded by well-manicured lawns, exotic gardens, and exquisite lighting, I can't believe a bachelor lives here.

We arrive at the front porch—I mean, a grand entrance with white marble pillars, impeccable tiles, and two elegantly etched-glass doors. The doorway is wide enough for two Victorian ladies in their hoop skirts to enter side by side without touching each other.

"I'll take Raffi," Clayton offers as soon as we get out of the car. The light is dim out here, and the inside is no different. I don't think anyone is in—perhaps not even live-in maids or butlers.

A bachelor he may be, but Clayton Hartley is not an ordinary one. Look at him, carrying my boy as if he did it every day.

I scoop Matty up in my arms, holding him gently so I don't wake him up. He is only a year younger than Raffi, but with my son being taller than most ten-year-olds, the youngest Hartley looks like the perfect little brother. His drool drips to my shoulder, and I know my life is going in the right direction.

## 19

## CLAYTON

Still asleep, Raffi clings to me as we head upstairs. For the first time, stepping into my house feels like coming home. I'm with my tribe, sharing the day—sharing the night.

"You okay?" I check on Isabelle, who's padding a few paces behind me.

"Yeah," she replies in a murmur, my baby brother firmly in her hug.

I nudge Matty's room door open, letting her in. "Here."

Isabelle tucks him in. She blinks at me when she notices Bjork.

I nod at her, whispering, "Yeah, that's the infamous teddy."

"So cute!" She kisses it, then tucks Bjork in, too, right next to Matty. My brother curves a smile, although he's still out with the fairies.

"Good job, Mama," I murmur as we head into the guest room. Damn, it feels good to call her that.

Raffi is still asleep on my shoulder. I catch her stealing a glance at me. Exactly the reaction I was hoping for: that I'm worthy of being her son's dad.

"What?" I tease her.

"Uh... um... He wouldn't have let me do that. Carry him," she replies, gazing at his son's arms around my neck. He is clinging to me tight.

"Well, if he was awake, he probably wouldn't have let me either," I concede.

She shrugs.

That reaction is even better. So she believes that Raffi would let me carry him even when he's awake? I very much like it to be true.

Despite riding on cloud nine, doubts are still hitching on me. Is this too good to be true? Or have I finally earned my right to become the man I've always wanted? When I look inside myself, I see winter is over, ice is melting.

I lay Raffi on the guest bed, and Isabelle spreads the covers over him, kissing him goodnight.

"Fancy some wine?" I offer.

"Sure."

Down in the living room, I serve us the same Kenyan red that we had for our first dinner.

Before she reaches for a glass, I pull her right hand, turning her palm up. I run a finger across the stitches. "What did you do?"

She clears her throat. "A mirror broke in my hand."

"Really?"

"Either it would've hurt Raffi, or this." She stares at her palm. "It was an easy decision."

I draw the delicate hand to my lips as if those scars are still hurting her, and my kiss will soothe it. She dips her chin, pulling her hand away slowly. I observe her fingers furling around the glass stem. After a brief pause, I raise my eyes to hers. "Tell me. What do you want in a man?"

She takes a nervous sip of wine. "Well, I can't remember the last time I asked myself that. It must've been when I was a teenager who still believed in fairytales."

"If you want a fairytale, I can't give you that."

"Oh, I think you can."

Now her answer takes me back.

"But I'm not a teenager anymore," she adds.

"Why do you think I can?"

She looks up, perusing the decorated ceiling and chandeliers. Her gaze roams the room as if trying to make sense of its size. "You see, Clayton. All these, they're like fantasy to me."

This is the second time she's said the word 'fantasy' when describing my life.

I let her scrutinize me while I'm unpacking the significance of her remark.

Fantasy was exactly my failure. It wasn't a shortcut to a man's success as I previously believed. It sowed seeds for betrayals. I let those who broke my heart believe that I was their fantasy come true because I gave them what they wanted. Pleasure, play, pay, and I thought—love, too.

But none of them had the guts to tell it as it was.

Like Isabelle just did.

Betrayals in my life came in many forms—thefts, lies, abandonment. Those who were driven by greed were the easiest to spot and deal with. But those who deceived me as if lying was their gift from God or those who discarded me like I wasn't even human? They hit me fucking hard.

Like Katie.

That name still makes my core blench. I didn't want to mention her name, albeit silently, but here with Isabelle, somehow I have the courage to. I adored Katie. She was a down-to-earth waitress at a café around the corner from Hartley

Marine. In her company, she made lone lunches somewhat fun. She put me on a pedestal as if I was the only one for her because of who I was and not what I had. I believed we were meant to be. Until—

Goddamn! Until my life stopped being her fantasy.

When Rob, Matty, and I lost our parents. When Matty needed us more than ever— that was when the lies started. She only wanted the thick. Or, well, maybe she tried to ride the thin with me, too, because she did stay on for a while. Maybe the line between her faithfulness and her betrayal wasn't all that straight. But in the end, she didn't have what it took. And instead of saying it to my face, she went behind my back—enjoying another main course while furtively pushing me like I was a side dish. What hurt the most, though, was that bitch dared to blame Matty for our demise.

"Clayton?" Isabelle murmurs, her hand on mine.

"Sorry," I sigh, recovering from my thought.

"Have I offended you?"

"No. On the contrary, you made me realize something. Now I do want to know, Isabelle. So you're not a teenager anymore. What do you want in a man?"

As if I've given her time to consider, she answers immediately, "I want to feel safe with him. I want to feel that I mean the world to him. And you? What do you want in a woman?"

I appraise her from head to toe, like I'd just seen her for the first time. "Genuineness."

She shifts back in her seat. "Is that why you persisted on me?"

"Yes." I take the wine glass away from her. She clutches it so tightly she could well snap the stem in two.

She nips her lip as if trying to contain something within her.

"Tell me, Isabelle." I put her hand in mine. "Do you think I can give you what you want?"

"Why the question, Clayton?"

"Don't look at what I have around me. Look at me. Look at the person in front of me." I place my palm on her chest, staring at her intently. "I'm not a fantasy. And tell me you're not either."

"No, I'm not. I'm real."

"So am I."

I claim her with a kiss, and she softens as if surrendering. She's still wearing her overalls, and I've been dying to strip her since she put them on, but right now, I simply want her lips to connect with mine, to be one with mine.

My palm coasts up to the back of her head, tightening our contact. My fingertips tingle, feeling the texture of her silky hair. Even after a long day out, I can still smell her iris scent, tempting me to consume her.

"Oh, baby..." she murmurs when we come up for air.

Oh, baby, indeed. If I ever had to walk away from her, I don't know if I could take it. With her, everything seems to be within my reach.

Too good to be true?

I'll take too good to be true if it's with Isabelle.

Starting with what's been taunting me all day.

I pull her up, forcing her to straddle me as I take her to my bed. As I lay her down, I keep my position between her parted thighs.

Her zipper purrs under my pulling fingers. It stutters as it passes the mound of her boobs, teaching me a lesson of patience. I know she's real—but God help me, Isabelle in her pilot overalls is an onslaught of vigor and female beauty which fits my fantasy to a tee.

I'm rewarded when her generous cleavage comes into view, and in return, I reward her with kisses—kisses that soon turn into me feasting on her smooth olive skin. I stop the zipper at her belly, then lift her singlet. She's braless, giving my mouth instant access to her nipples. They're brown like almonds, ample and firm. They rest on gorgeous areolas, which seem to be almost as sensitive. I swear their texture changes every time the tip of my tongue land on them.

My cock throbs from the sensation of sucking her. It fucking hurts. It begs for a release. I have to adjust my pants.

I take off the top part of her overalls and get rid of her singlet. I search for her entrance through the thick fabric—and her jeans shorts. She writhes with a restrained shriek. Perhaps I'm rubbing it too hard.

Seeing her agony, I unzip her all the way, yanking her overalls and shorts off her legs.

*Oh fuck...*

She's wearing a pair of thin, lacy panties that dip low, barely covering her sex. Her smell is destroying me—I'm not sure how long I can last.

"Clayton..." She stretches her belly, the start of her entrance peeking out of her panties.

I insert my palm under the lacy material, poking my finger into her. She moans—but she's not there yet.

The urge to enter her grabs me like a wave, but I keep my throbbing cock tucked inside my pants despite it precumming relentlessly. I've got to get her well-lubed, or I'm going to hurt her—too much. I spread her legs and press my mouth against her opening.

She squirms, shrieking, looking like she wants me off. But then she sighs—which I know is a plea for me to keep going. I'm toying with her, and I love how she responds. As she bucks, her boobs bounce in an enticing rhythm, hypnotizing me into ecstasy that I have no hope of resisting. While my tongue keeps glossing her opening, I reach for those magnificent curves. Cupping them, squeezing them, rubbing them. When they spill out, I greedily scoop them back.

The flavor of her sex is like raw honey at harvest time, and it consumes me, shredding my self-control.

"God, Isabelle..."

I've got to have her now, or I'm gonna waste this erection on myself.

## 20

### ISABELLE

Clayton scrambles to find a condom. Perhaps the foreplay has gone on a little too long considering the urgency he's trying to contain. His pants and underwear are still hanging on his knees when he starts penetrating me.

But the man can do no wrong. Just by witnessing his impatience, I'm aroused. I've seduced this might of a man to his limits, and I've never felt so sexy and powerful—and beautiful.

His cock strains me. This is only the second time I've been with him, but my body seems to recognize the sensation as if we had been partners for a long time. I'm sore, but I'm home.

He changes the angle of his thrusts, exploring a new place inside me.

Against my intention, I let out an obscene scream as his growing hard-on punishes me. But thanks to his earlier hustle to make my pussy generously drenched, his oversized flesh punishes me with pleasure.

"Baby, I'm almost there," he grunts.

He should've been there ages ago, but he has the presence of mind—actually, more than that, it's his affection—to hold and stay with my pace.

Now, his pace is my pace. I take him as he comes with a howl. We both pant, lying next to each other.

"This turns out to be some outing," he sighs, freeing his ankles off his rumpled pants.

I study him, recalling the way we've made love just now—or rather, how he started our lovemaking. So, it's not the nurse uniform, as I thought, but his 'thing' turns out to be a female pilot?

Clayton's gaze cruises my figure, his fingers stroking the contour of my hip. "Today meant a lot to me."

"It meant a lot to me, too, baby." I swipe his unruly fringe. I want to see his eyes—and the kindness behind them. "You're so good with Raffi."

He places a finger on my lips. I nibble it.

A carnal moan leaves his mouth. Is he about to fuck me again?

But he lets go of a breath, murmuring, "Can I tell you my wish?"

"Fire away."

"To one day be his dad."

Dead silence.

Until he shuffles his position as if wanting to start again. "Was I too abrupt?"

I trail a finger along his jaw, feeling his dark scruff. "No. It's a wonderful wish." No one else deserves to be Raffi's dad more than Clayton. Raffi himself would agree—hell, he said it once, that he wanted Clayton to be his dad.

A relief smile plasters his face. "And have more kids with you."

His eyes are filled with intrigue, perhaps gauging my reaction. I don't even want to speculate what he's noticing in me because right now, a tsunami of despair is swallowing me whole.

Not getting any response, he says, "Hey, don't look so worried. I'm not saying we procreate now."

I simper at him, masking the fact that I'm drowning inside. I wish Don would just go away—without Clayton having to become my protector, without Don having to come to him and do his worst. But Clayton's peaceful statement, ironically, highlights how hopeless my situation is, whether Don is in the picture or not. The wish he chose to tell me just now, which no doubt is the most important to him, is something that I can't give.

"It's a great wish," I conclude.

"Hey, relax." He shakes my arm as if sensing my guilt. "Really, that's just my wish. An end-of-the-rainbow kind of wish. Don't think I'm pressuring you. For now, let's have fun. Go with the flow." He rubs my arm. "How about you?"

"My wish?" I stretch, taking a glimpse of the carved ceiling spreading above me. Everywhere I look, I'm reminded of how lavish this house is. "For my son to be happy."

He cups my chin, stroking his thumb against my lower cheek. "I hope I can help give it to him."

That hurts even more. He wants to be in my life—in Raffi's and mine—and he sounds as sure as a man ready for a long journey.

'Genuineness.' When he said it, his eyes examined me—as if looking for clues. It's in me. I have nothing to hide. I simply want him. Not his money. Not his lifestyle. Not his status.

Still, my consciousness is far from clear. I'm here because of him, but I haven't forgotten that our togetherness happens because Don wants it to happen. So what does that make me?

I should be curling in shame now. But Clayton draws me closer, pulling my body flush against his, showering me with kisses of 'everything will be okay.'

"Goodnight, Baby Belle," he finally murmurs. That man has reached his limits. He's shattered.

I watch him falling asleep under my kiss. The day has taken a toll on him. But perhaps not as much as our conversation has allayed his uneasiness about where we're headed. He looks as peaceful as the two boys in the other rooms. He breathes softly, almost as if the sound doesn't belong to such an imposing man. But it's his—like the grace and tenderness he's made of. I can listen to it all night, but I've got to step out and entertain what the outside world demands of me.

"Clayton..." I check.

He doesn't respond.

I tiptoe downstairs to get to my phone. There are a couple of missed calls, but first, I check my text messages.

*Give me progress.*

The phone buzzes in my hand as if the caller could sense my presence. It's past midnight, but it's Don being my day and my night.

"Not a good time," I gripe. I'm still pulsing from my climax, but right now, guilt is mixing in, mulching my heart.

"I don't care! Time is ticking, Iz. Don't think I have patience for you just because you're the best person to get what I want."

"Start treating people like adults, Don, and perhaps your life will improve."

"My life is just fine, Iz. Tell me you're ready."

"I still need time. What do you need from him?"

"I want his access card," he reveals. "Before you tell me it's impossible, just remember what's at stake here."

I've noticed Clayton keeps a swipe card on his belt loop. Now it's even there for me to take, upstairs on his bedside table next to his wallet.

"Don, I'm not stupid, and Hartley is not stupid either. But

I've gained his trust. I know that much. Still, I can't just get into his pocket and steal his card."

"That shouldn't be too hard, should it? You've got under his pants how many times now?"

"He's going to take me on a tour of Hartley Marine. Trust me, when I have a chance to take his card, I will."

"Okay. You sound sure, but don't ever think of fooling me," he threatens. "Give me Clayton Hartley's access card by the end of next week, or else!"

Clayton is capable of defending himself physically. Don will have no chance against him. But I've seen what the Grim Reaper could do. He reserves his cloak and scythe for me because, against his enemies, he's hardly a confronter. He's a snake that comes from behind or under. When you don't know what you're up against, how do you protect yourself?

## 21

## CLAYTON

The weekend has ended, but I'm still relishing the aftermath of it.

I come into my office focused, chin high, and ready.

My new assistant Wanda is following me, reading me the agenda for today. She's replacing my long-serving assistant, who took her maternity leave and decided not to return so she could be a full-time mom. Wanda is only twenty-two, but she's a fast learner. Whatever Kylie, Rob's assistant, has taught her, she's put it to good use.

I hope she sticks around because apart from her bee-like efficiency, she's someone who's not afraid to tell things as they are and keep me in check. Her interview was an experience in itself. She was like nobody else in the queue of applicants. She wore a nose piercing and wasn't afraid to show off her arm tattoos. Perhaps looking at the well-made-up, model-like candidates in the room with her, she came in thinking I was some rich pervert looking for young blood. At the end of the interview, she told me, 'I'm here for a real job, Mr. Hartley. If you need someone who will accommodate you on the side, it won't be me.'

"You're late." Rob notices me coming.

"Oh, brother! I've been here since eight."

"It's all rainbows and bunny-shaped clouds in Clayton's sky then?" His lively expression tells me he knows something about the weekend. "My little informant told me."

That boy! He still has to learn about loyalty. "What did Matty tell you?"

"He said he had a great time."

"And?"

"You and Isabelle spent the night together at your house."

I try to recall whatever I did after we put the boys to bed. I'm sure I shut my bedroom door. Did I? *Shit!*

Rob chuckles. "Don't worry. You haven't destroyed his innocence."

"Clayton, General Adler on line one," Wanda calls.

"Geez, what's up with pilots being early today?" Rob remarks.

I give Rob a sign that I'll talk to him later and answer the call. "General, what can I do for you?"

"We've received the VesslScope updates and installed them. It took a while, but there wasn't a single error. You know I don't usually say this, but I'm impressed."

I clench my fist victoriously.

The general then reveals, "The testing has been brought forward. I need you at the base to start training our pilots."

"Of course. When?"

"Saturday."

It's the day I promised Isabelle that I'd take her to Hartley Marine. But, much as I want to put love first, when the highest-ranking US Air Force officer says he needs you, you say yes.

"I'll be there."

"Good man."

Adler ends the call. I get up from my seat, calling my big brother.

"He just went out," Wanda says, handing me an envelope. *Private and confidential.*

I take the letter to my desk. A subtle floral fragrance travels to me as soon as I tear the envelope open.

"Goddamn..."

So she did write it in a letter.

I read it with wide eyes, gulping at every sentence. She wants *that*? Never in a million years would I have guessed it! And the fact that she didn't hesitate to put pen on paper to tell me—she's gotta want it to come true. Pretty bad.

"Howdy!" Simon Blake knocks on my door.

I shove the letter inside my drawer, typing something into my laptop to cover up my increasing blood pressure. "Come in!"

Blake's bushy brows raise as soon as he sees me, and I know his nose is working keenly.

"What?" I glare at him.

"So, have you found forever love?" he asks in a neutral tone.

"You didn't get a scoop on that?"

"You didn't ask me to spy on you on your weekend outing. But, judging by your demeanor, I guess it went well?"

"It was great. That was why I called you."

"So, you've found the one, yet you still wanted me to investigate her?"

"Don't look at me like that, man."

Experience has told me not to be complacent, but I felt a bit of remorse when I asked Blake to investigate Isabelle again.

Blake affirms, "I've got nothing else on her, Clay. She's clean, apart from her interactions with Fletcher. Although he has been in and out of the country lately. The last time he was at her house was three weeks ago. There's no sign of him planning anything against her or her son."

Despite Isabelle's rejection when I offered protection for her son, I did get Blake to keep an eye on Raffi. As reliable as he is, neither Isabelle nor Fletcher knew about it.

I lean back on my chair, hands behind my head. "You're a one-woman man, Blake."

"I was. There was nobody else but Flo."

I motion for him to sit down. The man seems to want to move on this morning.

"Now I'm a no-woman man," he mutters. "What do you want from me with that question?"

Blake never wants to talk about Flo.

"What's your intuition on my choice this time?" I query.

"I know for a fact you're not like me. But I admire you, Clayton. You're still thinking with your head."

"You've known me for how many years, Blake?"

"Nine."

"How many women have you investigated for me?"

"A few."

"Do you think she's different?"

He leans forward. "Well, I think *you're* different. The fact that you fell for a woman who's a nurse, a mother, and seemingly wanting nothing of you at first—that's all *you*."

"I'm sure you've heard the results from the CIA about the last cyberattacks on Hartley Marine."

Their investigation confirmed that the culprits were from China. A known organization, apparently. But they couldn't find any connection to the Chinese developer associated with Fletcher.

"What about it?" Blake asks.

"Fletcher is behind it. He's got to be. The timing of the attacks was dubious. I mean, right after I caught Fletcher in Kenya? Trying to get his woman?"

"Maybe. We won't know for sure. It'll take some time to get to the bottom of it."

"Do you think I'm going to create a Trojan war here?"

"I'm just a PI, Clay, not a historian," he says, straight-faced. "Don't forget, those attacks happened not long after that sucker sabotaged us."

Following his failure to secure the contract with the US Air Force, Fletcher lodged an appeal, claiming collusion and corruption—knowing that I was close to General Adler. He lost the appeal, and then retaliated by attempting to sabotage Vessl-Scope, creating his own war with Hartley Marine. He and his company came out unscathed, and in the end, a rogue engineer took the fall. I don't know how his company is still in operation, but hey, I guess that's business. Super dirty.

"He's never a gracious loser," Blake adds. "So the reason for the attacks could be as simple as that—and not because you tried to steal his prized possession."

"Jesus, Blake! She's not his possession!"

"I know. But the man thinks so."

I sigh, "Fair point."

"Trojan war or not, if you love her, nothing else should matter. You've done all you can to protect yourself. A king who never leaves his castle will never find his queen."

I cackle at his seriousness. But it's actually not bad advice.

Blake clears his throat. "A word of caution. Fletcher's deals in Africa are falling apart. The Chinese developers, just like Fletcher, are bitter losers, and no doubt they knew who tipped off the CIA about the deals. I won't be surprised if they or Fletcher are planning more vicious attacks. I hope you're ready."

"We are," I declare. We have no choice but to be ready, but what it's going to look like—I don't know yet.

"Hey, I've got to go." Blake gets up.

"So you don't think love will be my downfall this time?"

He makes a slight detour to give my shoulder a firm pat. And in typical Blake fashion, he leaves me to answer my own question.

This game of 'yes or no' playing in my head is no good for anyone. I have to take the plunge. Isabelle isn't just some woman. She's a great mother and lover, and a person with the biggest heart I've known. Her son is proof. I don't have to look further.

I peek at her letter I shoved inside my drawer. It's facedown, but I swear I can read every word written on the other side. This fantasy of hers isn't going to be my demise. The lovemaking I have in mind—the kind she asked for and more—can only happen because of all the trust we've forged.

Adler has fast-tracked the second-phase testing of Vessl-Scope-AV, and Isabelle's confession is enough reason for me to fast-track a different kind of engineering.

**22**

_______

## ISABELLE

With only one doctor available, the ER is in utter chaos this morning.

"Where's Dr. Fawcett?" I ask around.

"He's gone home."

I'm trying to comfort an expectant mother who's been pleading with me not to send her away.

"I'm really not feeling good," she begs.

"I'll see what I can do." I approach my supervisor. "Please, you can't send her home."

"Dr. Fawcett had examined her. It's gastro. She doesn't have to stay here—we're short of beds as we are!"

"Her fever is a hundred and five! It could be sepsis. I've seen it before. Please, don't send her home."

"You're a doctor now, Martin?"

"A second opinion, that's all I ask. We can't risk it. Is Dr. Jacks in yet?" I insist.

My supervisor relents and manages to persuade the doctor, who has just started his shift, to diagnose the mother.

"Go home. You look awful," my supervisor tells me.

"I've just got one more thing to do, then I'll go."

I return to the bed at the end of the ER. A five-year-old boy has been lying there patiently, breathing through a tube. I promised to check on him one more time this morning. "How are you feeling, tiger?" I sit at the edge of his bed, caressing his arm.

"Better." He forces a smile.

Whether it's a smile, a half-smile, or a cry, what would the world be without children? It wouldn't be a world at all!

I hold his hand. This boy has a lot of recovery ahead, starting with him eating again. "I'm going to go home now. The other nurses will take good care of you, okay?"

The boy nods.

"I'm one of them." Bright-eyed Pippa joins me. "And I've got the book that you were asking for."

"Awesome!" He peruses the book with enthusiasm despite his lack of energy, no doubt immersing himself in the world of Peter Rabbit.

Pippa nudges me. "You heard about your USMLE?"

My lips flatten, recalling my dismal preparation leading up to the exam. Thanks to Don dragging me to Kenya!

Pippa raises a brow. "What's that look? Something happened..."

"I passed!"

She clasps her hands joyfully, then gives me a hug. "I'm so proud of you, Gizzy Belle! Six more years to go."

"Yeah," I hum. It's only my second year at med school, and then I'm going to continue my study to be a pediatrician. "Excluding any disruption."

"What do you mean? Something did happen!"

"Nothing happened. I'll see you later."

"What? Tell me!"

"Nothing, Pip. I've got to go."

I decide I'm going to have a shower at home.

Dr. Jacks calls me up as I'm leaving the ER. "Wait up, Martin."

"Doctor. What can I do for you?"

"Well done, you saved that mother's life," he praises. "I hope you're considering staying here when you get your medical degree."

"Absolutely. I'll see you tomorrow, Doc."

It's been one of those mornings where I finish my shift with nothing left in my tank. But, as Dr. Jacks said, I saved a life—in fact, two lives. So whatever else happens today, I can take it. First, though, I need some sleep.

But as soon as I arrive at the parking garage, I notice my Toyota is in the company of Clayton's red baby. I haven't been outside this morning, but gee, the driver's smile has got to be brighter than the L.A. sun right now.

"What happened to this weekend?" I challenge him as if his being off schedule is unacceptable—even though my heart is leaping with joy.

"Gee... you look—"

I complete his sentence with an 'I know' cock of my head.

"Jump in." He gestures to me, staying cool as if telling me this is how things are going to run this morning—his way.

"I have to—"

"You have to pick up Raffi for basketball, I know." He passes me a side smirk. "So that'll give us... four hours, give or take?"

Now my heart is racing for a different reason: his newly revealed authority and his mysterious expression. I'm not glad to see him anymore—I'm stimulated!

I hop in with him. It did cross my mind that I was going to sneak in a couple of hours' snooze this morning. But with this hunk smelling like testosterone sitting next to me, I'm as awake as an owl.

"I won't be able to take you to the HQ this weekend as I promised, so I thought I'd make it up to you now."

"You forgot you had another date?" I deadpan.

He laughs. "Yes, with a general."

"A Navy general?"

"Air Force, actually. He used to be my commander."

"I see. I thought Hartley Marine only did marine things." I pause, remembering what he once said about his business. "Well, I guess sea and air navigations aren't much different," I state as if the idea was my own.

"You paid attention, huh?" He starts the car. "Diversification, baby. That's the buzzword."

"Whatever. I guess it's lucky me. I get to see you three days early."

"Trust me, it *is* your lucky day."

"So what are we doing?"

"Do you always have to know?"

His eyes are full of wants. I know I'll get in trouble for not delivering to Don, but I can already smell Clayton's plan, and hell, I'm not going to say no. I have three days till the end of the week, and I'll sort out what I need to do then.

The destination of our drive isn't as mind-blowing as I thought. Still, his Beverly Hills mansion resembles a fairytale despite the fact that Clayton is as real as a prince can be. Under the sun, the façade of his classic Californian stone mansion shines like a happy castle. The vibe is uplifting, although I still can't fathom that only one adult and a boy live in it.

"Don't you get lonely here?" I query as we make our way from the garage to the main house.

"Sometimes," he concedes. "But on the flip side, I can do whatever the hell I want."

With that, he kisses me, and like a magician, a long piece of cloth is in his hands.

"You know what you're in for, aren't you?" he whispers, very close to my ear.

My legs start to wobble. Worse still, my core starts pulsing. I bet US Mail has delivered my secret safely to him.

He places the silk cloth against my fluttering lids.

Darkness deprives you of your sense of sight, but I've never anticipated it would heighten my arousal as much as this.

Clayton guides me, leading me down a staircase, holding on to my waist securely. A gentle master, if I may say.

It's warm in here, with a lavender smell everywhere. I think the scent comes from candles—a lot of candles.

We take a few steps, and then he stops, holding me in place. He grabs my right hand and then pulls it to stretch my arm wide, kissing the length of it as if it's his treasure.

Next, I'm cuffed onto something, the same with my other hand. I'm not against a wall. In fact, I don't think I'm near a wall at all. From the echoes of his footsteps and the chains hoisting my arms up, I think I'm placed in the middle of a room, a large room.

"You'll be uncomfortable for the next—well, I'll decide how long." He forces himself against me and slinks down to reach my feet. I can feel his sturdy fingers handling my ankles. Whatever he does, when he lets go, I can't move.

"Tell me you want this, Isabelle?" he grunts.

Too late for me to say no, but somehow his question reflects who this man is. Clayton will never ask or force me to do anything against my will.

"Yes," I answer loud and clear.

"I don't hold back, so you know."

"Have I ever asked you to?"

My legs are raised even before I finish my sentence. My wrists and ankles are raked as my body weighs me down. With nothing under my back, I'm now hanging horizontally in mid-air, completely helpless. This isn't part of what I wrote in my letter.

Clayton caresses my face, touching my clothes. His handling is feeble. I don't think he's going to tear it off.

No, he's not, because he's going to cut my uniform instead. With the crisscross sound of the scissors, without even seeing it, I know my uniform is no more. Top to bottom, I'm now only in my underwear.

Clayton's hand rubs my cleavage while the other removes my blindfold. The light from the candles shines on his V-shaped torso. That white underwear is impossibly tight and hides nothing.

I gasp, not only from the hanging position I'm subjected to but from the vibe he's giving me—sexual, carnal, and unstoppable.

He turns around, revealing his well-sculpted back. Better still, he then bends down, leaving me short-winded as I witness his ass jutting out to me. Following his movement, I realize he's picking up a bar from the floor.

Now, *that bar*—was my request.

"Welcome to your fantasy," he announces, rubbing the metal rod against my inner thigh.

I pulse, and he flicks his finger under my underwear.

Jesus... I'm so sensitive I clench hard like a sea clam protecting its pearl.

"You're wet already."

I have been since he blindfolded me!

Clayton secures the cuff at each end of the telescopic spreader bar onto my ankles. I move, and I'm stunned by how responsive the bar is.

"Remember, once you go wide, you can only go wider," he murmurs as his lips explore my shivering legs.

My body droops, snatching a painful moan out of my throat.

He keeps me that way and puts the scissors to good use once again, cutting my bra and panties.

Satisfaction mars his face. After letting his fingers travel the length of my body as if testing its readiness, he then pours oil all over it. He spreads his fingers and palms, lathering every inch of my skin with the oil, once in a while poking his finger inside my pussy.

"Clayton!" I scream.

My body droops even more.

He ducks to bypass the bar, then inserts himself in between my thighs. I pulse, and the bar extends, spreading my legs wider.

"Oh, Baby Belle." He feasts on my struggle. He trails his finger along the metal bar as if reminding me that every action will draw a reaction. Then he imposes even more torture by pressing his cock onto my opening. He's still underwear-clad, but it doesn't mean I can't feel what I'm up against.

Wild desire shrouds him as he pats my buttocks, kneading them slightly. With his hands still on my ass, he then lifts my body from sagging dismally.

"Ugh…" I pant, and my wrists and ankles are yanked slightly as one of his hands lets me go.

I've never been with a man like this. It's painful, overly arousing, but at the same time, it highlights my complete trust in him. And he doesn't let me down. Just before the pain turns into malignant torture, he pulls something from above, securing a loop around my waist like a girdle. This man isn't just well versed with female body, he's proficient in balancing pain and pleasure, and his timing is impeccable.

Now he can let me go completely without leaving me in grievous pain. I surmise that he wants me to last.

He saunters back to my gaping thighs like it was home to him. With the bar still attached to my ankles, preventing my legs from closing—not even narrowing an inch—he effortlessly slides his tongue between the lips of my sex.

"God!" The lapping feels incredible on my clit, especially with the vibration of his moan against my flesh.

After our last conversation, being this turned on feels like a violation of his trust. The realization that I won't ever make his wish come true should've been enough for me to stop him and confess my deficiency. Not to mention the Grim Reaper lurking behind me.

But this is Clayton Hartley. Like a wizard, he abolishes the negative vibes off me. He's licking my worries away, and my brain knows no better than my pussy. My cognitive ability has been short-circuited under the flood of his determination to please me.

He goes in deeper, and my legs start to kick around. I'm well aware of the consequences, but against Clayton's tongue, I have no hope.

Cruelly, he stops.

Before words of complaint leave my mouth, he takes off his underwear.

I growl like a wounded bear. Look at that magnificent flesh!

I'm a woman who doesn't put sex and physical beauty above all else. But shamefully, this morning, I don't give a damn about his eyes or his heart. His cock is what I want, and he's got plenty of it.

And he knows. He rubs it, shakes it, manipulates it.

"You said you wanted to watch, baby?" He stands tall, putting himself on display with no sign of restraint. "Then watch!"

Seeing a bondage scene in a movie is one thing. But living it with my man. who's no actor and whose assets no other men have, my frustration comes to a boil.

"Clayton..." I beg, writhing, squalling for him to come to me. The bar extends again, imposing more torture on my legs.

"Clayton, please!" I need to fucking feel him!

He keeps masturbating his massive shaft as if he can make it even harder. He moves in, presenting it awfully close to my pussy, only to withdraw.

I gyrate in protest—God, it hurts! The strains on my inner thighs, and the tightness of my ankles, are making me sweat like I'm being roasted alive.

Finally, he strides to my side. Passing the swaying flames on the candles, I can see the tip of his cock gleaming, covered in precum.

"Be careful what you wish for," he groans.

"Please... I want you."

Surprisingly, he gives himself to me—to my mouth. He brushes his wet tip against my lips, which I'm only too happy to taste.

"You want this?"

"Haven't I made myself clear?"

"I just want to hear it one more time, baby."

My restraints fail to contain my hunger.

"I want you!" I stretch my neck to reach him, then lick the delectable tip of his manhood, giving him no choice but to plunge his erection inside my mouth.

Blow jobs have been in my bad book because the man I was with never cared about his woman. Everything was all about him, for him.

But not this man. Not Clayton.

After all, I do care about his heart. Pleasing him is a privilege, and so is being pleased by him.

I work my mouth to the base of his shaft, greedy for his flesh. My hastiness doesn't help. The bar has stretched me so wide I can barely keep up. But nothing—nothing—will stop me from enjoying him.

"God, Isabelle..." His impressive wingspan effortlessly reaches between my legs, and soon his thumb finds my clit.

Along with my writhing, his moans get louder and coarser. He's close.

And he knows it. So he removes himself.

"Clayton..." I'm in pain, not because the spreader bar is at its full length, but because I want him in me. I can't wait any longer.

But instead of putting me out of my misery, he raises my legs higher, sending me to whimper and contort to no avail.

This man doesn't hold back, indeed.

My pelvis must be moving obscenely because he shoots an indulging stare at it. When he positions himself in front of me, it becomes clear that he *is* about to put me out of my misery. He's raised me so my opening is at the height of his cock.

He doesn't hold back, but he knows my limits. While my ankles and wrists are in agony, he holds my butt cheeks firmly, giving me that comfortable support just in time for him to enter me.

Despite his size, his entry is smooth, leaving pleasing trails on every inch of me. And when he increases the tempo—like now—it's heaven, hell, and earth all in one. My moans echo all around the room. That's the sound of a woman in immense arousal, and she's me.

He groans while shaking his pelvis to reposition himself inside me as if trying to find new spots. Then he carries on pushing.

"Jesus, Baby Belle... I've never been this turned on before." He eases his pumping, only to bend down and look at me. "I want you, Isabelle."

Hearing those words, with my body coated in wet heat thanks to his proximity, it becomes clear that this is more than just my fantasy come true. This is making love to a man as I crave it.

Even though his cock is raging, the man himself is pleasing me like he was born to be in me. Actually, because his cock is raging, I *need* to see his eyes—to affirm that it's not just sex. It's our bodies as much as our longing. He's real, and he reads me, and he understands.

"I want you too, Clayton."

He grips the base of his sheathed cock. Looking at me, he fiddles with the rolled end of the condom. He begs, "Can we not?"

"You want to do it without?"

"Only if you want it too."

"Yes. Clayton. Yes."

He showers me with kisses along my face, my lips, and my whole body. Only after he's satisfied that I'm well taken care of down there, that he enters me—his flesh against mine, bare, man to woman, like we're meant to be. Nothing comes between us.

Is there anything more liberating?

He glides his length inside me again and again.

Until something rolls over me. My four limbs pull at the restraints, my hands fist, and my feet contract.

Responding to my struggle, he releases with a loud growl.

In the throes of my climax, I let out a long moan. It's more air than vocal, as my throat is proven incapable of dealing with such force.

My hopeless state seems to spur him to do more. He pushes into me a couple of times, releasing again, groaning like he's given it everything he's got.

Palpitating, he lets himself fall on me without relinquishing his support of my body. I'm about to pass out, falling into a euphoric kind of unconsciousness. In the haze, I feel him lowering my legs. They touch the floor, but they might as well be still in the air, since I can't for the life of me stand on my own two feet.

"I got you." He frees my waist from the girdle and my wrists off the cuffs.

I surrender into the security of his arms.

With all the aches and pains wracking my body, like a child, I curl into his bounteous chest. The oil lathering my skin, mixed with his sweat, causes my body to slide down. But as he said, he got me.

Clayton always gets me.

We arrive upstairs in his bedroom, panting, huffing. He lowers me to the bed, and then he hurls himself next to me.

"God, Clayton..." My voice almost expires.

"You okay?"

"Yeah... I think..."

He smirks. I don't have to say any more. He knows I've just had the biggest orgasm of my life.

Now, the comfort of his bed and his hug are amplified after such a brutal passage of time.

"I didn't think you'd go all out on me like that," I quip.

"What can I say? I only offer the whole package."

He has certainly brought the meaning of 'the whole package' to a new level.

"Who installed all that? Did you swear them to secrecy?"

"Baby Belle, I build some of the largest yachts in the world, and I work with US Air Force's most advanced technologies. I fitted that room while I was having my morning snacks."

I giggle, curling under the covers.

"What can I say? You're my genie," I murmur.

He meets my lips, saying, "And I'm out of the bottle."

# 23

## ISABELLE

"Raffi, you're going to miss the bus!" I yell at my son. He's really slow this morning. Last night he spent time with Matty and Wyatt, the pilot—or 'tour guide,' as Clayton said—playing with his collections of toy planes and miniature trains.

"Coming, Mom!"

"You've got your lunch box?"

"Yes."

"Good boy." I give him a peck. "Go!"

"Bye, Mom!" He swings his backpack and rushes out the door.

I'd forgotten how long his legs are and how fast he can run. He gets to the stop before the bus arrives.

My landline rings. No one rings me on that phone except for telemarketers and the occasional overseas calls.

"Hello?" I utter my greeting suspiciously.

"Hey, it's me."

I huff. "Thomas?"

"I'm ringing you on a secure line, and I haven't got long."

"What's happening? Where are you?"

"Are you okay?"

"Yeah. Why?"

"Something's up. Something bad is up," he explains. "Look, I made contact with that passport guy. Just say yes, and you'll have yours and Raffi's in two days."

"Thomas! What did I say?"

"Right. So you haven't changed your mind."

"Get yourself one if that's what you want, and if you're absolutely sure you'll be out of Don's reach!"

"Iz, listen. I'm telling you this because you're my dear friend. If anything happens to me, you look the other way. You got that?"

His statement splits me in two. It's so real, yet I refuse to believe it. Maybe—just maybe—he's merely trying to sway me into taking the passports. "Don't you blackmail me, Thomas!"

"Shut up and listen. Don has planted a spy in Hartley Marine. I don't know the details yet, but I'll send them as soon as I know. I think Don's plan is to get that man to do the dirty work once you get hold of Clayton's access card."

The statement stabs my already struggling body. So this is it. Don is going all-out with whatever he's been planning.

Thomas asks, "What are you gonna do, Iz?"

"I don't know. I'll think of something."

But every time I try to hatch a plan, my mind is washed out with mud. For now, I have to know that my best friend is safe. "I owe you, Thomas. But you can't fucking say something's gonna happen to you! Take your passport, and go!"

"No. Once I know who this spy is, tell Clayton. No doubt Don will know I did it. But if you stay with Hartley, I'll know you're safe. Only then will I leave."

"Listen to me! Don't dig anything more. Don't wait for me. Just go!" I spell it out for him. "Clayton will figure out who that spy is after I alert him. Save yourself, Thomas."

"No. You and Raffi are our only priorities. Do you hear me?"

"Thomas! Leave now."

"Raffi is the brother I never had. And you, you're my best friend."

And he hangs up.

"Fuck!"

My day isn't getting any better when a couple of LAPD officers approach my car. I have a morning-afternoon shift today, and I left it on the street overnight to save time this morning.

"Miss Martin," one of them calls to me when I come out. They then introduce themselves.

"How can I help you, officers?"

"May I ask how this happened?" One of them rubs the dented corner of my hood.

I frown. "I don't know. It wasn't there when I drove home last night. Maybe someone hit it sometime between then and this morning."

"Were you driving along Hilgard Avenue at around seven a.m. yesterday?"

"Yes."

"Someone has reported a hit-and-run with your car details, including the exact registration."

Cold sweat coats the back of my neck. "It must be a mistake. I never hit anyone."

"Miss Martin—"

"I need to go to work. This is a mistake. You need to go back to your witness and ask them again."

"We can do it the easy way or the hard way." The officers stand in my way. "I suggest the latter. So come with us to the station."

I give in and go with them. Neighbors are watching as if I was a convicted criminal already.

This has got to be one of Don's tricks. Since he asked me for

Clayton's access card, I haven't updated him on anything. I haven't even tried to fish any intel off Clayton. I never intend to.

At the station, I'm placed inside a grim interview room, being asked the same question over and over.

"Lying to the police is a serious offense, Miss Martin."

"I know. But I haven't done anything wrong!"

"You admitted that you were driving along Hilgard Avenue at around seven a.m. yesterday. That put you at the crime scene."

"Who am I supposed to have hit?"

"You're a mother, Miss Martin. Surely, you remember that girl."

A girl? This is absurd!

"You're lucky she only has scratches and minor bruises. But what you've done is inexcusable, and you're not gonna get away with it!"

"I want a lawyer."

The door bursts open. "I'm he. Don't say anything else, Isabelle."

I've never seen that man before. He continues, "Your witness has just withdrawn their statement." He passes some paperwork to the officer interviewing me. "The plate number ends with an eight, not a three. My client has got nothing to do with the hit and run."

The officer studies the statement. He then gestures to his colleague to keep watch while he leaves the room.

Moments later, the officer comes back. "I apologize, Miss Martin. You're free to go."

Is that it?

I should be glad, but I'm so angry somehow, I'm expecting more confrontation from my supposed lawyer. He ushers me out of the station.

"Who are you?"

"Just follow me."

"I've got to go. I'm late for work."

"Follow me. It's not a request, it's an order."

And why am I not surprised? Waiting for me in his black BMW is the Grim Reaper himself.

"Today was an alleged hit-and-run. Next, it'll be a series of unfortunate events that you'll have no hope of recovering from," Don crows. "Get in!"

I join him in his car.

He throws me a sour look. "I still had the decency to do it after Raffi had left. Imagine if the boy had seen you being taken by the two officers. That would've been traumatic, don't you think?"

"You're a low piece of shit!"

"Language, Iz!" he warns. "Where's Clayton's access card?"

"He canceled on me. I didn't get that tour he promised."

"Why?"

"He had a meeting with the Air Force. With a general. Must've been something important for him to prioritize it over me."

Don lowers the window beside him and spits out his gum onto the street. He closes the window and then turns to me as if mulling over what I've just said. "Look at you. You think that's valuable information? Huh? Even beggars on the Hollywood Walk of Fame know the Hartleys are working with the Air Force!"

"I'm telling you what I know."

"I want his card."

"I haven't seen it on him."

"Isabelle." Don clenches my jaw. His anger collects at his fingertips, and they tremble against my bone. "Clayton Hartley is never without his card."

I fight the force, telling the Reaper, "Have you been in bed with him? I've never seen it!"

He studies my expression. "Perhaps he hasn't trusted you yet."

"Look, the tour will happen in a couple of days. Royalty is coming to Hartley Marine, and Clayton is taking me."

"Excellent. Now, surely, in his office, the card will be on him."

"Yeah. Can I go now?"

He grabs my wrist. "Not so fast. Do you know? I just made a substantial donation to support Social Services. One day, if I told them that the boy I've loved as my own son has been under the care of his abusive, murderer mother, they would believe me."

"Fuck you, Don!"

"Some details may be vague or contestable, but the stake's too high—they'll look the other way." His satisfied laugh slaps me.

"I will get that card for you, Don."

"Good. Because now you know I have my fingers in more than one pie." He pulls me by the throat, drawing me close to his face. His beastliness eclipses my vision.

"Then you'd better take it easy on those, or you might have a heart attack."

He scorns, "Funny. But you won't be laughing when things that you'll never imagine could happen start raining down on you."

"I've never fucked Hartley in his office," I flap. "I'm sure it'll be a mind-blowing experience for him."

He caresses my cheek. "You're a fast learner."

"I'll get his card for you."

"I don't doubt it. When you do, call this number." He sends me a text message. "I won't need the card for even more than an hour."

I bore into him, my teeth gritting behind my closed mouth. "Now let me go."

He unlocks the door, but he holds on to me. "I'll set you and Raffi free. But right now, you're on a short leash."

## 24

## ISABELLE

On a short leash—I certainly am. The man who arrives at my gate reminds me of it.

I stride toward his car before he has a chance to turn the engine off.

"You wanna take someone? Take me!" I present my wrists as if there was a pair of handcuffs waiting for me.

Don's bodyguard remains quiet. Even behind his sunglasses, I know he's not after me.

"He's not here," I snigger. Pippa had taken Raffi with her early this morning, even though my invitation to Hartley Marine was still hours away. I don't think the man anticipated that.

I rest my crossed arms against the base of his car window. "Think about your own son before you even think of taking mine. Do you hear me?"

He keeps silent.

"You know what I'm capable of." I show him the stitches on my palm. "Just think about it."

"Give Don what he wants, and no one will get hurt," he mutters.

I step backward, not taking my eyes off him until he drives away.

AFTER FERRYING me on his Porsche to the Hartley Marine headquarters, Clayton takes me on a scenic chopper ride over New Port.

The time stretches, but it hasn't helped me. There are two scenarios: I deliver for Don, or I don't. Whether I betray Clayton and hope the one percent chance of Don keeping his words will come true, or I face the possibility of losing Raffi.

I wish I didn't have to decide which scenario to test.

"You okay?" he asks, reaching for my thigh through my dress slit.

"Yeah." I look out the window. "The beach looks so beautiful from up here."

"Why am I sensing that you're not impressed?"

I turn to him with a neutral smile—or some kind of smile that doesn't constitute lying. It's not that I'm not impressed. I haven't paid attention to anything he was saying.

I don't know how long or far we're meant to fly, but Clayton makes a turn.

"Geez, your headquarters is huge," I comment as we descend into the complex. Only from the air can you actually appreciate the scale of the glass domes, which Clayton explained earlier, house their showroom, factory, and various offices. Extending to the marina and eventually the Pacific Ocean, it's as if Hartley Marine is inside a world of its own.

"We've got to have space to house some of our yachts. I mean, the ones that we can keep indoors. The big ones are out on the wharf. It actually looks even better inside," Clayton explains as we conclude our flight.

He takes my hand to help me disembark.

"Hey, you okay?" he asks again, probably sensing that I'm avoiding his eyes.

"Yeah, I'm fine. Come on, let's meet this prince then."

"He's not here yet, but all right, let's go inside."

Clayton entwines his arm over mine as we saunter along the tarmac. He reaches for his swipe card.

I've seen it many times, yet today it feels like my life is in it—implanted somewhere in the chip hidden behind the casing.

"You have to swipe in anywhere?" I ask casually.

"Pretty much. It's one of the most secure buildings in the country. My dear." He opens the door for me, letting me stride slightly in front of him. "Why does this dress remind me of Kenya?"

"Wasn't I wearing a yellow dress?"

He casts me a look as if telling me it's not what he meant. "What if I 'accidentally' snapped this?" His finger fiddles with the strap.

"Do it at your own peril," I murmur, masking the fright paralyzing me. How many more times will he need that card before I can snatch it and hand it to whoever Don instructs me to?

Clayton exhales hard as he inserts his hand from the side of my dress, obviously taking my quip as an invitation. My bare nipple stiffens under his palm. Feeling it and getting no protest from me, he massages my breast in a circular motion, not caring if he stretches or even tears the fabric covering it.

Pressing his lips against my lobe, he whispers, "You know, the prince is newly divorced. Please don't break his heart."

My hand reaches out to his belt, and the clip of his access card is on my fingertips. If there is a heart I'm going to break today, it'll be Clayton's.

I gulp air like it's acid. In the end, the only thing I manage to pull is his hand. I'm not going to snap his card off its clip, and I won't let him snap anything on my dress. At least for now.

"I intend to keep him as our customer," he jokes, oblivious to the battle raging inside me.

"Not my problem." I throw the responsibility back to him.

"Well, I'll make sure he knows you're off limits." He then leads me into the showroom.

"Wow!" I look up at the tall glass ceiling, gasping as if that would help me make sense of the immenseness of the space. He was right when he said it looked better from the inside. The color scheme, curvy layout, and the all-around glass make me feel that I'm truly in the ocean.

"Now you're impressed?"

I put a hand on his cheek. "Hey, I was impressed with the chopper ride. Sorry if I didn't show it. I just didn't feel like talking then."

"Don't fret, Baby Belle. All good."

We amble around as Clayton shows the Hartley Marine product collections.

"So this is what you do." I peruse the impossibly shiny yachts. "They look bigger when they're not in the ocean."

"They're actually the smallest model of each collection."

"Which one is the prince going to buy?"

"Not built yet. Today we're only going to show him the 3D model."

"I see. So which one is *your* favorite?"

He leads me to one with restrained enthusiasm.

"Welcome aboard the Pentela B5516." He takes my hand as we climb on board.

It feels like I'm stepping into a hotel lobby. "Marble, white leather, polished mahogany. No expense spared."

"That's the idea."

"So why this one?"

"Elegant, spacious, yet very intimate."

I peek into a stateroom and give it a pass. Clayton stands in front of me, nudging himself forward, giving me no choice but to backpedal into the room.

"Is this part of your spiel?" I helplessly ask.

"I'm a marketing man, not a salesperson."

"Oh yeah. I forgot," I giggle. "You kiss people's—"

He plunders my lips before I can finish my sentence. He keeps pressing on me until my back hits the bed, his erection crash-landing on me.

"*You* are the only one I kiss," he whispers as he stoops over me. My breasts spill out of my plunging dress, and he gives them a gander without shame. "So, where were we?"

Guilt soon overtakes passion. I was about to steal something from him, and now he wants to fuck me?

"Don't you think we should make our way to wherever the prince is?"

He muses. "Not in the mood?"

"Aren't we running out of time?"

Intrigue etches his features, but he doesn't question me. "All right, let's go then." He reaches out his hand apologetically, pulling me up.

The room isn't short of mirrors. Almost everywhere I look, I see myself. Perhaps they're there to give the illusion that the space is larger than it is, but right now, I loathe being surrounded by the reflections of me—like they were clones waiting to launch an attack on my conscience.

I tuck my breasts back behind my peek-a-boo bodice and fix my hair. I then smooth the creases we left on the bed.

"Do you make your and Raffi's bed every day?" he asks, watching me.

"Yes, I do. Do you do yours?"

"I used to. Though my discipline has dropped off since my

military days," he confesses. "But mornings when I make my bed usually turn out to be good days. You know, in the old days, the Navy SEAL's training started with making your own bed."

"Huh. Start with doing small things in a great way kind of message?"

"Pretty much. There's this well-known graduation speech from a former SEAL. Admiral McRaven, who said, 'If you make your bed every morning, you will have accomplished the first task of the day.'"

"I just like things to be tidy, that's all."

"Me too. But, consider this. He also said, 'If by chance you have a miserable day, you'll come home to a bed that is made.'"

Seeing my slight smile, he knows he's failed to fascinate me —just like his flying earlier. It's memorable wisdom, but I don't think a made bed would feel good to any of us tonight.

As he leads me off the yacht, his phone beeps. He keeps reading the text while telling me, "The prince is running late, and so are Rob and Amber. Come, let's wait in my office."

We take our time, meandering hand in hand through the rest of the showroom into another part of the headquarters.

Clayton lets me walk ahead of him, only to observe me. "So you like green? This is the second green dress you've worn with me."

"Jade color. It matches my bracelet."

"Of course." He extends his hand, and like a magnet, I take it without pause. He then draws me to him, kissing me even before he closes his office door.

"Ahem." A woman turns up. "Sorry Mr. Hartley. I thought you were in the conference room."

We say hello to each other with a handshake. Her name is Wanda. Clayton is not as predictable as I thought. I like this assistant already—look at her piercings and tattoos!

Clayton gestures to Wanda to leave us alone and closes the door behind him.

"Fancy!" I claim, my eyes roaming around the expansive room. He calls this his office? It's a fucking house!

He pulls me to his desk, staring at me as if he has a cunning plan. He clears his throat and then says, "Hey, let me show you something."

He takes a watch-like device from a drawer. I don't think this was his original plan, but I go along anyway.

"What is it?" I squint at the gold-colored object.

"I built it when I was a kid. Well, when I was in high school. I refined it over time. It's a very crude version of our current tracking system."

"A tracker?" I squint even harder.

"HartTracker."

"You're tracking people's hearts, Clayton?"

He pouts. "No. You can't track a heart. You know that." He places his hand on my left breast. Then he points at the device I'm trying to decipher, "This is just a toy. You can keep it if you want."

"So you know where I am at any time?"

"So you know I'm with you. That's *my* heart in there." He pulls me close, rubbing his chest against mine. "Well, it's off at the moment."

"How do I turn it on?" I flip the device, looking for a switch among the screws and buttons.

"See this lever here? You just need to flick it to the 'on' position—I mean this dot."

"Hmm... very intricate."

"I don't need to know where you are. Because I'll know." He touches his own heart this time.

I feel the device. The metal feels warm in my hand, like it has life inside. "I might just turn it on sometime for fun.

And to see if it is still working as you claim." I put it in my purse.

"It is still working, trust me."

Bit by bit, I slink out of his embrace, then saunter around the room, checking the ensuite, library, and closet. "You've got everything here."

"Yeah."

It's now or never. Whatever happens between us, however I feel about him and him about me, Raffi is still my priority.

I return to Clayton, pressing myself against him, kneading his ass. "So, where's the bed?"

"I don't have a bed here. But it doesn't mean we can't—" He puts his weight on me, forcing me to lay on his desk.

"You don't believe a good day starts with making your bed, then?"

He ignores me, pulling the pins that are holding my hair together.

"Clayton... I spent an hour creating that bun!"

A nonchalant smirk curves across his face. He then cups the back of my head, burying his hand in my hair—playful, like he's about to enter wonderland.

"Sorry, but not sorry," he hisses.

I pull the hem of his shirt, patting the waist of his pants. He's about to unbuckle his belt, and once again, his access card is within my reach.

"Mr. Hartley!" his assistant's voice blares from behind the door. "Rob and Amber are in the conference room. The prince is ten minutes away,"

"Fuck..." Clayton grumbles.

He tucks his shirt back in, telling me adamantly, "We'll have time for this. Well, I'll make time for this."

I get up from his desk, my hands trembling like I'd just crawled on ice.

He frowns at me. "Hey, you okay?"

Clearly I don't look okay, because this is the third time he's asked since he picked me up.

"Yeah, just nervous about meeting this prince."

"Don't be."

I flick my hair playfully, then put a hand on his lapel. "Damn, you look so handsome in a tux."

"You've only just noticed?" He starts fussing with my hair again as we embrace. "You should keep your hair down, Baby Belle. At all times."

"Your wish is my command." I tousle my hair, letting the texture brush his skin.

"You know, baby... when we were up in the air..."

He appraises me. I can still feel his bulge, but I think what's on his mind is about something that doesn't involve his cock. He puts his fingers through my hair, sighing. "Never mind. For another time. Let's not leave Rob high and dry."

Probably a good thing. I've got a feeling I'm not ready to hear it.

Clayton takes me to the conference room, his hand holding mine, calm—as if nothing happened.

"Rob," he calls. "Amber."

Rob and Amber beam at us. Their presence takes my breath away, more than the showroom did. I've seen them in photos—stunning couple, in love, made for each other. But in the flesh, they're simply real—real love, real connection, real them.

"Hey, brother! Hey, lovely," Clayton greets them, giving Amber a peck on the cheek. "Rob, Amber, this is Isabelle."

"Nice to finally meet you." I shake Rob's hand and then hug Amber—sideways because of her growing belly. "How far along are you?"

"We're almost there." Amber rubs her bump. "One more week."

I smile, mesmerized by the warmth they exude. Amber is so beautiful. With that magnificent mommy belly, I can't say anything else, but she is an angel. And Rob—Californians were right to award him their most eligible bachelor, however long ago it was. His gaze is deep but different from Clayton's. I don't think he's quite an extrovert like his younger brother. But if I have to sum up the way I feel about them, Rob and Amber are the couple I want to stay close to and chat with all night.

"The prince is here," Clayton's assistant Wanda announces.

"Amber-Rose and I will meet him at the front." Rob rounds his arm around his wife. "You guys stay here. Pour yourselves some drink."

"What would you like, Baby Belle?"

"Whatever you're having."

Clayton gets a couple of flutes and pours us some champagne.

Moments later, Amber, Rob, and the prince arrive in the conference room. He has a glass of champagne in his hand while Rob and Amber explain to him the Middle-Eastern-inspired cordial they're having. It appears both of them are teetotalers for the pregnancy. How sweet!

"Clay, my man!" the prince greets Clayton with open arms.

"Neo. Meet Isabelle."

Neo? I know his name is Prince Yiannis-Andreas from Greece, but how come Rob and Amber call him 'your highness' while Clayton seems to call him by his nickname?

"Nice to meet you, darling." The prince kisses my hand. "I really hope that man treats you well."

"He does. Very well. Great to meet you, your highness," I say, following Rob's and Amber's lead earlier.

"Call me Neo. Your boyfriend calls me that, so you call me that."

"Very well," I oblige. "Great to meet you, Neo."

"I know your Clay for a long time," he professes, looking like he's about to hand out some pearls of wisdom. "His romance timeline is like an erratic radio transmission. Up and down, up and down, and even a flatline. That was when he started to take Rob to parties as his other half because he ran out of dates. Then, of course, Rob found Amber, and he'd been a miserable bachelor ever since. Well, until now, apparently."

"I'm the luckiest man alive." He kisses me.

Lucky? He doesn't even know what's about to hit him.

Cold sweat spreads through me. Clayton will probably soon ask me again if I'm okay.

"Shall we?" Rob invites the prince to sit down, and soon the presentation begins.

The lights dim, and fortunately for me, Clayton's attention lands on the multimedia suite in front of the conference room.

I take a glimpse at his access card one more time.

Between love and reality, I make my decision.

## 25

# CLAYTON

As we've been informed earlier by Neo's PA, the prince is called to another event shortly after we conclude our presentation.

Rob, Amber, Isabelle, and I are now ambling back to the office area.

"Did you and the prince play basketball together or something?" Isabelle asks. In typical Neo fashion, during the presentation, he pointed out the absence of a basketball court in our model.

"Oh, you read about that, huh?" I hook my arm around her waist loosely, then move in closer to her, dropping my hand to her ass.

Jesus... I wish I'd insisted on bedding her in that showroom Pentela.

Isabelle raises her eyes to mine, and my hand coasts back up to her waist.

Actually, I'm glad we didn't fuck. If I'm to make love to her, it can't be just a five-minute blitz. I'm no good with quickies because I must give my woman good foreplay. She's got to be well aroused. Only then will I ask her to take me.

"Raffi told me. You and the prince played on one of your yachts."

I glance at Rob, and Isabelle traces my gaze.

"That hoop-off, it happened after his first date with Amber," I tell Isabelle.

"It wasn't just a date. Well, it's a long story," Amber gushes. "Right, husband?" She tugs Rob toward her, giving him a small kiss.

Isabelle drops her head onto my shoulder as if saying *I want that*—not just the story and the kiss, but them, what they've got together.

It's playing on my mind that the moment is coming for me to propose to her. Exactly when, where, or how, I don't know yet. I just want it sooner rather than later.

"Hey, why don't we show Isabelle the 'P'?" Rob suggests.

"What's the 'P'?" Isabelle queries.

"You'll see." I wink. We make a little detour to the speed wing. "I've got it!" I step ahead of the group and swipe us in.

"What is that?" Isabelle gapes at the vessel—its surface gleam under the spotlight.

I tug her so she can see the racing beauty closer. "This is the Peregrine. A hyper-speed vehicle made of airplane engines."

Isabelle furrows her brows. "But it's a boat, right?"

"It is a boat, my dear," I explain, patting her back and telling her it's okay to be confused. Truly, the 'P' looks more like a jet than a boat. "Rob broke the world record for speed on water with it. It's still standing."

"Impressive."

"He wanted to break another record, water speed at night, but—" I glance at Amber.

With delight, my sister-in-law chimes in, "By the time he thought he was ready, Graeme was born. So he put his plan on hold. And then the second time he was going to attempt it, I got pregnant again."

My brother kisses his wife. "I don't think I'm going to pursue that record any more, or any other record." He puts his hand on Amber's belly.

I angle a glance at Isabelle. She's smiling, but her gaze tells me her mind is somewhere else. What's the matter with her today?

I pull her close, and there she goes... she smiles again.

"Ugh," Amber pants. "I think I'm gonna hang around in your office, Rob."

"Hey, you okay?" Rob rubs her back.

"Yeah. I need to sit down."

"Come," Rob says. "Do you want me to carry you?"

"Don't embarrass me!" Amber tells her husband, then she turns to Isabelle. "We should catch up soon. Girls gotta stick together."

"And you can tell me all about your 'first date' with Rob." Isabelle winks at her.

After the couple leaves, I lead Isabelle into the engineering quarter. "I might as well show you the rest of the complex."

"Rob and Amber look good together," she comments. "So, your brother calls her Amber-Rose?"

"Yeah. Most people call her Amber, but he's special, you know."

Isabelle observes me. "Can you see yourself in his position?"

I stop, turn to her, and put my hand under her chin. "With a family of my own? Hell yeah. Imagine going back to the airbase with two or three more kids, queuing up to fly the jet."

Her features change, and I can feel her firm hold on my waist.

"Isabelle, is it bothering you? All this family talk?"

"No. No."

I look into her eyes, exposing her denial. "Hey, I can't help talking about it, but I don't mean to pressure you."

"I know." She looks at everything around her but me. "I'm fine. Come, show me what you wanted to show me."

I swipe us into the engineering quarter, and the doors slide open.

"Now, this is the heart of Hartley Marine," I announce. "And that man is the boss around here. Rocky, my man!"

Rocky takes off his visors and strides toward us. "Hi, you must be Isabelle. My name is Emmett, but people call me Rocky. It's my favorite movie," the man explains. "Hey, Stefan, come here," Rocky calls our newbie over to Isabelle. "That is Stefan Boss. Despite his name, he's actually my assistant."

She lets out a little giggle. "You don't look like a typical engineer."

"I'm anything but typical," Rocky raves.

"How do you do?" Stefan finally joins us after locking his plasma-cutting tool. He takes off his gloves and extends his hand to her.

She freezes for a second but then takes his hand tentatively, keeping silent.

Stefan continues, "Stefan Boss, no relation to Hugo Boss. It's a German surname, meaning tough. But as Rocky said, he's the boss."

Isabelle keeps smiling—and silent. I don't think she's paying attention to what he says. Evidently, she's still worried about the kid talk.

She then steps away from the two engineers, and I follow.

"Clayton, can we go back to your office?" she whispers.

She doesn't look right, and her hand is freezing!

"You okay?"

"Can we go, please?"

She follows me into my office, keeping me wondering. I

would like to think of her request lightly—perhaps she has some surprise for me? That she's going to turn into a vixen, and we'll pick up where we left off?

But as we arrive in my office, I know something is off.

"Isabelle? Are you feeling all right?" It looks as though the blood had drained from her face.

She bows her head. "Why me, Clayton?"

"You're still worried about the kids thing?" I invite her to sit on the couch. I hold her hands, which have turned even colder. "I want you because it's you. I've been screwed over by so many women that, at one point, I just gave up on my dream of becoming a father. But with you, I can't stop talking about it. I love kids. I want kids—but please tell me if you have something in your mind."

Her lips quiver. "I... I can't have any more children, Clayton. I can't give you the family you want."

I can't hide my disappointment, but I don't let go of her hands. Tears are brewing in her eyes, but she keeps her composure. The strain on her face—it's more than pain. It's like she's giving up on everything.

"I don't want to ruin you," she mutters.

The revelation hurts, but I'm sure separating from her will hurt even more. I've got to accept what she's told me. There are options. Perhaps she'll be open to them, and I can still be a dad, but right now, she's my only concern.

"I still want you," I maintain. "And you're not going to ruin me."

She tries to free herself, but I don't relent.

"Clayton... Raffi's younger sister." She gulps.

She had another baby?

I squeeze her fingers.

"I gave birth to her two months early. But the delivery was

too rough for her. So she didn't have a chance. She was stillborn. And my body didn't have a chance either."

That even makes me more determined. If anyone deserves my love and my life, it'll be her.

"Baby, I love you. If I can't have children with you, I'm okay with it. We've got Raffi. And Matty. It hasn't changed anything."

Unable to dam her unshed tears, she sobs. She hugs me, only to muffle her howl.

I've never been held like this by a woman. It's like her agony is melting into me. It's tearing her apart as viciously as it is me.

"Baby, tell me what's going on."

"Why do you have to be so goddamn perfect?'

"Isabelle?"

"Why didn't you just tell me that you didn't want to be with me because I couldn't give you what you want?"

"Because that's not what I want."

"You were upfront about it. I should've told you right from the start."

"I understand that you didn't tell me then. There were so many other things that were on our minds."

"I saw the way you looked at Rob and Amber. You want it so badly. Why? Why do you still want to be with me?"

"You and me—we're more than just my wish."

She grimaces in pain. Her lips swell from her cry. "Clayton... listen to me."

Her hands tremble in my hold like she's trying to contain a blast.

"Don sent me to get something from you."

A lump shut my airway. "What?"

"I never betrayed you, Clayton. I haven't given him anything."

"Isabelle!"

"I'm telling you now before things get out of hand between us."

"They already have!"

"He's implanting someone into your company. Stefan Boss."

"What the hell are you talking about?"

"He's Don's man. He was the man with the knife that morning. Remember that biker outside the hospital? When I pushed you onto the sidewalk?"

"Isabelle…"

"I saw a glimpse of a green tattoo on his hand. Stefan Boss—he has a big shamrock tattoo on top of his palm. It's him. He's going to sabotage whatever he's working on right now."

"Fuck!" Our alpha Rocky was right all along! That engineer is an imposter! But how?

Perhaps seeing me confused, she asserts, "You've got to believe me. I'm going to ring this number." She fiddles with her phone. "And I bet Stefan Boss will answer."

I let her go and call my brother. "Rob, where are you?"

"In my office, with Amber. You okay, man?"

"Call Rocky."

"What's going on, Clay?"

"Call him. Put him on a three-way call with us."

Rob releases a doubtful sigh. "Okay."

Soon I hear a beep of an incoming call. "Clay, I'm here." It's Rocky's voice—our real man.

"Rocky, tell me if Boss receives a call about…" I give Isabelle a sign to make the call. "Now."

Cold air creeps under my skin.

Then Rocky whispers, "Yeah. His phone is on silent, but he's looking at it."

I snatch Isabelle's phone and end her call to Boss.

"Rocky, lock that son of the bitch inside the stationery room. Take his phone, or phones, or whatever is on him. Don't let him talk to anyone," I blurt like a ticking bomb is about to explode. "Rob, call the police. Stefan Boss is Fletcher's mole!"

I turn to Isabelle, gripping her shoulders. "What does Don want?"

"He wants me to steal your access card and then give it to Boss."

Of course!

Only Rob's and my access cards can unlock the core software to VesslScope and VesslScope-AV. The engineers have access to it only when they're in working phase. Once each stable version is signed off, it's locked.

Isabelle shakes her head, apparently filled with a sudden thought. "Shit, that morning... Maybe Boss was on his motorbike, trying to steal your access card. Cutting it off your belt."

Everything in my body hurts.

She's telling me this because she loves me.

*Right?*

I take her hand, refusing to believe that she has malice in her. "Don't let Fletcher come between us. He wants my card? Here, give it to him!" I hand over my card to her.

But she throws it onto the table.

"It's too late. He'll know it's a lie. Not just because we've uncovered Boss, but he'll be able to see through me. What I feel for you is real, and I can't mask it no matter how hard I try. He'll take Raffi away from me."

"Do you remember what I said in the beginning? Let him come to *me*."

She shakes her head. "I'm sorry, Clayton. That can't happen. I'm not safe here, and Raffi is even in a worse situation."

"I'll keep you safe! Take Raffi to my house. I'll have security twenty-four-seven. No one will harm you or Raffi."

"No matter how many bodyguards you hire, it doesn't matter if you defeat Donovan Fletcher."

"It's a matter of when, Isabelle."

"If or when, it won't make a difference. At the end of the day, I still won't be able to give you what you want, what you dream of as a man."

"You have given me what I want. You. I don't care if we can't have children. All I want is you."

"I have too many secrets. I'm in too deep, and they're too painful to tell. I don't want to use you—you're too good for me. So please let me out. It's not too late to let me go."

Suddenly, we hear a scream coming from Rob's office.

"Wait here!" I instruct and rush to be with my brother.

"Clay! Where's Isabelle? We need her! Now!" Rob is holding Amber, who's lying on the floor. My God! She's in labor! "Ambulance is still ten minutes away. She can't wait!"

Isabelle is already standing by the door. "Let me help her." She darts to Amber's side, kneeling between her legs. I stand away from them, watching from behind.

"You're doing well, Amber," Isabelle encourages. "I can see the head. It's coming. Keep pushing."

"Rob..." Amber cries.

"I'm here, Amber-Rose."

Minutes later—a cry.

Isabelle takes the baby in her arms, wrapping it with a towel that I just handed to her.

"She's perfect," Isabelle cries, handing the baby over to Amber.

She's a beautiful girl, indeed, perfect as Isabelle claims—with very healthy lungs, too, judging by how hard she cries.

Rob hugs and kisses his wife, no doubt whispering words of love. The couple's new-parent smiles brighten the room as they caress their baby gently. Rob himself cries tears of joy.

I stand still, overwhelmed by my own tears. I want that—

there's no denying it. But there's no other woman I want in my life. I want that woman who just delivered that precious life.

Soon paramedics take over, and Isabelle slowly withdraws herself from the scene. But it doesn't go unnoticed by me.

"Isabelle!" I call her desperately. She keeps running, but I catch her. "It can't just end like this. *Us*—can't just end like this."

Her face crumples. She's fighting an agony that is bigger than herself. "I'm looking you in the eye, Clayton Hartley. I haven't betrayed you, and I will never do. So, let me go before I break my promise."

"You know, Isabelle. I've had a girlfriend forge my signature to steal a hundred grand from me. Then, hear this. My last girlfriend, whom I thought was my forever—do you know what she called me? A clinker in a million-dollar suit."

"I'm sorry, Clayton, but—"

"You're talking about betrayal. I *know* betrayal! Betrayal is stealing from me. Betrayal is putting me down, laying blame on me while you're cheating on me." My voice breaks. "You're not it, Isabelle! You'll never be it. I know I'm right."

"I'll never want you to be wrong, Clayton. That's why I'm walking away now."

"What you did back there for Rob and Amber, I won't forget it," I beg. "What we've shared together with Raffi and Matty! You've got to stay, please. Stay."

"I can't." Her eyes darken.

"You don't think I can love you?"

"I know you love me. But I don't want you to."

My feet seem to fix themselves to the floor. Numbness washes over me like what's happening is just a mirage. But there she is, running away from me, exiting the world I wish she was part of.

**26**

———

**ISABELLE**

The taxi driver keeps looking at me from the rearview mirror. It's probably not the first time he's had a crying passenger.

Yes, I was crying when I hopped in, but not for Clayton. My tears were for the life I just brought into this world. But with the state of my dress—and a common assumption—I won't blame the driver for thinking some kind of boy had just dumped me.

I tie my hair back in a ponytail. Responding to the driver's glance, I lift my chin up, showing that I'm composed. Then I wipe the smudges around my eyes with a tissue and reapply my makeup. My gaze strays back to the rearview mirror as if telling him the break-up is not going to bring me down, if that's what he's thinking about.

I'm grieving for Clayton, but it's really no time to cry for him. I'll have a lifetime to do it, but not now.

I refrain from calling Thomas. The last time he talked to me, he was on a secure line. For the sake of our safety, silence is golden at the moment.

"Can you go a little faster?" I ask the driver.

"I'm sorry, Ma'am. I can't. Speed limit."

I let it be. It seems that he's still scrutinizing me. I'm thankful that my dress is dark green. There's blood on it—from the delivery—but it appears like I'd spilled some red wine.

Being patient and composed is one thing, but time is ticking. This is ridiculously slow! I have to get to Raffi.

As we crawl along the highway, an idea springs out.

"I change my mind. Take me to LAX."

"Sure." The driver soon changes lanes.

I know how I'm going to spend Don's two-grand carrot, but I need more than that if my plan is to work. I call Pippa.

"Hey, what's up, Gizzy?" she answers jovially.

"Pip, is Raffi still with Wyatt?" This morning, I'd asked her to take my son to his house. There's no way Don's men will have the audacity to take Raffi from the former Navy pilot.

"Yes. Matty is with them, too. You okay?"

"Look. Pack Raffi's clothes, and take some of mine too."

"Iz? What's going on?"

"Just do it. The less you know, the better."

"That man who took Raffi that night when you were in Kenya. He wasn't your uncle, was he?"

"Pip! The less you know, the better. You're the only one who can help me now. Just do as I say, or you'll get us killed."

That seems to get her going. I can hear rustling near her, I think she's pulling my suitcase.

"Once you've packed up, get Raffi."

"What should I tell him?"

"When you pick him up, tell him I need him at home. Don't panic, and don't say anything else in front of Wyatt and Matty. And make sure no one is following you."

"Okay."

"When you're alone with Raffi, tell him that he and I need to get away for a few weeks and that I'll explain when he's with me."

Raffi will know this is no holiday. But out of any other

options, my plan is the gentlest way to take him away from the life he knows.

"Okay." It's a single-word answer, but I can hear her trembling. "Then what?"

"Meet me at Port of L.A."

My friend stays silent.

"Got that?"

"Yeah. Yeah."

I'm about to hang up, but then I remind her, "Please don't forget Mr. Oreo."

"Of course."

"Thank you, Pip."

Once I get to LAX,, I buy a couple of tickets to New York using my credit card, as well as a new set of clothes so I can get rid of my dress that's been making me stand out like a peacock. I get more clothes and supplies I may need for the journey until I max out my card. Then, I strip my two bank accounts bare. When you're on the run, cash is king.

No doubt Don will look for me, and I'm going to show him how I operate.

I throw away my phone.

I failed to get away from Nando three years ago. I'm not going to repeat the same mistake. This time, I will succeed.

## 27

## CLAYTON

A week after the police arrested Stefan Boss, detectives are still returning to Hartley Marine to get more evidence.

All productions have ceased—in fact, all activities in the factory are on hold except for essential services.

Rocky, our real man, is leading a massive operation to make sure Stefan Boss hasn't put his mark elsewhere and to flush out anyone else who may be involved. So far, though, the signs are promising that we've contained the damage. Boss had tampered with one of the engines designed for the Pentela Next-Gen prototype. The effect wouldn't have been immediate, but probably in a day or two, the damage would've sunk the ship.

Donovan Fletcher is back in Kenya again, perhaps intending to give the impression that it's business as usual for him, though the fires he's trying to put out in that part of the world are getting out of control. It's almost the end of the road for him, but he seems to insist on hanging on for as long as he can. Boss hasn't confessed to anything, so at this stage, the police can't link him to that stray cat.

I slump in my chair, aching from an attack that I never saw coming. When something looks too good to be true, chances are, it is. And in my case, that something was a woman I genuinely loved. Her green dress still flashes in my mind, but it looks bleak, like oil had been smeared all over it.

Never mind that my dream has been crushed, but being a fool again?

I feel like shouting it from the rooftop.

I made history, all right. In my war, Helen *is* the Trojan horse.

She said she had a lot of secrets. I don't doubt her.

But her smile, her affection, her hold on me, her moans— were they all lies?

And even my backup failed. How the hell did Simon Blake manage to be fooled too?

I scream to the wall, then wipe my desk clean with one sweep of my arms.

"Fuck!" I yell louder than the stationery and electronics battering the floor.

My assistant rushes in. "Mr. Hartley?"

"Stay out of this, Wanda. I mean it."

"Mr. Hartley, please."

"Wanda, turn around, and close that door!"

Pale-faced, Wanda backpedals, exiting quietly.

But soon the door bursts back open.

"I said—"

"Clay!"

I slump back into my chair, saying nothing more. I respect my big brother that much.

"Clay, talk to me."

My shoulders heave up and down like I was fending off an ogre coming out of me. I put my face in my hands. Now I can't even look at Rob.

"Take it easy, brother." Rob stands next to me, holding me. "Take it easy."

"What are you doing here? You're supposed to be with Amber."

"She's fine."

I pant. I'm happy for him, for his family. He deserves that happiness after all he went through.

But, that perfect picture in my head—what Isabelle, Raffi, Matty, and I, and the children I dreamed of, could've looked like —has been torn to pieces.

I simmer down, helped by the thought of the youngest Hartley. "Baby Mia?"

"She's doing great," Rob assures me. "But you're not, so I'm here."

I get off my chair and hug him. He never stops being my rock. Blood is thicker than water. Rob is proof.

"What the hell am I doing wrong, Rob?"

He pulls me to the couch. "Sit down." He then fixes me a glass of scotch, which I gulp in one go.

"I'm sorry, Clay. At least she confessed before Fletcher brought us all down. I know you're hurt—I've never seen you like this. But we have to move on. I need you."

I will fight for him, for us, but I won't let it slide with Isabelle.

My assistant's voice interrupts my chain of thought. She's trying to stop someone from coming in. "It's not a good time!"

The door clicks open, but whoever is behind it seems to heed Wanda's warning because he stops short of opening the door all the way. In a small pause, I hear Simon Blake announce, "Clay, it's me."

I refuse to look at the man. It's Rob who motions for him to come in.

"Hey, you okay, man?" Blake surveys the mess on the floor.

"The hell, Blake!" I shoot him a kerosene-charged scowl.

"Clay, calm down," Rob warns.

"How the fuck did you not know all that about Isabelle?"

The PI ignores my aggression. Not a strand of guilt is showing on his inscrutable face. God, I hate him right now!

"There's Isabella Martin. And there's Isabelli Martins. Isabelli Luna Martins," he explains.

"Are you saying you were researching the wrong person all this time?"

"No. They're the same person—same biometrics. But different criminal records."

My shoulders slump even lower.

"I swear, I've never seen these records before," Blake reassures. "It's like they just came out of the blue."

"So, which one is she?"

"Isabelli Luna Martins. Her parents originally came from Portugal before they settled in Brazil. Martins is a common Portuguese name, instead of Martin."

"So what has this Isabelli Martins done?"

Blake stops as if telling me I need another glass of scotch. "She killed her boyfriend."

My head might as well explode.

"Blake?" Even Rob stares at him in disbelief. "How could you have missed that?"

"I don't know, Rob. But I did."

"So her boyfriend didn't die in a car accident?" I ask, somehow hoping Blake had just gotten the facts mixed up and that he would change his statement.

"No."

"How did she kill him?"

Blake's shoulders slump slightly, then he reveals, "Stabbed him, nine times."

"Fuck..." I murmur. My energy has been sapped, I can't even swear properly.

So my girlfriend was a cold-blooded killer. This is some history I'm making!

She said she had a lot of secrets—never in my wildest dream I thought this would be one of them. Now it makes sense that she left. She couldn't live with her guilt.

Rob leans back, his head shaking repeatedly. He seems as hopeless as I am.

I put the pieces together in my head. Then I say it out loud, "So, Fletcher created Isabella Martin, the innocent woman whose boyfriend died in a car accident. And with that, he hid Isabelli Martins' hideous records. Then Fletcher blackmailed her to get to me. Now that she decided to come clean, he released those records."

"That'd be the likely scenario," Blake affirms.

"What else?"

Blake turns his head to escape two pairs of eyes staring at him.

"What else?" I repeat.

"She terminated her pregnancy not long after she killed him. Clearly, she didn't want anything more to do with her boyfriend. Even his child."

A boyfriend killer. Surprisingly, I still could take that. But killing an unborn child? Her own unborn child?

My limbs feel numb. I can't even feel myself breathing.

And she claimed that she couldn't have kids because she *lost* her baby? For fuck's sakes! She got rid of her kid!

That snaps awake an emotion that I thought was dead and buried. The bleakness around me turns into red-hot outrage. "Where's she now?"

Blake is about to shake his head, but perhaps seeing my confrontational intent, he dips his chin down.

I step toward him, not giving him any space to hide. My threatening groan prompts him to look at me. "Where is she?"

"Alaska."

"Where in fucking Alaska?"

"A CCTV camera caught her at Port of Ketchikan, but she hasn't been seen ever since."

"Rental car? Train tickets? Accommodation?"

"Nothing," Blake responds. "Yet."

"Find her! Then take me to her."

"Clay, she's out there because she doesn't want Fletcher to find her. She's—"

"You're on her side now? What the fuck is going on, Blake? Your loyalty is to us, to the Hartleys!"

"Don't question my loyalty, Clay!" Blake stands tall. "I'm saying that because I don't want you to do something you regret. You know what will happen if we lead Fletcher to her."

"If you can find her, Fletcher can too."

"Stop there!" Blake eyeballs me. "You hired me for a reason. Yes, I fucked this up big-time! I wish I'd known that Fletcher created Isabella Martin. I wish I'd known he hid Isabelli Martins' murder!"

"Murders. She killed two people!"

"As you say. But I'm asking you this, Clay. Have I ever failed before? Have I ever leaked anything? Has anyone else found out about what I found?"

"Clay..." Rob calls. "Take a breath. Think about this carefully."

I don't feel the need to be careful anymore, but I gesture to Blake to go on with his explanation.

"She's pretty good at making herself disappear," Blake restarts. "Alaska would be the last place anyone would think she'd go. New York or some city on the East Coast would be the easier option, seeing as she's from there. In fact, she bought a couple of tickets to JFK from LAX for herself and Raffi, but they never flew there."

"To fool Fletcher?" Rob asks.

"Yeah. She made all her card transactions in and around the

airport," Blake explains. "And smartly, she and Raffi went on a four-day cruise, just like normal tourists. Paid in cash, almost impossible to trace. I only knew she was in Alaska because *I'm* from there. I have eyes there."

"I'm going! I don't care if Fletcher follows."

"You do."

"I don't care about a damn thing! Whatever Fletcher will do to her, she deserves it."

"Clay, you didn't mean that," Rob asserts.

I bite my lip. I did love that woman. And she delivered my brother's baby, for God's sake! Despite my rage right now, I know I would carry eternal guilt if I became the cause of her demise.

"Listen to him," my brother adds.

"Once I know where she is, here's what we'll do," our PI says. "I will arrange for your flight to Seattle. There's a marine trade show coming up, which some prominent companies are taking part in. Of course, Hartley Marine won't. But we've got some of our associates involved in the event. You'll attend that trade show—which everybody, including Fletcher, will see as a gesture of goodwill. You'll only need a few hours there just to show your face. Then you'll sneak out, and I'll take you to her."

The bitter part of me is urging me to fire this man, but I know his plan is sound. "Fine!"

"Clay," Rob says. "There's another option."

"What is that?"

"Let her go." He pauses, assessing me. "With this intact." He taps at my left pec.

"I'm not chasing her, Rob. I just want to look her in the eye when I ask her why."

**28**

---

## ISABELLE

The past month has gone like a blur, with no time to think about what's ahead or to reflect on what has passed me by. It's like my body had been sucked into a tunnel and then spat out to this foreign land called Alaska. But inside, every cell in my body is stuck in California.

In Hartley Marine, to be exact. The breathtaking ocean-on-land complex, the pinnacle of Clayton's empire, and the place where things fell apart for me.

There, I shook hands with my enemy. The shamrock tattoo on Stefan Boss has become the dire symbol of what I had brought to Clayton and his family. Donovan Fletcher has set out to bring down his rival since a long time ago. I was never the cause, but I was the enabler—I was the reason Don dared to make his move.

I would've sacrificed everything I'd got to make it right with Clayton. God, even before I'd known him, I was prepared to take a knife for him! And having tasted his love, I would've done it again in a heartbeat—even if the danger was more lethal than a knife. But that wasn't what he needed from me.

I know what 'worst' can look like when Donovan Fletcher's

name is attached to it. But Clayton is capable of defending himself. With the manpower and resources at his disposal, he'll be able to crush the Reaper sooner rather than later.

What Clayton truly needs, I can't give. And I wouldn't be able to live with myself had I stayed.

The desperation and sadness in his eyes when pleading with me is the regret that I haven't come to terms with. Perhaps I never will. At that last moment, a revelation was spread in front of me. The man loved me unconditionally, no sliver of a doubt.

But love isn't everything. In any relationship, if a party's needs aren't fulfilled, it's not going to last. And when a man's need is as primal as having his own children, there is no substitute. He may not want to admit its significance, but had I clung to him, my deficiency would become a thorn that eventually severed our bond.

The Hartleys are a family with hearts despite their power and wealth. I've done enough damage. They don't deserve further woes and misfortunes because of me. For that, my decision to leave was justified.

Despite the wrongs, somehow, Hartley Marine epitomizes redemption. It came from the tiniest yet mightiest form of miracle—Rob's and Amber's baby. Her cry was the most beautiful sound I'd heard in a long time. Knowing that my hands were the first thing she felt when she was born into this world gave me peace, a sign that the universe still regarded me as a worthy person.

I rub my forearms, tingling from the thought of baby Hartley. I wonder what they named her.

"Mom!" Raffi calls, pointing at a creature floating in the water. "Look, sea otter!"

I smile at my constant miracle. "Cute, huh?"

The boy eagerly points his phone to take photos—well, technically, my new phone.

"Can I go there?" He gestures to the hull of our whale-watching boat.

"Of course. But don't run, and make sure you hang on, okay?"

He throws me an 'I'm a big boy' look before disappearing.

Alaska is a change of scenery, for sure. Sometimes I convince myself that our time here is truly a vacation. It helps—because what you believe always translates to how you look on the outside, what you do, and what you say. I need to make Raffi feel safe, however I do it. While I stay vigilant, I try to give him as many positive distractions as possible.

I lean on the railing, watching the endless blue stretch before me. There are only a handful of people around in this part of the boat. The hull seems to be the place to be right now.

The stillness stirs the lingering grief I have for Clayton. Yet I can't speak about it, not even a murmur in my heart. And the goddamn tears that I supposedly had a lifetime to cry never came.

But I miss him for everything he was. As a man, a friend, a lover, and a partner.

A man who reads you before you tell, a man who satisfies you even before you ask, a man who doesn't play games and isn't afraid of showing how much you mean to him—is a man who will cherish you forever.

Yet, I had to run away from him.

I watch the clouds move, imagining one of them is hiding him as he flies his aircraft wherever he's going.

*My* Clayton.

Our story is over, and there's nothing I can do now.

The boat sways after the captain stops the engine. He's probably looking around for a sign of whales. I reach for my wallet, drawing a round, golden object from one of its sleeves. I don't even know why I'm still keeping it.

Maybe it's time to forget.

My hand forms a fist around it.

The boat's engine whirs back alive under my feet. Apparently, the captain has decided to move on.

It's time.

I extend my arm. My hand trembles, but my fingers keep clinging to it like another force is controlling them.

*Goddammit!*

I stare at my own fist, the ocean wake in the background. My fingers start unfurling in the wind.

But among the noise of nature, I hear a whisper.

*Baby Belle.*

It's my own whisper, but it makes me withdraw my arm.

And for the first time, I cry for him.

Our story is truly over. This golden object, the HartTracker, is the only thing that's left of him. And he said it was his heart. Maybe it's true, because the metal feels warm in my hand.

With tears streaming down my face, I clutch it and press it against my beating heart.

I miss him so much.

Because nobody hugs like Clayton Hartley.

Nobody kisses like Clayton Hartley.

Nobody keeps me safe like Clayton Hartley.

"Mom?" Raffi takes my hand that's holding the railing. "Are you going to get sick again?"

"Hey baby, no. I'm fine." I sniffle.

"Are you sure? Don't puke here."

I chuckle. "No. I'm fine."

Soon the captain announces we have a humpback surfacing at two o'clock.

"Go!" I say to Raffi to grab a spot so he can take pictures.

But my son tugs my hand. "Come on, Mom! It's a huge whale!"

I follow him, standing behind his frame, which, no doubt, will grow taller than me one day soon. The whale is breaching, making everyone gasp. The magnificent scene makes me forget about things for a second, but just like the creature disappearing into the blue, my attention lands back on Hart-Tracker. I open my wallet, inserting it into the sleeve where it belongs.

We see two more humpbacks as we make our way back to the bay—to a small coastal city called Homer, which we've now called home for the last couple of weeks.

"So, you didn't get sick on a smaller boat, but you were terrible on that big boat when we left California," Raffi recalls as we drive home in an old Suburban, which I've borrowed from a local.

"I know. It's weird, right?"

"It is!"

"Maybe I was nervous then," I justify.

Our house is a twenty-minute drive from the wharf. After moving from place to place, having this modest but beautiful spot to settle in is a nice welcome. Every transaction I make is cash, and I'm lucky that I can pay my landlord under the table.

We share the two-bedroom house with a girl from Seattle who, just like a lot of people in Alaska at this time, is a seasonal worker who earns her keeps from tourism activities. The twenty-year-old has been here since early spring, and she'll be returning home around mid-fall. I really hope my life will be back to normal by then—wherever it may be.

"Did you enjoy the cruise?" I put my arm around Raffi as we step into the living room. This kind of excursion usually gets his mind off things, especially since there's been no school for him since we left California. I homeschool him a couple of days a week, but without his friends and his basketball, I know it feels like an exile for him.

"The whales were so cool. I enjoyed it. Thanks, Mom." He gives me a peck on the cheek.

This sweet child. What would I do without him?

"Fancy seeing some bears next week?" I suggest.

A smile paints his tired face. "I wish Matty was here." Raffi looks out the window. It's an overgrown garden, but with the mountain surrounding us, it's actually not a bad view. "Imagine if there's a bear that looks like Bjork. He'll go crazy!"

"I know, baby." I put my arm around his shoulder.

"Mom..."

"Yes, Raffi?"

"Why are we here?"

I study him. "Come, sit down with me."

We sit on the old leather couch.

"You're a big boy," I say. "So I'm going to tell you the truth. We're running from Uncle Don. He was going to hurt us, and Clayton too, if we stayed."

Raffi shifts himself gingerly. "Really? Is Thomas going to hurt us, too?"

"He's good, he's on our side, but he can't do anything."

"How long are we going to be here?"

"I'm hoping only for a few more weeks."

"Then we'll go back to California?"

"Maybe."

"I will protect you, Mom. I'm strong now." He shakes my arm as if trying to prove his case.

"I know, baby, but we can't risk it. Uncle Don is a powerful man."

"So... that night... when we... when we lost baby Caili, Uncle Don wasn't helping us?"

We haven't talked about it since the Grim Reaper took us under his robe. It hurts that my son still remembers. "No, he wasn't."

"We need to go back to Clayton. Yeah. We must!" His head nods furiously.

"We can't."

"But he's a kind man."

"That's why I don't want anything to happen to him. It's just us now. We can't involve Clayton anymore."

"Will Uncle Don hurt Matty?"

Bless the two boys. It was cruel of me to separate them, but I hope someday they can see each other again. "No, baby, he won't. Uncle Don wants me."

"So... this is why you've been practicing shooting?"

When it's only the two of us, I can't hide what I do from him. Raffi has seen me handling a gun, and that's just the way it is. I have to be able to defend myself—and him.

"Yes, baby."

"I want to learn too!"

I've seen that determined face before. It was when we decided to give it a go registering him with the Junior Clippers. He doesn't know what danger really is, despite having been in the thick of it when he was really young. But I admire his determination to protect me.

"No, Raffi. You're not old enough. And I won't let you anyway. A gun is not a toy, understand?"

"But I want to protect you."

"You can protect me another way."

"How?"

"By standing by me and listening to what I say."

"Okay." He stares at his own lap, thinking.

"I love you. You know that, right?"

He's the only one I've got, and I will protect him with everything of me. I tidy his hair, smelling it. "Go and take a shower. You smell like seaweed."

Raffi rubs his head, laughing.

"Mom, can I call Dime? Just five minutes."

Dime, his good friend, who I still like to call Eric.

"Not yet. I'll tell you when you can start calling your friends, okay?"

"Just him."

"Not yet."

He sighs out his disappointment and goes into the bathroom in silence.

As I hear the water running, I see a shadow move outside on the west side of the house.

"Bree?"

It's not my housemate.

I take my gun, rounding the house. If someone is looking for me, there are only two possibilities: the Reaper who won't hesitate to swing his scythe, or the stranger in the dark who's still insisting on me. Whatever his reason.

Either way, I'm going to confront him.

After prudently taking my steps along the side wall of the house, I peek out. There's a man, and he's just about to leave.

"Hey!" I point my gun at him.

He swiftly pivots and jumps over a fence with his long legs, then sprints across a yard next door. Not to be outdone, I work my gazelle limbs to keep on his tail. I can't let him get to his car. If he's here to get me or Raffi, I'm going to send him back to Don with something missing. And if Clayton had sent him, I've got a message for him.

The man manages to get to his car, but the road is narrow here. He can't just maneuver it around. He drives straight on, but I change direction. I'm going to catch that son of a bitch around the corner.

And there he is.

I shoot at his windshield, and he stops.

I know I haven't shot the man himself, so I keep pointing my gun at the car. He's stepping out now.

"Who sent you?" I follow his movement. "The scumbag or the fool?"

The man takes off his sunglasses. For the life of me, I hope he's with the good guy. Am I so deprived of good people that my exhaustion has distorted my view of men? Because my stalker doesn't look like someone who would harm anyone. He's not a Donovan Fletcher. He's not a Stefan Boss. The man's gaze is tempered, even kind. Kind? Yes, like Clayton, only not that intense.

"Neither," he answers in his deep voice. He must be in his early forties, and he's dressed just like the locals here.

"Who sent you?" I cock my gun.

"I'm Simon Blake. Clayton Hartley sent me."

"So, the fool." I rue the fact that Clayton is stupid enough to follow me after what I've done.

"Make no mistake, Miss Martins. Mr. Hartley is not a fool."

*Miss Martins.*

This man knows about Isabelli Martins.

I tighten my grip, pointing the barrel at his head. I had told my shooting instructor that I didn't want to shoot to kill—which he laughed at. 'You wouldn't just shoot to wound, young lady,' he said. Perhaps he was right, because in reality, it feels stupid to aim low.

My stalker, whose name turns out to be Simon Blake, mumbles, "He just loves you too much." He almost makes no sense, as if something has interfered with his vocal cord.

I stop breathing for a few seconds. After all, I haven't got what it takes to take a life. Especially after hearing the word 'love.'

"Put the gun down, Miss Martins." His normal voice returns. He's so calm, I consider if he actually wanted me to catch him.

He's right, too, that Clayton Hartley is not a fool. And with what he's got, he won't hire a fool, either.

I slip my gun in the waistband of my jeans.

"Talk to him," he urges.

"Go back to California! Tell Mr. Hartley that Isabelli Martins never met him."

"He really wants to talk to you."

Something clamps my throat. The air has changed, just like the PI's expression. "Then where is he?"

He doesn't have to tell me. I didn't even have to ask.

"I'm here."

## 29

## CLAYTON

I glare at her.

But my desire to lash out at her dissipates. I hated her for fooling me, but I can't deny I still love her. My feelings can't just disappear even though my heart has shattered to the sharpest shards.

Regardless, I shove away anything that resembles affection from within me. I've come here motivated by anger, and I've chosen to be with her now because I'm seeking the truth.

"A gun? Really, Isabelle? Is that how much guilt you're carrying?"

"What do you want, Clayton?" she challenges.

"A reason."

A figure approaches me from behind. "Clayton!"

I turn around. Now that is the person that will never ever see my anger.

"Raffi, go back inside!" she orders, trying to shield her son away from the scene—including me, Blake, and his shattered windscreen.

"But, Mom..."

"Go back inside!"

I refuse to look at the boy, and my gut sinks like I'm committing the worst crime. I miss him. Matty misses him. It's the world at its most unfair.

After making sure he's nowhere around us, I ask Isabelle, "What did you tell him?"

"I told him Don would hurt us, and if we stayed around, he would hurt you too."

There is still a fair distance between us, but I hear her loud and clear, and her face doesn't seem to try to hide anything.

"Sounds noble."

"It's the truth," she grits. After seconds of scorning at me, she softens her stance. "How's bab—"

But she stops. In a situation like this, only a baby would make her soft like that. But no, she's not going to ask how Rob's daughter is doing. Not now, and she knows it.

"So, who are you?" I confront her.

"Isabelli Luna Martins."

"What are your secrets, really, Isabelli Luna Martins?"

"I killed my boyfriend, Raffi's father."

At least she's not trying to beat around the bush, although she stops short of explaining how. "In cold—"

"Self-defense!" she cuts.

"By stabbing him nine times?"

"I stabbed him with a piece of broken mirror. About four inches went into his body. As for the rest of it, it broke in my hand, Clayton." She extends her arm, showing her scarred palm.

Jesus…that was how she got those scars. Still, it doesn't mean she didn't kill him in cold blood.

She continues as she steps closer. "So tell me, how could I stab my boyfriend nine times?"

"You tell me."

"No, I didn't, Clayton. But I guess I was so good that I got his heart with my first and only blow."

There's no emotion in her statement, but it sounds so real, I feel it in my chest. "Are you saying what they accused you of is not true?"

"That night, you asked me how I got these scars. I told you the truth. I let the mirror hurt me so my boyfriend couldn't get to Raffi. He had his belt in his hand, ready to beat the life out of him."

My gut flips over. *Raffi.* What Isabelle does is always for her son. I should've known. And it turned out it was his own father who abused him. But before I surrender to my guilt, there's one more question that needs to be answered.

Isabelle shakes her head, taking my pause as something else. "I guess you've already made up your mind. Once guilty, always guilty. Why are you even here?"

"Look me in the eye, Isabelle. You remember what I said when you were leaving Hartley Marine? I've been betrayed and ditched like an old shoe, and I'm not going to let this slide with you," I retort. "Tell me the truth. Why did you lie to me about your baby?"

"Clayton?" Her eyes are on fire as if some kind of revelation is rattling her. I came with anger, but this woman is burning with rage. "What did Don say about my baby?"

I stand my ground despite her hostile vibe. "Why did you terminate her?"

"You believe what Donovan Fletcher claimed?" Her rage shakes her.

"It's in your health records!"

"You'd rather believe your enemy than me? Some man you are!" Her lips tremble so hard, I'm surprised she still can speak. "Tell me I'm a cold-blooded murderer, but never, *never* accuse me of killing my own child!"

Something in me gives way. Call me a fool who never learns, but that is a pain that you can't create without a cause.

She's a mother, and a great one, too. How could I have doubted her?

"She was inside me for more than seven months," she cries, her hand clutching her belly.

I stride forward, reaching out to her. "Isabelle..."

"Don't touch me!"

"Isabelle... I'm—"

"I'm looking you in the eye, Clayton Hartley." She stares into me. "That night, I lost a part of me that I'd cared for, loved, and adored for all her life, and you're questioning it?"

I gulp. My tongue never tasted so foul. What have I done?

"My boyfriend hit my stomach with a bedside lamp, then pressed my belly against the wall."

Her words shatter me like an earthquake decimates a city. No one has ever made me realize how blind I've been. And this time, my blindness has devastated our lives.

She carries on. "When he was running to unleash his belt on Raffi again, I stopped him. He pushed me against a mirror. But I'm a mother, and I had to do all I could to protect my son. So I stabbed him. *Once*."

"Isabelle... I'm so sorry." This time I ignore her gestures to repel me. I take her in my arms.

She pushes me back with a deep groan. Her biceps swell, and her power is unbelievable. I sway backward, offering no resistance.

"Clayton, look at me. Look at me!" She keeps her distance to make sure I see the whole of her. "My boyfriend hurt me here. Right here." She presses her palm on her belly. "I could've had a chance to save my baby. Don left me bleeding while he was leisurely looking around the scene, planning what he'd do to me.

"By the time I got to the hospital, it was too late. I tried to fight for her... I tried, but my body didn't have a chance, and neither did little Caili. Blame me for that! That I failed to protect her, but don't tell me that I got rid of her!"

"Isabelle, I'm so sorry."

"I bet you are!" She stares at me with her tear-laden eyes. "I've never betrayed you, never cheated on you, and even though I want you to leave me now, I'm not ditching you like an old shoe. I'm getting rid of a thorn in my vein that is you."

She backpaddles.

How could I do this to her?

For the first time in my life, I'm riddled with guilt and shame so vast I might as well perish.

"Isabelle, I'm so sorry. Come back to me. Please, come back to me!"

"I won't be here, Clay. Tomorrow or the next day, Don might've burned down the house, but I won't be here."

"Where are you going?"

"That Simon Blake will tell you, won't he? You can track me all you want, but I'll keep running away from you, and there's nothing you can do to stop me."

"Isabelle, wait! I'll make this right. Look back. Please look back on what we had. I'm begging you to forgive me."

That makes her sob, her frame shrinking as if she's going to disappear right in front of me. "Clayton, years from now, I don't want today to be what I remember of you. And I don't want you to remember me as the woman who robbed you of the family you've always dreamed of."

"No, we're none of that, Isabelle! I've made a mistake."

"Goodbye, stranger in the dark." She pivots, not even sparing me a look as I wilt into the ground I'm standing.

Donovan Fletcher has played me, and I gave into his lies.

How the hell am I going to get her back?

Do I even deserve her?

**30**

---

## ISABELLE

We packed our bags and hit the road again the day after Clayton and his PI paid us a visit. I don't think any of them followed us—at least not Clayton because I swear, I'd be able to smell him if he was close.

No one has ever torn me to pieces like he did. He might've branded me a boyfriend killer. I could take it. But that vindictive look when he was accusing me of terminating my unborn baby? It was more than a bitter pill to swallow. It was like gulping a handful of hot sand. And to know that Don had won at that moment, it felt like the sand was going straight into my heart, clogging and burning every ventricle.

Yet, above all that, I had forgiven him even before the word 'sorry' came out of his mouth. It hurt to see his anguished face agonizing over his own words. I'm sure that hurt me because I loved him.

In fact, I still love him.

What I have with him can't just be erased by a few painful events—especially ones that were orchestrated by a despicable snake. Regardless, I've strayed too far from him. I don't know if there's a way back.

Raffi and I have stayed in Anchorage for a couple of weeks. I decided that what my son needed wasn't another excursion or animal encounter but to have interactions with other kids and stay in a place that somehow resembles a city. So I signed him up with the local YMCA basketball club.

"Yeah, Raffi!" his coach cheers as the boy manages to steal the ball from his opponent.

Most of his teammates are twelve, but Raffi doesn't seem to have any problem fitting in.

"Pass it, pass it!" the coach instructs. "Good job!"

I clap as Raffi completes an assist, resulting in another two-pointer. Even I would struggle to move like that. I can only imagine what Clayton would say if he were here.

I've tried to push the thought of him from my mind, but that name will never be erased. He's a part of me who will never be a part of my life. Yet, I'm clinging to him, like I'm clinging to the small paper bag in my hand, creasing it.

Raffi joins me after the team's debrief. That is some serious sweat. Exactly what the boy needed to release his pent-up energy.

"Whoa, that was a close game," Raffi pants.

"You did well." I pass him a towel.

He wipes his face and then takes in his energy drink. "Hey, Mom. Did you buy me the deodorant?"

"Yeah. Do you need it now?"

Raffi tosses me a 'D'uh!' look.

I smirk. "It's only me for the rest of the afternoon. Do you really need it?"

"Mom, come on."

My son has never asked for deodorant before. I suspect those teenage teammates of his gave him the idea. It's kind of a good thing, I guess, that the boy is keen on maintaining his hygiene.

I rummage into the creased paper bag I got from the

chemist, careful not to show Raffi its content—because there's more than just kids' antiperspirant in there. "Here."

"Cool." He rolls it on his armpits as if it'd been part of his post-practice regime forever. It just shows how fast kids learn, especially from other kids.

"Come, let's go home."

It's not exactly home, but our uptown Airbnb condo is comfortable enough to be our home away from home, and this time we're not sharing it with anyone. Privacy is easy to sacrifice when you're strapped for cash, but boy, I'll never take it for granted again.

Raffi keeps smelling his armpits as we drive.

"Do you like the smell?"

"Not bad." He reads the deodorant label. "Gummy burst? No wonder I smell like watermelon."

Watermelon is always better than old socks, which, admittedly, is how he smells sometimes. Chuckling, I mess up his sweat-laden hair.

"Mooom!" he protests. Probably he's going to ask for hair gel soon.

I pull into our garage, looking left and right, ahead and behind. I usually stay close to Raffi even after we've entered the building, along the stairs and hallway to our apartment on the fourth floor.

"When are we going back to California?" Raffi stomps his way up the last flight of stairs with his head down.

"Soon, baby." I unlock the door with Raffi shielded behind me, my hand inside my bag, ready to pull out my gun. But the boy slides past me, entering without care.

He shakes his head behind the basketball spinning on his finger. I know he thinks our getting in and out routine is silly, but I can't take any chances.

"I mean, playing at the club is nice, but it's not the same." He bounces the ball on the floor and starts dribbling.

"Raffi, don't do that. Neighbors will complain."

He grumbles, throwing himself on the couch. "I miss our house in L.A. I know it's Uncle Don's but, you know—it was a house."

"I know." Guilt piles up in my chest, and I can't even look him in the eye.

"I understand we have to stay safe, away from him. But...I'm bored."

We can't be on the run forever. I was hoping that by this time, I would've had a clear view of how to beat Don. But no option seems to be feasible.

"I'm sorry, baby." I join him on the couch, telling him what has just hatched in my head. "Do you remember New York? Did you like it there?"

"Hmm... don't really remember. What's wrong with California?"

"Let me think about it. Go and have a show—" I leave him mid-sentence and run to the only bathroom in the apartment.

Holding the eruption of my stomach in my mouth, I barely make it.

There goes my lunch.

"Mom, are you okay?" asks Raffi from outside the door.

"Yes, baby. Go and watch tv."

When I come out, Raffi is there waiting for me by the door. He peruses me with concern. "Would you like me to make you some tea?"

"It's okay. I can make it."

"No, no, Mom. Sit down. I'll make it for you."

"Thanks, Raffi."

The boy has never stopped to amaze me with his care and

attention. Perhaps channeling his inner big brother that can never become a reality.

Or can it?

My ass falls onto the couch like a stone. I lean back, huffing.

"So it wasn't the boat?" Raffi hands me the cup.

"Apparently not. Maybe I ate something bad."

"Well, you ate what I ate, and I'm fine." He stares at me. "I'm sorry, Mom. Am I upsetting you?"

"No, no!" I rub his arm. "I'm not upset. I'm just a bit sick."

"You miss Clayton."

"Raffi!" I almost choke on the tea I'm sipping.

"Why? If we go back to California, we can be together again, and Uncle Don won't come to us. Clayton will protect us."

"Please, no more Clayton talk."

Raffi lets out a growl.

"Look, Raffi. I know you're tired and you're bored. Please, give me a couple of days to think about what to do."

His lips stay pursed.

I pull him close. Sweat and all, he's my life, and I will truly die if he's not with me. I give him a kiss which he almost turns his face away from.

"Hey, can't I kiss you now?"

He twists his lips, I'm sure telling me *I'm too old for that.* Really, those teenagers at the YMCA basketball club seem to have made my boy grow up a few years in just a matter of weeks.

"You have a shower first, Mom. I'm still sweating." He shakes the neckline of his singlet.

I smile, agreeing with him. I usually warn him not to have a shower when he's sweating like that. Clearly, today he remembers it better than I do.

"Mom..."

"Yes, Raffi?"

"Can I call Dime?"

A pang of guilt stings my chest. He and his best friend haven't spoken since we left California. I've kept denying him a call, delaying his frustration.

"Of course. Talk to him. Just don't tell him where we are, okay?"

"Okay," he agrees. "Can I call Matty after that?"

The two had grown close. Back in California, they talked and played online almost every day. Since we ran away, Raffi has hardly complained. Only now it dawns on me how much I've disrupted my son's life. "Of course, baby. Call Matty."

Instead of heading to the bathroom, I scan the living room.

"What are you looking for?" Raffi asks.

"Oh, um, the bag from the chemist."

"Didn't you put it in your handbag?"

"Oh, of course!"

Raffi watches me marching to the bathroom, clutching my handbag.

"What is it, baby?"

"I need your phone."

"Oh, of course! Sorry."

Raffi smiles tentatively when I toss him my phone, perhaps unsure how to react to my scatteredness today.

I poke my head out of the bathroom door, saying, "Don't forget to put it on the charger after your calls."

With the bath running, I sit on the toilet seat and pull the pregnancy test kits out of the paper bag.

With the injury I sustained from Nando's attack that fateful night and the aftermath of losing Caili, doctors told me that it was impossible for me to have another child. My endometrium simply can't sustain another pregnancy. Since then, my period has never been regular. So I shouldn't be concerned that I've missed it two months in a row.

Yet, I am.

I brace myself to drench the tip of the test stick with my pee. My eyes slam shut, refusing to see whatever change is happening. I can't take it. I can't.

Abstract shapes play behind my closed lids, like luminous jellyfish swimming in dark water. It could've been two minutes, it could've been fifteen, but when I open my eyes—

My throat is choked with tears. I hush my sobs, telling myself not to get carried away. There's a reason why I bought two different brands. Just in case. *Just in case.*

Never have I been so desperate to make myself do a back-to-back pee. I furiously gulp water from the tap.

This time I watch the test stick as if someone would've tampered with it if I didn't.

Two lines.

On both of them.

I smile to heaven, tears wetting my face in an instant—maybe more furiously than the streams of pee I had produced to get to this point.

I step into the bath, immersing myself in the bubbly water—jubilant, humbled, and playful. "Hey, baby..." I caress my belly.

So there is such a thing as a miracle. And this miracle might just answer two of the most important questions of my life: what would it be like to be a mother for the second time? Should I go back to California?

The second question is really: Should I go back to Clayton?

Raffi will like my answer. Hell, I love my answer!

There's no hiding the fact that I wish the man himself were here. Just there in the living room, perhaps reading a magazine, unaware that I was going to give him the surprise of his life.

My hand stays on my belly as I whisper, "You'll see Daddy soon. I promise."

I put on a fresh t-shirt, but I have to settle with wearing the pair of jeans I've been wearing for weeks. Even though it's light here almost twenty-four hours a day, I still haven't caught up with all my washing.

I dab my hair. Then, with the towel spread on my bed, I lie back. I laugh at the ceiling, hands on my belly, just behind the jeans fly. I'll have to buy a new pair soon. In fact, I'll have to buy lots of new clothes. Mine and the baby's.

Raffi's room is open, and he's awfully quiet, as if he's still on the phone with either Eric or Matty.

"Raffi?" I call out when I can't find him in his room. How much privacy does the boy need to have his call?

I comb the whole apartment, my heart throttling into fifth gear.

When I can't find him anywhere within the building, I run out, checking the yards and garage.

"Raffi!" I shout.

What is that boy doing?

Perhaps it's anxiety, or even exertion, but my stomach starts cramping. I need to take the car.

"Damn!" I complain, unable to find my car key in my bag.

I rush back upstairs and find the door ajar. It wasn't like that when I left.

Entering quietly, I pick up my gun from my handbag.

A shadow moves in the kitchen. It could be Raffi grabbing a bowl of ice cream in between calls, but there's no way it's my son. It's big, and it moves like a thief. I doubt Clayton will have sent another Simon Blake.

That leaves only one other possibility.

The intruder is walking into my room now. I can see he's wearing black clothing, leather gloves, and a dark cap that's drawn really low. Curiously, his gun is still in its holster. Well, that man will soon learn about his lack of preparation.

I join him in my room and shoot his thigh.

"Bitch!"

Before he can reach for his gun, I point mine at the back of his neck. I train to shoot to wound despite my instructor's reluctance, but it doesn't mean I can't or won't kill him, and he knows my intention.

He puts his arms up, but he's still standing.

"Where's my son?"

"I'm here to take you. I don't know of no boy."

I think he's telling the truth. But where is Raffi?

The man turns, grabbing my wrists like eagle talons seizing prey. My hands tremble in the wrestle, but I refuse to let go of my gun.

He's still not interested in drawing his own. Either he's confident that he can subdue me without firing a shot, or he has been ordered not to shoot me.

Not expecting such resistance from me, he swings his healthy leg while leaning on the wall behind him, so his wounded leg doesn't have to bear his whole weight.

*Hell, no!*

I'm not going to let him touch my belly, let alone hurt it.

As he gives himself room to complete his kick, his grip loosens. It's slight but enough for my finger to pull the trigger.

First, his hands let up, then his leg falls mid-kick, and finally, his body slides down the wall he's leaning on, leaving a trail of blood. As if the man was going to get up and haunt me, I throw a sheet over his body.

I puke once more. I'm still groggy from the scene I've just left in this Airbnb master bedroom, but I've got to find my son.

"Raffi!" I search the apartment again, hoping he's back after a walk or something.

The front door creaks open.

"Raffi? That you?"

My split-second of ambivalence gives my uninvited guest a chance to stop me in my track. In that split second, all I thought about was Raffi. What would my son think if I had pointed the gun at him? Even worse, what if I'd accidentally shot him?

*Fuck!*

Don's bodyguard is trying to disarm me, although I notice no sign of a weapon on him. So Don has instructed his men not to shoot me?

My hand is folded right in front of me, his clenching hands wrestling with my gun. I could do the same as I did to his colleague—but as I learned fast, destroying a stranger is not the same as killing someone I know. I'd killed someone I knew well. It was justified, but I never intended to do it again. I'd taken a life barely minutes ago. It was also a justified killing, but my heart is screaming at me to stop.

I let Don's bodyguard overcome me. This may be my demise, but my conscience is clear. There's no way on earth I could knowingly kill a man with an infant waiting for him at home. I have to survive Don another way.

I offer no resistance when he ties my wrists. I can't afford to get hurt.

As if knowing that everything is under control, Don himself enters.

"Hello, Iz." Whatever his plan, he's wearing an ensemble that makes him appear like an actor auditioning for *A Walk in the Woods*. "Paz!" he calls out—it must be to that dead man. He then takes over me and instructs his bodyguard. "Find the boy!"

So they really have no idea where my son is?

I feel like a terrible parent, yet I'm glad that Raffi isn't here. When the boy doesn't want to be found, he'll find a way to stay hidden—I'm hoping this time that it'll be long enough for Don to give up his hunt, at least for now.

The bodyguard scours the house, room to room. When he steps into the master bedroom, I hear, "Jesus Christ!"

"What?"

"Paz is fucking dead!"

Don turns me around, forcing me to look at him. "Shit, Iz! So you did shoot that fucking gun? Well, I guess Paz wasn't your first kill. Getting an upgrade, were you? From a broken mirror to a—" Don peruses my gun. "Glock 43x? Nice to grip."

He puts it away, then continues, "I shouldn't be surprised. It's always been here!" He slaps my chest. "Your killer instinct."

"I did what I had to do."

"Now that—" Don points at my bedroom auspiciously. "That will land you in jail for a long time. You know Raffi wouldn't survive as an orphan."

An orphan? That was exactly the threat Fletcher Senior posed on my parents before he got us out of Rio. I was in his clutches while my mom and dad begged, guns to their heads.

"Don't you fucking dare!"

"Or what, my darling?" he snorts. "Don't you worry. I'll take Raffi under my wings. He'll most likely forget about you. If you're lucky, maybe he'll visit you in jail. But soon enough, he'll realize what kind of mother you are. Do you think he'll still see you after he graduates from high school? From Uni? Or when he's getting married? I doubt he wants his fiancée to know what you've done."

"Well, as you can see, you've won, Don. You've won," I concede, and bitterness coats my lips. "Now, what do you want from me?"

"I could ask you to try again with Hartley," he suggests. "But it's too late for that."

"He still loves me. I can make up a story, and he'll buy it."

Don shakes his head. "Too late, Iz."

His bodyguard comes back. "The boy's not here, sir."

"What do you mean?" Don gripes.

I glare at both men with disdain.

Don clutches my jaw. An old threat, but this time he does so tightly that he may break half my face if he goes on long enough. "Where is he?"

I slant my head, and one of his fingers slips enough to let me utter a few words. "What can I say? I'm a bad mother!"

Right then, Don strangles me. "You're my whore. That's all you are, and all you'll ever be."

He lets go and points my gun instead. "The jail thing... that was a bad idea. You're well past your used-by date, and you're getting too dangerous. You need to go, Iz."

I throw him a glare—not a blink, not even when I hear the gun cock.

"Nah!" He cackles and withdraws. "I'll kill you another way."

He hits my head.

## 31

# CLAYTON

It's eighty-five degrees outside. Even my running-addict brother almost gave me a raincheck. But here we are, pounding the streets of Newport for the sake of fitness and venting out—the latter is just for me.

"I envy them," Rob remarks as we pass a café.

"Sweat and fried muscles are what we need, brother. Not iced coffee."

"Iced coffee would taste fucking great right now," Rob laments. But we move on. "So, what have you decided?"

"Status quo," I deadpan. My trust issue is a hard habit to break, and dismally, it was a habit that broke me. "I accused her of killing her unborn child. I believed Donovan Fletcher instead of her. I'll never get her back, Rob. It's over."

Rob speeds up. I must admit my brother seems to run faster as he ages—or it must be his 'cheetah' wife that has kept him elevating his game.

"Don't tell me that! You haven't even tried," my brother replies. "I've been there, Clay. I'm sure you remember. I lost trust in Amber-Rose at one stage."

We've both had a fair share of betrayals and embarrassment. Trust doesn't come easy for us Hartleys. Now I realize our cautiousness can also serve as our downfall.

Rob wipes beads of sweat off his forehead. "But when you're meant to be, if you dig deep enough, you'll find a way to leap over whatever is burning under your feet. You and Isabelle can't just end here."

I fling my head up toward the heavens, forming an image of what could've been. "I looked her in the eye, Rob—as I'd wanted to. There's no way anyone could lie like that. What's killing me, though, is the fact that I might just be the worst asshole she's ever known. Fletcher may have done bad things to her, but he wouldn't have broken her heart. Because it's evil's work. I'm not evil—well, I hope I'm not—"

"You're not evil, Clay!"

"But look at what I was capable of. I hurt her. Bad."

"We'd been blinded and fooled," Rob pants as we make the last turn before going back to our HQ. "It wasn't your fault that you dug into her past. It was your right. Yes, your judgment was skewed—hell, *we* got it wrong. Blake and I never saw it coming. You hit a wall, but—"

"I don't even know if I want her to forgive me."

"Well, that's *your* problem then. Do you want her? Or do you want to punish yourself?"

"Both."

"It's an 'or' question, Clay. You can't choose both."

Out of the blue, I feel something, someone, coming toward us at speed.

"Jesus! Blake!" I didn't know he could run like that—in his suit and perfectly-polished loafers too.

"Clay, something's wrong," Blake pants.

"What? What?"

"I just got a call from my friend in Anchorage—my detective friend. He's with Raffi."

"Raffi?"

"He came alone to the station."

My already increased heart rate blows off the charts. "How?"

"Apparently, he was borrowing her mother's phone. He wandered off to look for better cell reception while Isabelle was in the bathroom. It turned out the local cell tower was under maintenance, so he kept going. He wanted to call his friend, and Matty."

Persistent sweats drip off my lids. But I don't even have the will to wipe them. The effects from my running and my verge-of-insanity emotions all mingle into a huge ball, inflating my chest cavity.

We huff our way back to Hartley Marine.

"Did he ring Matty in the end?" I query. "What did he say? Why didn't Matty call me?"

Blake explains, "The phone ran out of battery. But that smart kid went to the police. I was told, from the state of him, it looked like he'd been running quite a distance. My friend recognized Raffi from the CCTV footage from Port of Ketchikan when they first arrived. He's still with Raffi, so he's safe."

"Did you speak to Raffi?"

"Yes."

"Is he okay?"

"He didn't talk much. I think he's just shaken."

"I'm gonna take the plane," I say to Rob.

"Get Wyatt to fly you."

"I don't have a need for speed, Rob. I *need* speed right now."

Wyatt is a very capable pilot, but he won't be able to fly faster than I do.

"Take Wyatt," Rob insists.

I know he's worried I'll do something stupid—which, there's a high chance that I will.

*Do you want her? Or do you want to punish yourself?*

The answer is clear, and I don't have a second to waste.

## 32

## ISABELLE

The blow to my head hasn't made me unconscious, but it has subdued me. The dizziness sends me swaying, and my legs have given up. And I can't do anything when Don's bodyguard ties my wrists.

Then, like a rolled rug, I'm carried out of the building and tossed inside the cargo space of my borrowed Suburban.

"Get rid of Paz and his car, then fetch me as planned. We haven't got much time. We'll find the boy later." Don gives instructions to his bodyguard as he towers over the trunk. He then turns to me, zipping up his puffer jacket. "Meanwhile, I'm going to take Miss Alaska hiking."

Filled with pride, he shows off the gun in his hand—my gun —his other hand hanging to the open hatch.

I've known this Reaper and learned his limited facial expressions since his parents came into my family's life. This time his smile is all teeth, full of menace. It's not his happy face when he's itching to clean up someone's mess and take control of their life. It's Don when he can't wait to eliminate someone.

"Oh, come on, don't be so naïve. Everyone is disposable, Iz. You've become too dangerous now. I must admit what you did to

Paz was a surprise. But with the existence of this—" He shows me my own gun like it was a symbol of my stupidity. "—boy, the sky's the limit. You know I'm a cleaner. I can create any scene I want. And I'm willing to bleed a little to play the part, if you get my drift."

Don levels a grossly cunning smile.

"Your luck will run out, Don. And I've got a strong feeling this is gonna be it."

"See you soon, darling."

The hatch drops with a thud. I inspect the space around me —there may be a way out. But the car is gathering speed, and even if I get out, Don will find me again sooner or later.

Having canned my intention to kill him in that Airbnb apartment, I told myself I'd survive the Reaper another way. With my hands tied like this, placed in a space that might as well be a coffin, what can I do? That man has defeated me twice—when I lost Caili, and when Clayton fell for his lies. The third time may be the most devastating of all.

Raffi.

If there's a time that I need to stay alive, it's now.

Once again, I close my eyes, letting fluorescent shapes play in my blackened vision. Stars, rings, blobs.

Rings.

Circles—white, golden...

With a gasp, I stare at my jeans. The pair that I've worn for the last few weeks because I haven't caught up with my laundry. That means my wallet is still in the pocket!

The car hits a rough patch, causing me to bounce. Once the drive becomes steady again, I turn sideways, stacking my left hip up. Yes, my wallet is in there.

I stretch my arms behind my back, twisting them so I can reach past my ass into the side pocket.

*Come on! Come on!*

I bite off the pain as the flexicuffs dig into my wrists.

My left fingers barely reach the edge of the wallet. I lengthen my limbs, even if I dislocate something, I've got to have it in my hand.

I scratch at it, scrambling to fish it out. The leather zip puller slowly spills out of the edge of my jeans pocket.

*Come on!*

I pinch the leather puller attentively, bit by bit drawing the wallet out. It's out, but the car hits a bump, and I lose my grip.

*Shit.*

Worse still, my sickness catches up with me. Having almost zero energy left in my tank, I'm forced to lie on my own vomit. But I have no time to dwell on the grossness of my situation. Don may stop at any time now. We've been traveling for a couple of hours, for sure.

I gyrate, trying to find where my wallet has landed after that bump. I can feel it behind my knees. I keep my head lifted to avoid the mess around me getting into my eyes and mouth, and then I turn my body so I'm facing it. Then I drive the wallet up with my thigh.

"Come on, baby, come to mama." I manage to get it close enough to my mouth, allowing me to open it with my teeth.

The golden object pokes out of my wallet sleeve, beaming at me.

*Clayton's heart.*

He has never left me.

He's a home that I have to get to.

We hit another bump, but I keep my open wallet in my bite. Then I set it down, clipping it between my cheek and the floor of the cargo hold. With my teeth, I pull the HartTracker out just enough to expose the switch. I can't muck it up now. Even though my instinct is telling me I'm running out of time, I take it slow, pressing my tongue against the tracker's base, and push the switch to the 'on' position with my front teeth.

Nothing happens.

No beep, no light, no nothing.

I've done all I can. The only thing I can do is hope that it is still working, as Clayton claimed.

We're slowing.

I quickly close the wallet and push it down, so I can reach it again with my hands when I turn around. Don can't see it at any cost. I have to put it back deep into my pocket.

We are almost at a crawling pace. And after surviving a few bumps, my stomach starts cramping up.

The sensation takes me back to that night when I fought Nando.

*Jesus... no, please. Not again!*

I pray hard that I'm not going to witness another living being die today.

And I pray just as hard that my Raffi is out there somewhere.

Safe.

**33**

---

## CLAYTON

"Faster, Wyatt, for God's sake!"

"This is why your brother insisted," my pilot contends. "We're not in Cuba's airspace, Mr. Hartley."

"Fuck, Wyatt. Have you forgotten why we're flying? We could be above 1965 Vietnam for all I care!"

"I'm doing you a favor, sir. We're almost there."

Meanwhile, Blake is sitting quietly. It's as if he hasn't changed his posture since we took off.

We land in Anchorage in less than five hours. It felt like forever, but that was actually a pretty good time.

A rental car is waiting for us, and we head straight to the Anchorage PD.

"Crawley," Blake calls a man who's just come out of a door, clearly expecting us. He's in plain clothes, and they soon hug each other. Blake told me he and the detective had been friends since they were teenagers. While Blake moved on, Crawley stayed on with the Anchorage PD.

Blake introduces us to the detective, "This is Clayton Hartley and our pilot Wyatt Grimes."

"Gents." Crawley ushers us. "Come. Raffi is in a conference

room with my colleague. She's great with kids. Rest assured, the boy has been well taken care of."

"Did you find out where his house is?"

"No. What I told Blake on the phone, that was all he said. The kid is scared. We've asked around the neighborhood, but no one recognized him."

As soon as I enter the room, Raffi runs to me.

"Clayton!" He clings to my waist. He's wearing his basketball gear, but someone has put a police jacket over him.

"Hey, pal. I'm here." I kneel so he can rest his head on my shoulder.

"Clayton…" His grip is even fiercer now. I don't think he's ever going to let me go. The boy has proven himself tough, just like his mother. But he's a ten-year-old, after all. It won't be his fault if he breaks down now.

"Are you okay?"

He nods, trying to hide his cry.

Crawley gestures to the policewoman who's been accompanying Raffi to step away, and in turn, Blake tells his friend to leave us be.

"What happened, Raffi?" I ask when it's just the two of us in the room.

"I don't know. I don't know." This time he cries in my arms.

"It's okay, pal. Take your time." I wrap my arms around him, rubbing his back, telling him I've got him. "We'll find your mom."

I offer him water, but he refuses, looking down like he's about to fall.

"Hey, come on." I lift him up while keeping him close. I'm not going to pretend that I'm his father, but what's driving me is, I'm sure, nothing short of a fatherly instinct.

Raffi seems to be receptive to my gesture. Isabelle once said the boy wouldn't have let her carry him but hinted at the possibility that her son might let *me*. And she was right, and I'm humbled.

I set him down on a chair. "Take a deep breath," I say, holding his fisting hands. Then I offer him some water again. This time he takes a couple of sips. "Tell me what happened."

His fingers unfurl. "I borrowed Mom's phone. I wanted to ring Dime and Matty," he confides. "But there was no reception around the building. I knew I wasn't supposed to go far, but—"

He pauses as if regretting what he'd done.

"It's okay, Raffi."

Upon a deep sigh, he continues, "I hate it here. I hate that apartment. So I just kept going. In the end, the battery died anyway. Then I walked back. But when I got to the building, I saw Uncle Don with his bodyguard standing near our car."

Stray cat is too good a name for him. I don't know what Fletcher is, but how dare he!

I look away, concealing my anger only because of Raffi. Then I ask him gently, "Did he take her?"

"I couldn't see. The garage is far away from the front gate. I wanted to come close, but I was scared. I know I shouldn't have left her. I was supposed to protect her."

"Hey, it's not your fault."

"What if he killed her?"

He leaves his seat and falls into my arms, trembling.

"Hey, easy, Raffi." I stroke his back, leaning my face onto his head. "Your mother is strong. She wouldn't let anyone kill her, not even Uncle Don. Good thing you didn't approach him. He didn't take you, so you can help us."

"I didn't know what else to do, so I ran here. We passed this station a few times when we went shopping. But Clay, I shouldn't have come here." He shakes his head repeatedly. "I should've found a phone and called Matty, and then asked Matty to call you."

I slowly pull him away from my shoulder, so he's facing me. "Listen, Raffi, you did the right thing. Where's your apartment? The detective said you couldn't remember."

Raffi bows his head. "I lied to the policeman. I said I got lost and didn't know my way home. Every time he asked something, I said I don't remember." He wipes his snort on the sleeve of the Anchorage PD jacket he's wearing. He then scratches his index finger. "I didn't want anyone to see the apartment. I don't know what Uncle Don has done. I don't want Mom to get into trouble. She's been practicing shooting."

"Practicing shooting isn't a crime. Your mom won't get into trouble."

He scratches his finger harder. "Am I going to go to jail?"

"No! Raffi, of course not." I cover his hand with my palm, stopping him from scraping his finger.

Raffi then adds, "Uncle Don may lie to the police. Then they'd take me away from her."

"No one's going to take you away, Raffi."

"Clay, what if she's dead?" There're no more tears in his eyes now, but he looks to be bracing for something horrific.

"No, she's not. I promise you."

"How do you know?"

I kneel down and pull his hand to my chest. "I know it here, Raffi. I know she's still alive."

Raffi curves a tiny smile, then nods.

"Now tell me." I rest my hands on his shoulders. "Where's your apartment? No one else will know. Only me, Wyatt, and Blake."

He whispers the address to me.

"Wait here." I then fetch Wyatt and Blake from another room. "Blake, I don't care how you do it. Get the Anchorage PD off this. And the Alaska Troopers or anyone else who might want to take an interest in this. Do you hear me?"

"Not a problem, Clay," Blake assures me.

"We'll go to Isabelle's apartment, just Wyatt and me. You stay here with Raffi, okay?"

"Got it," Blake affirms.

I go back to Raffi. "I've got to go, pal, but Blake will stay here with you."

Raffi blinks at me, hinting at my PI. Perhaps he hasn't forgotten that his mother shot the man's windscreen. "Clay... can Wyatt stay with me?"

The last thing I want is to scare the boy who's already terrified.

Blake senses it. He suggests, "Let me talk to Crawley again."

"All right, you do that," I tell him. Then I turn to Raffi. "Blake's my friend."

"But I don't know him, Clay. Please, I want to be with Wyatt."

"Okay, pal." I then glance at Wyatt, checking if he agrees.

"I've got you, young man," my pilot says to Raffi.

The boy implores, "Promise me you'll find Mom."

"I promise." I hug him.

Like the world is on my shoulder, I pull myself up. Blake stands by the door, telling me he's got things under control with the Anchorage PD.

"Go!" Wyatt says—vigilant, guarded. Raffi is in good hands, indeed. No one dares to cross Wyatt when he's like that.

"Jesus, the boy did run far!" Blake comments as we drive to the address that Raffi gave me.

It's a seven-story condominium complex. I won't be surprised if someone can pull off a murder inside one of those units without anyone noticing. Sounds may not travel far, especially with the concrete construction and each unit having only small windows.

It's still bright, like it's in the middle of the day. I'm thankful that the sun doesn't set until almost midnight during summer in this part of the world. In saying that, no matter how dark the day gets, I have to find Isabelle tonight. Tomorrow will be too late.

Blake and I head to the fourth floor. He opens the door, which turns out to be unlocked, while I point my gun, ready to shoot.

"Clear!" my PI declares.

We sweep the kitchen and then a small bedroom, which looks to be Raffi's. Someone has turned this room inside out, probably looking for the boy.

I turn my attention to the larger bedroom, which I'm sure is Isabelle's.

It's clean—too clean, and I can smell bleach.

"Something happened here," I murmur. There's a towel on the bed, and some strands of her hair are still there. Did she wash her hair before Fletcher took her?

Blake continues sweeping the bedroom while I move on to the bathroom. It's like I can smell the trace of her scent.

Her t-shirt and underwear are on the floor. And next to it, there's a bin, and like a beacon, a couple of sticks catch my attention. One pink and the other one white.

"Isabelle..." I whisper to myself as I pick them up.

Elation, disbelief, regret, and anger roll into me. She and her baby had better be alive, or I'll go on a rampage!

I clutch the test kits. These are the closest thing I have of her in so long. I know in my heart she hasn't been with another man. I'd bet on my life! But it's not the time to pause and cry tears of joy, although I desperately want to. By the grace of God, I'm about to be a dad!

I put the kits inside my pocket and move on. Two lives are at stake—I can't let emotions slow me down. Every fucking second matters!

"Clay!" Blake calls.

I join him. Still in Isabelle's room, he has just pushed a dresser aside, revealing a corner of carnage.

A sick feeling sinks into my stomach.

Blood.

Whose blood?

Someone tried to clean up, but it looks like they ran out of time. There were still faint splatters on the wall, and the stain on the carpet hadn't been touched.

"It's not hers." Even the ever-certain Simon Blake's voice wavers because he can't fucking guarantee that!

My breathing speeds up. I'm at a loss, but no matter how flimsy Blake's theory is, I have to go with it. I hold my shirt pocket, feeling the pregnancy test kits. It can't be her blood. I've promised Raffi his mom is still alive. And her baby?

I pace around the house, questions swirling in my head. One persists. Did Raffi witness something that led him to conclude that Isabelle was dead?

No. It was just his fear. He would've told me if he'd seen something. He would've.

I march back to the bloody scene, squatting in front of it. Everything blurs, and my eyes get filmed out by the tears I don't want to shed.

"She's still alive." Blake crouches beside me, peering at the same bloodied patch of carpet.

I can't afford not to believe him. So I refrain from turning—because if I do, I'll see his doubt.

"She's pregnant, Blake," I confess. I can't bear the news alone, and somehow I'm seeking his assurance that he meant it when he told me Isabelle is still alive.

"Clay?"

I show him one of the pregnancy tests, and the man turns to hug me. Apart from Rob, I've never had a guy instilling strength in me like this. He doesn't have to say anything more to convince me that we're not too late.

"Come on," he presses. "We've got to find her."

Rob calls as I step out of the room. Without wasting time on greetings and preambles, he blurts, "Clay, what happened to your HartTracker?"

It's as if a fist had just clouted my chest in a good way. "I gave it to Isabelle."

"You won't believe this, but we've got a signal from it."

"No fucking way!" I exclaim. "It's gotta be her!" Although the question remains—is the device on her or on her dead body?

From the corner of my eye, I see Blake returning to Isabelle's bedroom.

Rob adds, "The laptop that you swept off your desk, Wanda found it beeping. So you can thank her."

Blake soon comes to me with an object—or half an object— in his hand. It looks like a broken piece of a cap's snapback strap, bloody and dented. "Hang on, Rob."

My PI interprets the finding for me, "Whoever was bleeding there wasn't Isabelle. Why would she be wearing a cap in the house? After a shower?"

I flash him a praising smile. Now his theory might not just be a theory anymore.

"Is everything okay there?" Rob asks. "Who's bleeding?"

"Long story, Rob. Where's she?"

"She's moving north, approaching a town called Cantwell."

Keenly listening in, Blake comments, "He's taking her to a trail, probably Denali or even further north."

"We're still in Anchorage, Rob. How far is she from us now?"

"Two hundred miles."

Blake and I glance at each other. We've got to fly if we want to save her.

"Rob, I'll call you back!" I turn to Blake. "Let's go to the airport and see what our options are."

As Blake takes the wheel, I steal a few minutes to digest what has happened and to convince myself that Isabelle is still alive.

She is. Too much is at stake for her not to be alive.

"So, suppose that cap belonged to a man, Don's man, then he was shot, yes?"

"Yes. Likely in the head. That was why the strap was damaged. Or in the face, and the bullet exited behind his skull," Blake proposes.

"And she did that, yes?"

"She shot my windscreen, and I'm the good guy." His eyes cross to me, provoking a thought.

Of course she did it!

My head falls back, bouncing against the seat's headrest, wishing she was in my arms right now—right at this moment. I would kiss her. I would tell her how much I love her.

I let out a harsh breath.

"You okay, man?" Blake asks.

"Yeah. Just keep driving!"

She was protecting her baby. That was how Isabelle garnered the grit to kill Fletcher's man that way. She was protecting two people, and she simply had to destroy him. I wish she had done that to Fletcher, too.

"We need Wyatt," Blake says.

"He needs to stay with Raffi."

"You'll need another pair of hands, Clay, I can assure you."

"You are that other pair of hands, Blake!"

"Whatever we can find at the airport, someone needs to fly the fucking thing, and it's not gonna be you."

"I'll fly it!"

"Wyatt will!" He sounds like Rob now. "When we find Isabelle, you will be with her. And then, I'll be your extra pair of hands."

He's right—and I guess this is why he's by my side, my voice of reason.

"But I'm worried about leaving Raffi alone. That boy is traumatized."

"I know. But we can't go without Wyatt."

"Do you think Raffi will be okay with Crawley?"

"I've asked Crawley to reassure Raffi that neither he nor his mother is in trouble. I'm certain he's told Raffi that by now."

I call my pilot. "Meet me at the airport."

"Sure, Mr. Hartley."

Blake speaks into my phone. "Get Crawley to take Raffi to his home—his wife and son will be happy to keep him company."

"You hear that, Wyatt?"

"Yeah. I'll relay that to Crawley. Raffi will be fine. He and Crawley have been spending hours together now."

"Let him call his friend, or Matty," I suggest, thinking it'll help the boy to feel at ease.

"Good idea."

Wyatt arrives at the airport almost at the same time as Blake and me. After asking every aviation company around here, we know we're running out of options.

We end up standing hopelessly at one of the piers in Lake Hood, staring at the rows of idle seaplanes around us. From what we know so far, where Isabelle may be taken to is nowhere near water.

Rob calls again. "They're still on the move, Clay. And there's a storm coming, so you know. You may be able to outfly it if you're quick."

"Okay."

"And..." Rob pauses. "I've got a Thomas Matheson here."

"Thomas?" Why the hell did that kid come to Rob?

"He's Isabelle's friend. Well, he claims to be, anyway."

"Take a photo of him and send it to me."

"His face is messed up, but here it is."

Jesus Christ! He is messed up. His right eye is barely open as deep purple surrounds it, his upper lip is split, and his left cheek doesn't fare much better.

"Let me talk to him!" I tell Rob.

"Clay!" Thomas's calling my name is barely audible behind his heavy breathing.

"Where's Don taking her? Tell me!"

"I don't know, but I know that Don has booked a chopper from a company called Ilya-Pavel. Somewhere in Alyeska. You can't find them in the Yellow Pages, but they're there.

We speed up to Alyeska, and in the meantime, Rob shares with us the tracking data from HartTracker, overlaying it with a map of the terrains. Whoever did it is a genius.

With the terrain that we'll be up against and the rescue that we'll need to pull off, we definitely need a chopper.

"Hey!" I nudge Blake. "Recognize that man?"

The man in the suit hops out of a Land Rover, then prowls toward a small yard. If we were in California, he would blend in. But here, his figure sticks out like a sore thumb.

"Shit! That's Don's bodyguard!" Blake whisper-shouts.

The same man I saw in Kenya.

We follow him into a hangar.

I nod at Wyatt and Blake. "Gents, let's keep this hijack quiet and quick."

**34**

———

**ISABELLE**

The noxious face of the Grim Reaper greets me when the hatch lifts open.

"Jesus fucking Christ!" Don glowers at the mess I made. He drags me out of the cargo space, pouring water all over my face and hair to wash off the remnants of my vomit.

"What are you gonna do?"

He cuts my arms loose. "Taking you for a hike, as I promised." He then appraises my expression. "It's not that hard. Even a ten-year-old can do it."

Has his bodyguard found Raffi and taken him here too?

Don lets out a mocking laugh. "I like it when you're afraid. I mean, piss-in-your-pants afraid." He's been holding my gun, and now he's pointing it at me. "Walk!"

We follow a trail that winds through a forest of aspen and spruce trees. I'm thankful that my stomach cramps have stopped.

Don gazes at the sky, then at me. "Hurry up! What happens to your gazelle legs?"

"I need a drink, Don!"

He tosses me a bottle of water. "Keep going!"

I drink as I go, twigs snapping under my feet. Then my steps start squelching muddy ground as we move in deeper.

Fatigue sets in. But I have to keep going—with a positive mind. I can't afford to be handled or hurt by this man. Besides, if Raffi is here, I want to be with him—conscious and with enough in the tank to defend my son and myself.

Don suddenly whistles. "Wrong way!" He nods to his left.

"Where the hell are we going?"

The direction that Don wants us to take is overgrown. We are in a remote area, but the main trail isn't that hard to find, so I'm not surprised that his plan includes a route that will make a search that much more difficult.

"The unknown can be scary, can't it?" Sarcasm dribbles out of his speech. "Like that night in Kenya when I was about to fuck you bareback."

He stops walking, prompting me to look back at him. The bastard simply wants to watch my reaction. He then blabbers in amusement, "No, I'm not gonna fuck you here, if that's what you're thinking. After that cunt Hartley dumped his filth in you? Jesus, no!"

I maintain a straight face.

Getting nothing out of me, he motions at me to keep moving. Although the vegetation is thick, we are following an existing path—narrow nonetheless, our two feet hardly fit its width.

After about a couple of miles meandering the tiny trail, we tramp on what's seemingly an endless incline.

I must give it to Don. Without his ED pills, his stamina in bed was minuscule. But out here, he's keeping it up despite the terrain and distance.

And he keeps on gabbing. "I really thought you would've been more thankful, Iz. When a notorious Brazilian overlord put a price on your head, it was certain death. But my family stopped that. Not only saving your dad but his wife and his young child."

"What a pair of saints!" I mock, wiping sweat off my forehead.

"You're such a condescending bitch—just like your parents were. You know, Isabelli Martins, getting your family out and taking you safely into this country was no easy feat. My parents spent money and resources, not to mention risking their own lives."

"My parents didn't owe you anything. Fletcher Tech earned millions off them. Your father enslaved my family. Just like you did me. And we both know what your father did to mine."

In the months leading up to his death, my dad had turned into a human statue—distant, silent, bereft. Although there was no proof, I have no doubt Fletcher Senior caused my father's heart failure in the end.

I stop and turn to face Don. "We, the Martins, didn't owe you nothing!"

He sneers, indulging in my anger. "Our parents may have broken even. But you, lady, *you* owe me. I saved your life. I cleaned up your mess." He gives me a few seconds to consider. "Oh, don't look at me like that! Yes, I introduced you to that fool Nando. But you, falling in love with him? It was your choice. It was your most fucked-up decision, but hey, you had Raffi."

Don waves my gun that has become his now. "Keep walking!"

He wasn't wrong—I have Raffi, the only good that came out of all the disasters the Fletchers had imposed on my family. But with every step I'm taking now, I question my son's future. I will keep defending him, but for how long?

I stop to catch my breath. There's a ridgeline ahead, and Don gestures to me to keep going toward it. I stomp ahead of him—Raffi may be there waiting.

Don follows leisurely, seemingly happy to be a few steps behind me. But out of the blue, I feel a thump behind my knees. Then he swiftly charges at my back. As soon as I lose my balance, he smashes my shin against a rock on the ground.

I scream like I've never screamed before, staring at my mangled limb.

"I'm sorry it has to end this way, Iz."

I wail, rolling on the forest floor in agony. What the hell is he trying to do? Is the Reaper finally going to swing his scythe now?

"It doesn't have to be like this, Don," I beg.

"Get up!" He hauls my arm like I was a sled. My uninjured leg kicks the ground as I try to push myself upright.

"Don! Please stop!"

"Keep walking!"

"I can't! You broke my fucking leg!"

"Keep walking, or you'll never see your son again."

Everything inside me dwindles. "Raffi!" I yell. But only the echo of my voice returns. "What did you do to him?"

"God, Iz. I get hard just by looking at you scared." Don picks up a fallen tree branch and tosses it over to me from a distance, the gun firmly pointed at me. "Come on, keep walking, and don't do anything stupid!"

The stick helps me walk, but the pain in my leg is almost unbearable. I limp my way up as Don watches my back, keeping his distance, aware that I'm holding a potential weapon.

Yard after yard, we arrive at a narrow clifftop, very rocky, with tall grass, shrubs, and trees scattered around.

"Raffi!" I call desperately.

The Grim Reaper's laugh returns. Facing a canyon, it sounds like he is the ghost that haunts this place.

"You will see him again, I promise you," he tells me. His face is not that of amusement. There's irrationality oozing out of his aura. This man will do anything to eliminate me—and entertain himself.

"What are you trying to do, Don?"

"Gee, Iz. One simply needs to use his imagination. Well, actually, you don't even need imagination. You're not a well woman. What mother in her right mind would suddenly disappear with her young son who was thriving at school and his sport? From Los Angeles—out of anywhere in the country—to Alaska? One of the states with the most hiking accidents?"

"You want people to think I'm crazy?"

"You are!" He almost spits at me. "You tricked me in L.A., I must admit. But you, looking lost and out of place around LAX, dumping that bloodied green dress of yours—you really didn't look well there, Iz. You'd gotten rid of Nando's baby once. After your relationship with Clayton fell apart because of your past, you couldn't bear it. You simply wanted to remove any trace of Nando from your life."

"Son of a bitch!" I lunge at him, but he puts me back in my place with a mere push.

"You were here, hiking with Raffi, but who knows what your real intention is. You broke your leg. Well, accidents happen, don't you agree? It's a nice touch to make all this look candid, and—I just wanted to hurt you. Anyway, you kept going because you were so determined to finish it all."

"Well, you've just confessed that your plan has been fucked up," I mock. "Raffi isn't here. If you haven't found him by now, you won't find him ever."

He grins as if trying to convince himself everything is still under control. "I'll find him. And once I've dealt with both of you, here's what I'm going to tell the police. I love Raffi so much that I tracked you down. I tried to save him, but you shot me—then him, then yourself. Make no mistake, I'm not afraid to shed a little blood for the sake of a perfect scene."

"You fucking snake!"

"That's one scenario. I mean, I liked that boy, and I wanted to take him under my wings. But what would I need him for?"

"You do whatever you want to me. But don't ever hurt Raffi!"

He keeps pondering. "Maybe you end up pushing your son over the cliff?"

"You sick bastard!"

"I haven't decided, Iz, so don't curse me yet. You'll see how things end for you both when I'm back here with him. Maybe tomorrow or the day after."

The slices of pain keep me grimacing, but pride and anger help me gather back my composure. "No one's gonna buy that story, Don," I sneer. "You won't find my son! They'll find out who did this to me. Clayton Hartley will never let you get away with this."

"I'll make time to deal with that cunt Hartley, don't worry about that."

"You'll leave traces. Even your feet are doing it at the moment."

"Thanks for reminding me. I'll clean up after myself. Oh, actually, this part of Alaska is due for some rain, I heard."

He nods at the distant clouds as if inviting me to let the dire situation sink in. A moment later, he drags me to a tree and then takes out a length of rope.

"You'll stay here for a day or two. Some animals might decide to have a taste of you. Perhaps a bear or a wolf. They might not finish you off in one go, though." Don snatches my wrists. "If you're lucky, you might still be alive when I bring Raffi to join you."

"You won't get away with this!" I gyrate, but Don overpowers me without even breaking a sweat.

He barely ties one of my wrists when a distant whir disturbs the air—and it's not wind or thunder.

"You hear that?" he gloats. "That's my ride!"

He runs away from me, standing on a small patch of clearing —the only clearing on this clifftop. He looks up at the sky, waving for someone to notice.

Don spins around, losing sight of the aircraft.

It gradually sounds closer, but the sky is empty.

Out of nowhere, a helicopter raises in front of us—as if the canyon just lifts it up from the bottom.

Don's joyful face turns outrageous. He takes cover next to me as a couple of bullets land next to his feet.

"Fuck this!" He cuts the half-done bound on my wrist and uses me as a shield.

The chopper flies closer, its nose turning, revealing its wide-open side.

That's my man—focused, resolute, and battle ready. No doubt, the HartTracker has led him to me. Precisely, his *heart* has led him to me.

Don is clutching my hands behind my back, covering every inch of him with my body. "You want her, Clayton?" he yells. "Get your ass over here and claim her like a man!"

"Clayton! Just shoot!" I yell.

Cornered, Don starts firing back as he retreats closer to the edge. The pilot maneuvers the chopper away.

"Fuck!" The gun in his hand stops firing—he's run out of ammo.

Don is never graceful in defeat, but this time—as the chopper makes a turn toward us—he puts his all-or-nothing decision on display.

Still hopeless in his clutch, I feel my feet lifting off the ground.

Between the chopper blades whirring, Don screaming below me, and Clayton's desperate yells from the air—and my own cry—I find myself in no one's grip.

And at the mercy of gravity.

## 35

## CLAYTON

"Isabelle! Nooo!"

My bullet hits Fletcher's neck—one millisecond too late.

It severs his spinal cord—two fucking milliseconds too late!

Donovan Fletcher is a man who makes terrible decisions under pressure, and this time his decision may have left devastation on a scale even he would've never imagined possible. That monster has an easy death. His mouth still gapes from laughing when he hits the ground.

I've seen wars, I've seen despicable things done to human beings, but how do you deal with this? Witnessing a victory of an enemy who may have single-handedly taken everything from you?

No. Donovan Fletcher hasn't won!

I won't let him, and I won't pay attention to that carcass anymore.

"Where's she?" I shout, looking around.

"Clay..." Wyatt's voice hints at how desperate the situation is, but I know he's still fighting alongside me. He's flying the chopper along the outline of the cliff.

"Where's she!" He'd better not say that she's at the bottom of the canyon.

"Clay!" Blake calls. "Over there!"

I see her clinging. Although the cliff is almost vertical, the surface is uneven, with big rocks and vegetation scattered around. That appears to have helped Isabelle to hang on.

"Isabelle! I'm coming!"

Her frame looks so fragile among the vast wall. But if anyone can do it, it'll be her. She knows. A mother knows what her survival means.

There's nowhere the chopper can land, but I've got to get to her. "Wyatt, fly closer."

I don't know how he'll do it, but we've got to try.

Fletcher hired this helicopter to fetch him from this risky spot, so it's equipped with a winch-fed cable. It's not made for a cliff-face rescue, but it may just help us.

I hook the cable onto my harness.

Wyatt steadies the chopper a little bit on an angle so he can get close to the cliff face.

I jump, lowering myself toward Isabelle. The cable starts to spin as the length grows, and the brutal wind sways both the chopper and me.

"Clayton..." I barely hear Isabelle's voice.

She's still way beyond my reach.

"Isabelle, hang on."

There's a length of rope attached to her right wrist, and somehow it gets caught on a bulb of tussock grass. It's not suspending her, but I think it helped slow down her fall, allowing her to grab hold of those rocks she's hanging onto now.

"I'm coming, baby."

Isabelle clings with her two arms, supported by one foot which only her toes perching on a small rock. Her other leg is dangling precariously. Looking at the state of it, I think it's broken.

Seeing I'm still struggling to reach her, with the cable swaying almost out of control, Wyatt flies closer to the cliff, tilting even further.

Isabelle screams, the muscles on her arms swelling as she holds onto the rocks with all her might.

This is a terrible mistake!

"Wyatt, abort! Abort!" I yell, waving vigorously at the pilot to fly away from her.

"Clayton! Please, don't go!" Isabelle cries desperately, clearly aware that I'm moving away.

"I'll come back, baby. Just hold on. I'll come back for you. I promise." I don't think she hears me, and with her facing the cliff, she certainly can't see my face. But I have to do this for her. I look up. "Blake, haul me up! Come on, haul me up!"

The winch slurps the cable to bring me back up, with Blake controlling it, stopping it from spinning excessively. It feels like forever. Once on board, I unhook the cable but keep my harness on.

"We can't get close to her," I tell Wyatt. "The downwash will suck her out of her grip, and she'll fall."

"What do you want me to do, Mr. Hartley?"

"Fly to the top of the cliff. Keep the altitude. I'll jump."

"Clay, no..." Blake throws me a disapproving look.

I ignore him. There's no other option. By this time, Wyatt has already executed my order.

I take another harness with me. "Have we got ropes?"

We look around, and we have about twenty yards of climbing rope. It'll do. It'll *have* to do.

Wyatt approaches the cliff away from where Isabelle is hanging on. From here, we can see the dead body of the monster that doesn't deserve to be described or named. Even a stray cat has more dignity than he did.

I scan the ground while Wyatt steadies the chopper. As soon as I'm down, I'll have to know exactly where I need to go and what to do.

We're hovering at twenty-five, thirty feet. I was never a paratrooper, but I've learned to perform a landing fall—and my training soon kicks in. My body buckles almost automatically, absorbing the impact, thus protecting my spine. Not a perfect ten landing, but I swallow the impact pain and get back on my feet. I rush toward the tree closest to the edge of the cliff. I secure the climbing rope around it and then fasten the other end onto my harness.

Wyatt is keeping a distance. Although having my team close by would've been my preference, with the wind from the weather already swirling, he knows the presence of the chopper will only make it worse.

The other harness which I've reserved for Isabelle is hanging on my shoulder. I haven't got much rope, but I'll have to make it work. I don't care if I have to get to her upside down!

"Isabelle, I'm coming!" I yell as I descend along the cliff wall.

"Clayton... I can't hold on much longer."

The strain on her face tears me apart. When she says she can't, I believe her. She's been hanging on for too long!

"You can, Isabelle. Hang on. Please, hang on."

She howls in agony. I peek down. Shit! Her only leg that was supporting her has slipped. Her arms are now the only difference between survival and falling.

I'm running out of rope, but I can get to her with just enough slack. I anchor my footing on a couple of small but stable rocks, so I can use both arms to reach and secure her.

"Isabelle. Baby, I'm here."

I can see every vein and muscle swell on her hands and

arms. There's no way I can put the harness around her when she's clinging like that.

How the hell am I going to ask her to let go?

I've held her so many times, but at this moment, what's at stake is no less than her life. I put my arm around her waist, holding on to her with all I've got. If she falls, I'll go down with her.

"Let go of the rocks, baby."

"I can't." Her voice tears from her mouth painfully. "I'll fall."

"Trust me, Baby Belle. I've got you."

Her head carefully deviates from the rocks, and she releases her grip. She dips. But my arm banding around her is unmoved. Not even Earth's gravity can take her away from me.

"I've got you." I breathe on her crown while planning my next move. Somehow I'll have to put her legs into the harness loops.

The rope Fletcher tied around her wrist is still there, but I'll have to ignore it for now. While my foot is still planted on a rock, I turn her so her back is leaning against the cliff face, balancing her on an indent.

Her every limb is trembling, but she clings to me, her face buried in the curve of my shoulder. With one arm still holding her, I reach down to lower the loops of the harness, and then, one by one, I slip her legs into them. Her teeth grit, stifling her cry as the strap travels up her broken leg.

"Sorry, baby. I'm almost there."

As soon as the harness is secure on her, I clip mine onto hers.

"Good job, good job." Relief fills me. We're linked—whatever happens to her will happen to me. "We're gonna climb now, okay?"

As if the worst has passed, she wastes no time coming on to me. "Clayton..." Her sobs vibrate in my ear. "I'm pregnant."

We have to keep going, but I let the moment take me as I

sob with her. Surely, heaven would grant me just a few seconds with her to celebrate a miracle among the devastation around us. "I know, Isabelle. I know," I murmur over her cheek.

"I don't want to lose the baby, Clayton."

"No. You won't," I vow. "Now, we have to go. It's gonna hurt. But we've got to climb up."

She pushes herself despite her broken leg. With that, she straddles me close, and her arms never leave me. The more secure she is on me, the easier it is for me.

Painful groans escape her throat as I start the laborious ascent.

"Hang in there, Isabelle."

"I lost Baby Caili... I can't go through it again," she sobs. Her fear thickens as she feels herself sagging.

In a bid to calm her, I pause, wedging her gently between the cliff face and my body. My eyes find hers. "You won't lose the baby. We won't lose the baby. I promise."

She tucks her face against my chest, holding on to me even tighter. From here on, I plant kisses on her crown with every foot of height I gain.

Until we make it to the top.

She keeps herself glued to me even when she feels solid ground under her. I stay in this position, signaling to her I'm not asking her to let go.

We're still linked, and we will be until we're safely back on the chopper.

"We must find Raffi," she pants as her eyes wander to Fletcher's lifeless body, lying not far from us.

"He's safe. He's with Blake's police friend. It's over. No one is going to harm him, or you." Then I place my hand on her belly.

She beams like I've never seen her before, inviting me to kiss her. And I do her lips, her face, her tears, her pain. I then get rid of the rope that's tied around her wrist—the last remaining sign of Fletcher's reign of terror.

I give a signal to Wyatt, who's been flying the chopper in place about half a mile away from us.

"Hang on to me one more time," I beg Isabelle as the rain starts to pelt down on us.

Her pain is visible, but calmness radiates out of her as she readies herself for the extraction.

Blake lowers the winch-fed cable while Wyatt maintains altitude to keep minimal downwash. I hook us up, and soon we leave the ground. I say in her ear, "Actually, hold me like this forever, and I'll be a happy man."

She locks her lips onto mine. Gentle but firm—loving beyond anything I've ever felt.

Thunder and lightning crack around us.

"Come on, guys! We've gotta get out of here!" Wyatt shouts as Blake hustles to get us on board.

"Be careful. Her right leg is broken," I warn Blake when he takes over Isabelle. "And she's—"

Blake smiles against the wind that's battering his face. Of course, he knows.

"I've got you, Isabelle." Blake holds her by the armpits, then hauls her to the middle of the chopper.

"Let's go!" I instruct Wyatt. We've got to outfly this storm.

I watch Blake unclipping Isabelle's carabiner off mine, and I see blood.

Is this not over?

I jump next to Isabelle, who is now secure in the back seat, patting her all over. "Are you bleeding?"

"What?" Her eyes immediately drop to her pelvis. "No."

I keep patting her, looking for any sign of a wound as she continues scanning herself.

"It's just my leg, Clayton."

I place my lips on her forehead, exhaling deeply. I've promised her everything will be okay—I can't break it now.

If Isabelle isn't bleeding, and I'm not either, then there's only one person that blood could belong to.

I turn to Blake. Goddammit, it's his hands!

"Man... what the hell?"

"I'm fine."

I inspect the cable that hauled us up.

"The brake on that winch was dicey," he comments as if it was nothing.

Jesus! All this time, he was controlling our extraction with his bare hands?

"Clay, I'm fine. Don't look at me like that." He dismisses my concern, helping me get out of my harness.

"You're gonna have that checked out!" I give him a stern look. He'll probably opt for self-medication, but those are serious cuts!

Wyatt makes a swift turn to Anchorage.

Blake kneels in the narrow space between the back and the co-pilot seats, facing us. He then looks at Isabelle. "Told you."

That earns a smile from her.

"What did you tell her?" I ask him.

Blake shrugs.

I let it slide, tapping his shoulder. "I owe you, man."

"You, finding your queen, makes it up for it. And I can tell you, it wasn't a Trojan war. It was just how you were meant to fight for her." Blake winks at me, then dives into the co-pilot seat.

"Baby Belle..." I call her among the noise, leaning into her ear. My hand lands on her belly again. "Are you all right?"

She puts her hand on top of mine. "Sore, but I think I'll be okay."

I comb her wet fringe back using my hand, nuzzling her

forehead to take in her scent. It's sweat and dirt, but she still smells sweet.

I'm a man of science. Perhaps it was biologically or physiologically impossible for her to bear another child. But this woman was born to defy the odds. After the ordeal that rocked us and almost broke us, she beat all the odds in ways that I'd never anticipated. She fought on that cliff. Fletcher threw her, but she hung on! And I ought to thank her for that, because I don't know what I'd do had I lost her.

Now we can look to the future. She's carrying our child, and beyond her agony right now, she's beaming. Look at her face—it's glowing!

We land at the Alaska Regional Hospital heliport after Wyatt takes the chopper on a flash flight, almost getting into trouble with the Alaskan aviation authorities for the speed we traveled in.

"We'll take care of her, Mr. Hartley," the doctor says.

"Clayton," Isabelle pleads, refusing to let me go.

"I'm here, baby." I keep up with the medical team as we rush to the ER. I angle my shoulder, so the doctor notices me. "She's pregnant, Doc."

Her hand falls limp.

"Isabelle?"

The doctor stops me from following her further.

I watch as staff positions themselves around her, obscuring her features. All I can do is gaze at her dangling hand and the jade bracelet around her wrist. We've come so far since that Kenya night. We can't falter now!

## 36

## CLAYTON

I pace the length of the waiting room.

I'm rewinding the event over and over, from the second I saw Fletcher hurling her over the cliff to the moment she was leaning on me, next to me inside the chopper. What have I failed to do that now nobody—*nobody*—is able to tell me how she is?

A nurse finally approaches me. Her expression doesn't give anything away, but what's in her hands makes my stomach clench.

"Mr. Hartley," the nurse calls.

"How's she?"

"The doctor will see you soon. In the meantime, you may want to hang on to these." She hands over Isabelle's bracelet and wallet.

I hold them in my hand while giving her a blank look. Why is she giving me Isabelle's belongings?

"How is she?"

The nurse takes a breath, then says, "She's having delayed shock symptoms."

Delayed shock symptoms?

Pilots can suffer mid-air shock, for whatever reason, from

environmental factors to extreme distress. But they're machines. They're supposed to withstand such a thing. To a mother with child? What will shock do to them?

And the fact that it's delayed? That's even worse! That means her injuries had done damage long before she felt the effects.

"Wait!" I catch the nurse, who is now leaving the waiting room. "What... what does that mean?"

"The doctor will explain, sir."

I return to the room where a few people blatantly scrutinize me. I throw myself into a corner couch, sinking as the cushion fails to support me.

"Clay!"

The voice I've been waiting for, the person I desperately need.

I hug my big brother.

"How is she, Clay?"

"I don't know. All they gave was these..." I show Rob what's in my hand and an object slips out of her wallet.

The HartTracker. It's still in the 'on' position. It was supposed to be merely a toy, but it did bring me back to her.

"So that thing worked," Rob nods at it.

"The battery would've probably run out." I clench a fist around it, sighing, "Why the hell am I holding her things, Rob? I don't do hospitals, so I don't know their procedures. Does it mean that she's dying?"

"Hey, of course not! They just wanted you to keep her belongings safe. That's all. Sit down." He picks a better couch this time. "Coffee?"

"Ah... yeah, thanks, Rob!" I take the cup.

"Alaskan espresso. Sorry I couldn't bring Mama's coffee."

I curve a reminiscing smile. Amber's mother's coffee is the best. I have even forgotten that I'm more than three thousand miles from home. I guess the coffee wouldn't survive the journey here.

"The nurse just now told me Isabelle is having delayed shock symptoms. Was it her fall? Did I pull her too hard? Why didn't they treat her for shock right from the start? Why does it have to be *delayed*?"

Rob takes the cup away from my hand. A good thing, because I'm about to drop it and spill it all over the floor.

"She hung on for a long time, Clay. Her body just needs time to recover. She'll do it again. She has you, and she has Raffi and the baby. She won't quit."

"You know, Rob. That day when everything happened," I say. "When Mia was born, when Isabelle ran away, it did cross my mind that I was going to propose to her. I mean, I wasn't going to do it that day, but just a thought—how beautiful would it be to hear her say yes? I didn't know how I'd do it. I still don't. But I knew it'd be beautiful."

He keeps quiet as if giving me more time to imagine it. Then he looks at me playfully. "You're not going to upstage me, though."

I chuckle. Rob's proposal to Amber was spectacular—I've got to hand it to him for his ingenuity. Just like the love story between him and her, there's no way I will ever upstage it.

Rob pats my shoulder. "Keep it simple, brother. There are more important things you two need to think of other than a few seconds of you on your bended knee."

I nod at his wisdom as I reach for my coffee cup, taking a couple more sips. "I've said a lot of despicable things to her. I just hope she can forgive me. I mean, I don't think she'll leave me, but—I don't want our fallout to resurface in the future. You know, when things aren't going so well, and we look to the past for some kind of justification."

"Come on. She doesn't seem to be the type who holds grudges."

It never crosses my mind that she is. Rather, it's me who needs to hear from her that I've been forgiven.

It has to wait. In the meantime, I ask Rob about her best friend. "By the way, what happened to Thomas?"

"That kid was tortured by Fletcher's man back in L.A. They believed he knew something about Raffi's whereabouts. Apparently he had a new passport with him, ready to leave, but he stayed on for Isabelle."

"That kid!

"And he can prove Fletcher's tampering of her health and criminal records."

"Thank God for Thomas!"

"Indeed. And he's a wiz!" Rob admits. "I mean, he transformed your old HartTracker software in less than an hour. Did you see the terrain overlay that he did?"

"It was him?"

"Yeah."

"Poach him."

"Already have!" Rob gushes. "Fletcher Tech will be no more anyway."

A man who looks like Stanley Tucci makes a beeline toward us. He introduces himself as the hospital's head of trauma. A doctor at last!

"How is she?" I ask him.

The doctor grants me a reassuring smile. "The worst has passed, so she's on the mend."

I release a long breath. Rob stands closer to me.

The doctor explains, "Her blood pressure and heart rate are still low, normal symptoms for delayed shock. What she went through was traumatic. Her body had sustained an extended period of 'survival mode,' so to speak. And once she left that mode, her body reacted—hence the delayed symptoms."

Why was it so hard for anyone to explain it to me before? Perhaps she did go into a rough patch.

The doctor adds, "We'll keep her under close observation. Her right tibia is broken in three places. We've performed surgery on it. It will heal; it's just a matter of time and therapy. For now, she's comfortable and recovering well."

"The baby?"

"The baby's just fine, Mr. Hartley."

My legs almost fail to support me as relief washes through me. It's only because Rob is next to me that I don't crash to the floor. Could this be the delayed effects of my distress? It turns out I still have a lot to learn about strength.

"Miss Martins is ten weeks along, so the pregnancy is still young. Considering her previous pregnancy and historical trauma to her uterus, she will need a lot of rest." The doctor pauses, assessing my reaction.

He's got to know I'll do whatever it takes, give her whatever she needs.

"Can I see her now?"

"Sure. For now, keep it to light conversations. Don't make her excited or emotional."

I nod, although I don't feel that I have control over it.

"This way, Mr. Hartley," the doctor points ahead.

I step into her room, very light on my feet, not wanting to wake her up. I take a seat next to her bed, observing her. I don't even dare to touch her anywhere. She's weak, I understand. But looking at her peaceful face, I can't believe she was suffering from shock. And the only sign of her injury is her cast leg, suspended in a sling.

Then I hear her moan.

I shift in my chair, pushing myself as close as possible to her without disturbing her.

"Clayton... is that you?"

No matter how stealthy I am, she knows. "Hey," I caress the top of her hand.

Her eyes are still shut, but a small smile forms on her features. She sluggishly turns her palm up, squeezing my hand.

"The doctor said I shouldn't make you excited or emotional."

She chuckles, and this time her lids flutter open. "Too late for that," she murmurs.

Of course, she's already excited to see me. How I miss those blue eyes looking back at me with love and admiration.

She shifts herself up, and her suspended leg shakes.

"Hey, take it easy. What do you need? Just tell me."

"My back... it's itchy, right in the middle."

I turn her slightly and then give her a few scratches. "That better?"

"Thanks."

I release an amused chuckle. These little things become significant when I'm with her.

"Ugh... why am I so tired?" she sighs.

"You need to rest, baby. Go back to sleep." I get off my seat, my lips reaching hers.

Isabelle welcomes my kiss with a soft pucker. Our kisses have been passionate, naughty, intense, and everything in between. But right now, this kiss simply tells me she will be okay.

"The doctor said your blood pressure and heart rate were low, but—"

She flicks her eyes half-open, blinking at the monitors next to her. Of course, she's a nurse. She knows how to read those numbers.

"They just shot up a bit after that kiss," she quips.

I place my hand on her belly. "I guess you know that the baby is doing fine, too."

She puts her hand on top of mine, pressing it just a tad. I lay my head cheek-to-cheek with her, absorbing the moment. There are a lot of things I want to tell her, but they can wait.

After she falls asleep, I doze off, too.

A long beep from the machine rouses me back to alertness.

"Baby Belle?" I pat her hand.

"The vitals clip just slipped off my finger. I'm still alive, don't worry."

A nurse comes in to check on her but soon leaves us be when she sees Isabelle is okay.

I stifle a yawn, unsure how long I was asleep. I glance at Isabelle. She looks way brighter than me, which reminds me of something. Her middle name, which I like very much but hasn't been on my mind. "Baby Moon Belle?"

Her smile widens. "Moon?"

"Yes, Isabelli Luna Martins. It's a quarter moon outside, but it's very bright."

"Ah, the moon. When I'm at the hospital, I usually think about the sun. Because of my graveyard shift, I guess. I was always looking forward to sunrise," she reveals, one hand caressing my cheek. "Are you okay?"

"I'm supposed to do that to you," I tease her, kissing her palm as I take over being the caresser.

"Something bothering you?" she asks.

"No. I'm happy."

"Come on, Clayton. Talk to me."

"I don't want to make you emotional."

"Try me."

With that solemn gaze, I find the courage to tell her, "I'm sorry about what I said. I made a terrible mistake with what I accused you of."

"I can't remember what you said."

"Truly, Isabelle, I need you to forgive me. I was cruel. I wasn't myself then. Fletcher certainly took advantage of it, and I fell for it. That's not how I want you to remember me."

Her eyes glisten, soft and understanding.

I add, "Hell, I'm not myself whenever you're not by my side."

"I forgive you, Clay. I've forgiven you right after you said it."

"I love you, Isabelli Martins. With all of me."

"I love you too, Clayton Hartley, a stranger with a heart. This —" She caresses her belly. "—is how I'm going to remember you. Every baby is a miracle, but this baby is more than that. It's proof that we're meant to be."

I kiss her deeply. To hell with making her emotional! What we're sharing is an emotion that will heal her.

As a response, Isabelle presses her lips against mine as if saying, 'Who dares separate us!'

Clayton the bachelor didn't know where his heart belonged. Now I do—its place is with this woman in my arms. Of course, I still have love for others—my family, those kids in Oltepesi—but her? She has my whole heart.

I sit back on my chair, observing her cast leg.

"By the way, the doctor also said no telescopic bars for the next few weeks."

She laughs. "That's bad advice."

37

―――――

## ISABELLE

After weeks of being confined to bed and bringing my right leg back to health, Clayton proposed to me at the Franklin Canyon cottage—on the same boat that had taken us to the middle of the lake, gotten us soaked, and led us to our first surrender.

With my conditions, being the responsible man that he is, he went through everything with my doctors—the shoulds and shouldn'ts, the okays and not okays. Needless to say, he had to can the skydiving and mid-flight proposal ideas he'd conceived prior to knowing my pregnancy.

It was a down-to-earth engagement, just how I loved it. The water was calm, allowing him to get down on one knee and present me with a stunning emerald platinum ring.

It wasn't just a proposal. The big man, on bended knee with sincerity in his eyes and a firm hold on me, gave himself to me. I wish I could've knelt in front of him, too, because I would give myself to him for all eternity.

But the life growing inside me made up for that missed chance—I'd already given myself to him long before that moment.

Today, as our pregnancy enters our last trimester, we're about to seal our promise with our vows. And we're back to where we started.

The Franklin Canyon cottage lakeside is lined with tables intricately dressed in white and purple. The only exception is my and Clayton's table, which is covered in a stunning traditional Kenyan cloth, gifted by Mr. and Mrs. Makena, who have flown all the way here to attend our wedding. Only when Clayton and I were sorting out our guest list did I finally find out who he was dining with that night at the Giraffe Manor.

My husband-to-be may be a billionaire, but I'm relieved to hear that he was looking at a low-key wedding. Truly, I had no fuss about how it was going to be as long as Clayton and his family are here. But knowing I wouldn't have to deal with hundreds of people I don't even know, I'm a calmer bride.

With my growing belly, Amber lent a hand in choosing a dress for me. It's a Verona gown with a divine empire line overlaid in delicate lace. Who knew that she herself was five months pregnant when she married Rob? What is it with the Hartley boys and their timing?

"Stay still, babe!" Thomas commands as he fixes my veil, helped by Pippa. "What do you think?" he asks her.

"A bit more to the right, maybe?" Pippa proposes. "The middle flower isn't centered."

"Well, the pin is asymmetric, babe. I think it's perfect like that," Thomas insists.

"Okay... you're the expert," Pippa relents.

"I think it looks great like that." Amber shows it to me in a mirror, seemingly happy to be the deciding vote.

Pippa helps me stand up, watching me striking a pose—as elegantly as I can with my bulging belly. She then starts crying. "Look at you, Gizzy Belle."

Like a domino effect, Thomas sheds errant tears. "I wish you were my bride..."

"Easy, babe. Just remember that I stole your soulmate."

Thomas giggles, sniffling away his cry.

Amber looks out the door and then says to me, "It's time."

As soon as I step out of my room, Simon Blake greets me. He doesn't usually give away anything with his blank paper expression, but this time his smile widens as he presses a gentle kiss to my forehead. "Damn that boss of mine is a lucky man."

He's not old enough to be my father, but as I found out, he was a faithful advocate for me and Clayton, even when we were at our lowest point. That's got to be a good enough reason for him to give me away. Besides, in his police uniform, he looks sleek—like Tom Ford runway sleek.

"Wish me luck," I whisper to Thomas, who leans on Pippa, still in tears.

"You've got a gun concealed somewhere?" Blake teases me as he takes my arm. "Clayton had better behave today!"

I chuckle. "I'm a peaceful mother now, Simon."

As we stride forward, I can't take my eyes off of the man waiting for me at the end of the aisle. Clayton Hartley. He looks dashing—oh my, I'm weak all over seeing him in his Air Force uniform—but he is the home where I belong. There's nowhere else I'd rather be.

He takes my hand, presenting a platinum band to me. "Isabelle... I've flown high, I've roamed wide, but I've never found another person whom I love more than you. Now that we've found each other, fallen for each other, and bound to each other, I promise I'll be your pilot and navigator of our life's adventures and be the wind beneath your wings when you need me. I love you, Isabelli Luna Martins. From now on, and for the rest of my life, you will have the best of me without reservation."

He places the ring next to the engagement ring. It's written there, so I will forever carry his name.

"Clayton... my fierce, limitless, and unending feelings for you cannot be adequately described by the word 'love' alone. You know my flaws and faults, yet your heart and arms never fail to provide me with the gentlest safety and constant affection. I have no doubt that same heart and arms of yours will provide such safety and affection for our children." I glance at Raffi and then put Clayton's hand on my belly. "Through life's ups and downs, I'll never be your enemy, but rather, I'll fight beside you. Because, Clayton Faber Hartley, you're the only man I cherish, and I will do so for the rest of my life."

We kiss, following me putting my ring on him.

"God, you look stunning," Clayton murmurs. His lips are still hovering over mine.

"I'm yours, husband."

We leave the ceremony, passing a saber arch formed by six Air Force men, arranged by Clayton's former commanding officer, General Adler.

Then we pass our own guard of honor, including Clayton's former SEAL brother Rob, Wyatt the retired Navy pilot, and Blake the retired police officer, and General Adler himself. All of them in their full uniform.

My bouquet goes to my best girl Pippa, uncontested. Most of the ladies in the party have married their other halves already!

I melt all over when I'm greeted by the clapping hands from the kids, all tuxedo-clad. Raffi and Matty, and even little Graeme, throw rose petals—no doubt they've been herded well by Thomas, who's standing by behind them. But even before the petals hit the ground, Raffi and Matty abandon their posts, running to me and Clayton, giving us hugs and kisses.

"Mom!" my son hugs me. "I'm so happy for you."

"Thank you, baby."

"Sit down, Baby Belle." Clayton helps me maneuver myself onto a chair. He even arranges the skirt of my dress neatly.

"Clay!" Matty jumps up at his brother. "You did it!"

Clayton carries him. "Yeah, pal. *We* did it." They give each other a fist bump.

"Congratulations, you two!" Rob and Amber soon join in, taking turns hugging us.

"So, when I grow up, who's going to be my wingman?" Matty asks as he jumps down from Clayton's hip.

"Hey, where did you learn that word from?" Rob queries in a suspicious tone.

Matty glances at his middle brother with wicked eyes.

"I'll be your wingman, buddy," Clayton claims.

Matty tinkers with the idea. "Can a wingman be old?"

Rob, Amber, and I restrain our laughter as we wait for Clayton's reply.

"As long as you're handsome, it doesn't matter if you're old or young."

"Huh!" Matty scoffs, still thinking.

"Come on, Matty." Rob takes his little brother's hand. "Let's get you some food."

Raffi walks to Clayton who opens his arms wide. "Now, don't pick me up, okay? I'm too big for that."

Clayton grins. It almost looks like a brotherly grin. "Come here!" The two boys give each other a hug.

"So... my name will be Rafael Hartley?"

As soon as Clayton and I got engaged, we discussed Clayton adopting Raffi.

Clayton crouches in front of him. "If you still want it."

"Of course!" Raffi affirms.

Hell, yeah, he's a Hartley, all right.

"Wait..." Raffi ponders. "That means... Matty will be my uncle?"

We burst out laughing. We'd thought about it, but hearing it from him, it sounds hilarious.

"Nah. He's your brother," Clayton says. "He loves being your brother."

"Do I have to call you 'Dad'?"

"Not if you don't want to."

"I'll decide later," Raffi says lightly.

"That works, too," Clayton replies.

"But I see you as my dad. You know that, right?" Raffi looks up at him, then me. "I've never seen my mom this happy before."

"Thanks, pal." Clayton rubs his eye.

"Go and play with Matty," I tell Raffi. I want time alone with my husband now, my husband who's—I study him. "Are you crying?"

"I'm just happy."

"Thank you for everything," I murmur. "Thank you for taking me here, again and again."

"Baby Moon Belle, you don't have to thank me for our wedding. I know how much you love this place," he acknowledges with a soft touch on my hand. "I told you my father initially built that cottage for my mother?" His gaze shoots up to the top of the hill.

"Uh-huh."

"I was never close to either of our parents. Rob was extremely close to our mother, but he had a love-hate relationship with father. This place used to be just a holiday home. But you know, being here with you, I feel something has just been brought to life—a connection of some sort."

I nod, telling him that was exactly what I felt when I first set foot on this place, and continue to do so. It's not just the beauty. It's the spirit around it.

"Do you want to live here, Baby Belle?"

"No, not really. I love your Beverly Hills home. It's not a

lonely house anymore. In saying that, this place will always be part of us."

In the distance, Simon Blake raises a glass to us.

"He's been quiet," I comment.

"He's always quiet at parties."

I was honored that the man agreed to give me away, but right now, I realize how little I know about him. "I didn't realize he was single. Was he ever married?"

"More than married, baby. He was utterly devoted to her."

"What happened to her?"

"She was killed."

"Oh, God. In Alaska?"

"Yeah. He was a PI with one of the diplomats there—a controversial one. Things got ugly. Flo, Blake's wife, was shot in revenge gone wrong."

"That's so tragic."

"You know, you're the only person he investigated who found him out—in his whole PI career with Hartley Marine. Let alone shot at his windscreen!"

Oh, the madness! I can't fathom I'd ever do that again. "I think he wanted to be found out." I defend Blake, keeping my attention on him. "He looks so sad."

Clayton nudges a finger against the side of my jaw, softly asking me to stop glancing at Blake. "He's a melancholic guy."

"He never intends to remarry?"

"He's a one-woman man. It will take the universe to shake to change that."

I really hope the universe does shake for him one day. If anyone deserves a second chance at love, my vote will go to him.

Without warning the heavens open.

"Come on, guys, inside!" Rob announces, getting the guests to line up as he's waiting for me and Clayton to make our move.

We grin at each other.

It's a perfect day. Rain or shine, this place will always be beautiful.

My husband warns me with his eyes of what he's about to do. I'm not wearing high heels, but I welcome his sturdy arms as he carries me all the way to the top.

To the warmth of the cottage.

**38**

# EPILOGUE: CLAYTON

I'm glad to find my Baby Belle asleep when I get home. She's lying sideways, cuddling her special pillow.

Occasionally I do get jealous of that pillow. But I'll have my cuddle time back after the baby is born—or that's what I'm hoping. Rob has given me a lot of tips about fatherhood, including the infamous sleep deprivation. But I'm up for anything!

"Clayton..." Isabelle murmurs, her arm flailing to find me.

I sit on the edge of the bed next to where her ass is. I softly peck the side of her neck. "I'm just going to check on the boys and then join you. Okay?"

She hums and then adjusts her position. Literally a second later, I hear her purring away.

It's past ten o'clock. The meeting with General Adler and his team went overtime, as we're preparing for the next phase of testing—real combat scenarios over a longer period and distances.

I have a quick peek at Raffi's bedroom and then Matty's. Both boys are fast asleep.

Thomas is still awake, though. He's Hartley Marine's Enterprise Digital Security Manager, but once he's swiped out of the office, he is Raffi's and Matty's official babysitter—our own Care Bear. Just for a few days. Isabelle is due anytime now, so he's only too happy to hang around our Beverly Hills home until D-day.

"Nothing to report on?" I query as I land downstairs.

"No. The boys played hard during the day, so by the time they finished dinner, they didn't have much energy left to create trouble," he says. "You had dinner?"

"I did. I'm gonna turn in now."

"Played too hard?"

"Way too hard. Good night, Thomas."

"Night, Clay."

I keep my steps light as I return to our bedroom, staying as stealthy as possible even when I have my shower. Isabelle moans when I join her in bed, but she's still out.

As I lay awake, something is nagging me from the inside. I might wake her up and undo my effort to keep her asleep, but I need to get close. It's not because my wife is hugging her pillow like it was her new man. I just have to feel her.

I nudge myself to spoon her. Luckily, she doesn't stir even though the mattress jolts.

But there's something unusual. It might be why my sixth sense told me to get close to her. "Baby Belle?" I touch her shoulder. Now I want her to wake up.

"Clayton?"

"Baby..."

"Huh?" She isn't still quite with herself—she must've been in a deep sleep just now.

"Sweetheart, I think your water broke."

That wakes her up. "What? Really? Turn on the light, baby." She observes the wet patch under her. "No blood? Did you see any blood?"

"No," I reassure her.

"Jesus! How did I sleep through it? How come you knew?"

I smile proudly. "Must've been all the bump-talks."

She laughs, then places her hand on my cheek. "I'll get dressed."

"I'll help you. You okay?" I observe her grimacing.

"The contractions have started."

"Wait here. I'm gonna wake Thomas up, and then I'll come and get you."

"Clay..." She squeezes my hand.

She never said it, but I know she's still traumatized by her last pregnancy. It's my turn to be her rock now. "Everything will be all right, I promise."

I knock on Thomas's door, and as soon as I tell him, the man cries like he's going to be a father himself. Isabelle told me about the night she lost her baby—how Thomas stayed by her side and comforted Raffi while apparently Don was fast asleep in his home. And that boy was still eighteen at the time!

I give him a reassuring hug. "Hey, she'll be okay."

"I know! I know!" He sniffles. "I'm just so happy..."

"You keep an eye on Raffi and Matty, okay? Call me if there's anything."

The time passes, dragging on and racing at the same time.

Now I'm waiting for her to come out of the C-section surgery while Rob is keeping me company, this time with a thermos full of Mama's coffee.

"How did you do it with Graeme?" I say to him as he refills my cup. This waiting is driving me nuts.

"I was going crazy, if you remember. I'm kind of thankful that Mia didn't give any of us a chance to get nervous like that."

Mia's arrival was quick, and thanks to my Baby Belle, it was safe, too. That's what I remember that day by—not the other noises.

The doctor comes back to us earlier than expected. "Congratulations, Mr. Hartley. It's a boy. One impatient baby, but he's healthy."

My head falls on Rob's shoulder.

"Well done, Clay!" His embrace never fails to remind me that, despite life's many changes, we are forever brothers. Nothing will replace or alter what we have together.

"How's my wife doing?" I ask the doctor.

"She's ready to see you, and the baby is with her."

I hold Rob's shoulder. "Hey, man. Isabelle and I have decided, if it's a boy, we'll name him Faber Robson Hartley."

My brother grins, pride and joy painting his face. Trying to fight tears pooling in his eyes, he trembles, "He'll be more handsome than his dad. Hell yeah." He taps my cheek. "Go. Send them a hug from me, will you?"

I pat his shoulder hard as if he wouldn't feel it if I didn't.

"This way, Mr. Hartley," the doctor gestures. If he looks this happy every time he delivers a baby, I don't think he'll ever age. "Your baby has a healthy appetite, that's for sure."

A hospital is never anyone's favorite place, but seeing Isabelle and Faber in that room, surrounded by white, I feel like I'm in heaven.

I wrap Isabelle in my arms, showering her with as many kisses as I can muster. And right now, words simply escape me. All the things I was planning to say, I can't get them out. I weep as I rest one arm around her waist, and the other reaching out to my son, caressing his rosy cheek.

"It's daddy," Isabelle says. "Faber, it's daddy."

"He's perfect." Finally I can utter something.

"He is." Isabelle reaches for my lips to give me a proud-mama kiss. "Hold him."

My heart bursts inside my ribcage with emotional confetti, my head overloaded with thoughts—how should I cradle him? How firm? How soft?

But as soon as he's in my arms, everything falls into place.

Fatherly instinct? It's more than that. What I'm feeling is an immense sense of humbleness, devotion, and protectiveness.

"Hey, Faber," I murmur as I kiss his little forehead. He may not hear me, but we've known each other for months now, so he's got to feel me. I know the bond between us will last a lifetime.

I turn to Isabelle, who's wiping tears of her own. I ask, "How are you feeling?"

"A little exhausted, but I can't be happier. It feels weird not having a load, though." She observes and rubs her belly. Then she turns to me with a naughty gaze. "You know, Clayton, I'm gonna miss your massages."

I chuckle.

"Seriously!" she adds. "You've got the best hands!"

"Here, hold Faber." I hand our baby back to her. The boy seems to be content commuting between his parents.

"Oh God…" Isabelle moans as I massage her shoulders. "You keep doing that, and everybody will think I'm having an orgasm."

"You're allowed to enjoy it," I justify my continued massage. But hell, she is moaning like my cock was in her. She didn't do this at home. "Tell me, Baby Belle." I hope my next question will settle her vocal somewhat.

"Hmm?"

"Can I ask you if you want another one?"

She casts me a sweet, shy smile. "I do want another one, Clayton."

"Um… I'm going to ask you this. Because you're my wife and I know you'll understand my question. You want a girl?"

She breathes out her last moan as I stop massaging—only because I need to see her expression.

"Every child is a blessing," she says, tenderness and longing in her voice.

"I know. But, admit it..." I wink at her.

A lovely scarlet flush colors her cheeks. "Yeah... a girl would be nice, but really, I'll be happy with another boy if that's what life gives us."

"We'll try, Baby Moon Belle. I promise we'll try."

She stretches her neck to reach my lips. "You know me too well."

"Because you've let me."

She gives me a nod. "Clayton. I've been thinking." She caresses Faber's hair. "I'm not so sure if I want to finish my degree."

I put my hand on her shoulder. "Hey, what brought that on?"

"I don't know... I kind of want to be a full-time mom." She gazes at Faber—her motherly love shines through. You could almost touch it.

"Whatever you want to do, I'm behind you, okay? Personally, I think you should complete your degree. Many kids will thank you for it. And you won't be short of subjects to practice your skills on," I quip. "Matty, Raffi, Graeme, Mia, Faber. Our next baby."

Her eyes light up, hearing those names. It's like they're her world, and she's the sun, so she's got to keep shining.

I continue, "Besides, Rob and Amber are planning to have at least one more."

She slants her face to me and grins. "Okay. I'll think about it."

"I'll be a stay-home dad if that's what it takes. Whatever you want, baby."

Faber soon cries. "Hey, Mommy's here," Isabelle murmurs.

I admire the perfect form in her arms, suckling hard at her nipple.

Isabelli Luna Martins. She turned my life upside down, only to fill my heart with riches beyond what I thought possible. Many times I reflect on her vow—that her feelings for me are more than love.

She's right.

Love is too soft, abstract, and prosaic to describe us. We're two souls forged in fire and bonded by strife. She's the better half of me whom I will cherish forever.

THANK you for reading *Cherish Me Forever*.

Grab the next book, *Embrace Me Forever* (coming soon), and find out what awaits the Hartleys' faithful PI, Simon Blake, when danger and a second chance knock at his door.

If you haven't already, pick up the first book, **Hold Me Forever**, and discover how Matty's teddy bear kicks off the love story between Rob and Amber—and read all about his spectacular proposal!

Join my newsletter for release updates, free books, and more → alessakelly.com.

# ALSO BY ALESSA KELLY

She's ready for a soulmate. He's sealed away his heart. When attempted murder brings them together, can they survive long enough to find love?

## Longing for You: From Secret to Fearless Lovers

He's a notorious mercenary boss, she's a no-nonsense oil tycoon. When legal entanglements take them on a collision course, will they rise to beat unsurmountable odds?

### ***The Hartley Brothers Series***

## Hold Me Forever

She's a traumatized survivor. He's a closed-off veteran. Can two lost souls find safe harbor together?

## Cherish Me Forever

Two wounded hearts. When unexpected love comes within their grasp, can they learn to trust before it's ripped away?

### ***Standalone***

## Protecting Her

He's a disgraced ex-cop. She's on a mad quest for justice. When they're trapped in a deadly game, can they escape into each other's arms?

Join my newsletter for release updates, free books, and more ➜ alessakelly.com.

*For my family, my biggest supporters*